NO RESERVATIONS

A JAYNE STANFORD MYSTERY, Book 3

BY L. A. KELLER RAGER

Published by Lacoursiere Publishing
Copyright © 2024 L. A. Keller Rager
All rights reserved.

ISBN: 978-0-9961487-5-7
ISBN: 978-0-9961487-6-4

DEDICATION

This book is dedicated to the man who gave me
the love I waited a lifetime for, my husband,
Sterling.
Thank you for keeping me motivated, inspired,
and laughing daily.

ACKNOWLEDGEMENTS

Thank you to my editor, Carolyne Ruck for not only helping me write a better book. but also, for her friendship.

Thank you to my amazing artist and friend Lona Bates for designing the cover. Your creativity and talent are beyond what you realize and your friendship is a gift.

To all my friends, near and far, who have stood by me with love, laughter, and endless glasses of wine, this book is as much yours as it is mine. Your presence in my life is a gift beyond measure, and I am eternally grateful for your friendship.

Thank you to my sister, Laura who is always my first reader. Thank you for being not only my sister but also my trusted confidante and cheerleader. Your support has been a constant source of inspiration, and I am profoundly grateful to have you by my side.

Thank you to my readers and supporters who kept me going despite the long break in my writing. There were so many days I thought this book would never be finished, but because of you, I focused and here we are.

CHAPTER ONE

Three hours and twenty dollars—that's all I had to get my life in order. I clutched hastily written instructions in my sweaty hand. I repeated the most important part - be at the airport at nine a.m. and not a minute later.

My name is Jayne Stanford. I hope to someday describe myself as a "restaurant server extraordinaire" but in reality, I'm average. I make enough to pay my bills with a small bit left over for a pair of shoes or a squeaky cat toy for my senior rescue kitty, Bugsy.

I'm a server at the Wild Bronco Steakhouse in the small town of Cave Creek, Arizona. I picked this town for its motto, 'Where the Wild West Lives' because all my life I dreamed of living surrounded by horses, cowboys, and history. Let's be honest, I picked it for the cowboys.

Since moving from the small beach town in Maryland where I grew up, I've been on a collision course with trouble. Police charged me with the murder of the town mayor, which, of course, I didn't do. Sadly, the actual killer escaped and may come back to get revenge on me. Most recently, I helped solve the mysterious deaths of seniors at the Sunset Elderly Living Facility, where I work part-time.

Thirty minutes before my panic set in, the barking ringtone on my prepaid flip phone woke me at a quarter to *too early to be awake for a night shift worker*. I recognized it as my best friend Bailey because she was the only one who would program that sound into my phone and laugh when I picked it up.

"Hey, Bailey. Did we have plans today which I slept through?"

"We didn't have plans but I hope we do now."

I pushed Bugsy off my chest so I could crawl out of bed. "Am I going to need to get my caffeine fix for this?

"Probably. No, definitely."

I trudged the ten steps from my bedroom to my kitchen, careful to step over a pile of laundry that might have been clean or might have been dirty. An advantage of first-floor apartment living was that it didn't take me long to move from room to room. I popped the top on my first Diet Mountain Dew of the day and plopped food in Bugsy's bowl so he would stop sending me death rays with his eyes.

"Okay, are you ready for this? I booked several days at a spectacular mountain resort in Colorado."

"That sounds fantastic. But, uh did you have to call me so early to give me this cheerful news?"

"Yes!"

I heard the bangles on her wrists clang as she bounced around in her excitement. She loved riddles and, obviously, she wanted me to guess this one.

"You get to go hiking in the bitter cold and maybe get frostbite?"

"Yes, to the hiking, no to the frostbite. There's skiing, snow-shoeing, snowmobiling, and a first-class spa."

"What made you decide to go?"

"I was contacted by a potential new client who will be in Colorado with his entire team. He said if I was available, we could meet to discuss a project. This has the potential to take my business to the next level. I've been working so much, and I desperately need a break this weekend. Since it's a long drive from the airport to the resort, and the meeting will only last an hour or two. I'm hoping you will join me."

"It sounds fantastic but I'm dancing on the edge this week and I will have to pay my rent late if I use my reserves for a trip.'

"You don't have to pay. My client paid for the room. I'll use miles for the airfare which I would lose soon anyway, and the rest is my treat to thank you for going with me. I travel for work alone all the time and it's not fun. This weekend is on me, and I could use your company."

My internal voice said no. Bailey has done so much for me in the brief time I've known her. It wouldn't be right to let her pay my way. But the bad Jayne in me said go for it. I needed a break too. Lately, things had been strained with my boyfriend, Jonas, and working two jobs was tough.

"I will only say yes if you let me make it up to you. I could clean the horse pens and weed your garden for a month."

Bailey had been one of my first friends when I moved from Maryland to this little cowboy town. We shared a love of animals, except for her rescue rooster, who loved to chase me around her mini farm. I considered myself lucky to have such a kind and generous friend who was always there when I needed her. I needed her a lot these days to rescue not just animals but myself as well.

Bailey laughed, "Neither is necessary. I need fun girl time, and this seems like an opportunity that I can't turn down. Say yes."

"Yes!"

"There is one tiny little catch."

"Uh-oh."

"The flight leaves in two hours."

I chewed on a fingernail, a habit that disgusted me but I couldn't stop whenever stress reared its head. "I don't know if I can get my shifts covered and find clothes in time."

"You can do this," she shouted.

"I can do this," I whispered.

We hung up and I bolted into action. Unfortunately, I'm not the most organized person and most days I struggled to find

3

something clean to wear from the pile on my bedroom floor. I was fairly sure I wouldn't be allowed to board the plane sans clothes.

On my budget, most weeks it's difficult to afford groceries, let alone buy a winter wardrobe. My Arizona-warmed body was not accustomed to any temperature that fell below sixty. I needed to beg, borrow, or steal, well not steal, but purchase at a super fair price, everything.

I gulped the rest of my super-strength energy soda and hit the road on a mission to find appropriate attire for the wintry weather.

I started with my friend and co-worker Emmett because he had a two-bedroom apartment, one bedroom which was used exclusively as a closet. It's not as if we were the same size but if he didn't have something, he would know who would.

Emmett has been my mentor in the restaurant business since I started a year ago. More significantly he was my closest guy friend and the big brother I never had. His model-good looks and impeccable taste made him my go-to person if I needed to dress better than my usual wrinkled capris, t-shirt, and flip-flops.

I dashed up to his second-story condo and pounded on the door. It was only six-thirty a.m. and we both put in a late shift the night before. My last party stayed two bottles of wine too long, which meant I didn't cross my threshold until well after one a.m. I knew Emmett, being a complete social butterfly, wouldn't have crawled between the sheets until much later than me.

Emmett opened the door with a scowl. "I swear if you aren't already bleeding it's dangerous for you to be banging on my door at this hour."

"No blood, but it is an emergency."

He gave me that look that said, *girl, I may wring your neck* but I ignored it as usual.

"What can you want that got me out of bed this early? Seriously, it better be life-threatening and please don't tell me you have been accused of murdering someone—again."

4

I shook my head. I didn't want to serve that dish again in this lifetime. Not that I was ever involved in the murder part, more of an '*it wasn't me situation.*'

"Nothing like that at all. In fact, it's better than good. It's fantastic. Bailey has a meeting in Colorado and she's taking me."

"You could have called me when you got back and told me all the details. Have fun." He started to shut the door but I was on a quest with limited time to accomplish my goal so I shoved my foot in the doorway.

"I need a favor. Well, a couple of favors."

"No." He nudged me back and shut the door. I could hear him chuckling on the other side.

"Come on Emmett. You owe me. You wouldn't have met your dream guy if I hadn't found him." I pressed the doorbell.

Steve Morgan was a famous actor who had a place outside of Cave Creek. I came across him by accident and, long story short, now he and Emmett were dating.

The door opened a crack. "Oh honey, I know! Too bad you cashed that ticket in."

"One small favor and then we're even. Actually, two itsy bitsy favors and we're even."

He opened the door and waved me in. "What do you need?"

I resisted a chuckle because he and I both knew this wouldn't be the last favor I would need. Emmett was all talk. His heart was as big as his New York attitude and for some reason, I couldn't explain, he never said no to me.

"I need to borrow winter gear. Oh, and I need you to cover a couple of shifts."

"The clothes I can do but the shifts are impossible. Steve and I have plans. He's booked us a romantic getaway to Cabo."

So much for the never saying no theory. Not having my shifts covered put a serious crimp in my plans. I was determined not to miss this trip. Bailey could go alone but she didn't drive, and the resort was two hours outside of Denver. Without Emmett, I would have to beg the only other available server, Sue. She and I were at opposite ends of the server world.

I called her Slutty Sue, not to her face, of course, because she could kick my butt in a fair fight. Sue cut corners when it came to her share of side work at the end of her shift. That made me stay late to polish extra glasses and silverware. She made a habit of not telling guests the price of specials, something I would never do. As a result, her checks were higher and so were her tips. But even more, because she used the restaurant as her personal dating app, even if she was perky and cute, it annoyed me to watch her work guests like a chef works the grill.

Emmett led me to his spare closet and tossed clothes at me. Sweaters, faux fur-lined leather gloves, winter socks, and a hat with ear flaps.

"These belonged to a guy I dated who was shorter than me." He handed me a pair of bib-top ski pants. "They might fit you but if not check out that secondhand store on Easy Street."

"I knew you would come through. Now I just need to get my shifts covered. Would you call Sue and ask her for me? She likes you."

"Everyone likes me but I'm not calling her. Put your grownup girl panties on. Rumor has it she wants to buy a new car so she'll take your shifts."

I hugged Emmett and lugged all my borrowed goods into my little rickety car I called Betsy. When I got this car, it appeared she may have rolled off the assembly line when Betsy Ross was sewing the flag.

I do know automobiles weren't invented back then but she seems that ancient. She ran and never complained about low fuel or how I went from gas pedal to brake quickly. Or the time I used her to play dodgeball in the desert with cacti and a dry wash. Or the one night when I was mad at my boyfriend Jonas and ran over his trash cans. Then there was the time I drove her down the Scottsdale airport runway and almost connected with a plane coming in for a landing.

I preferred not to think about those times and gave her steering wheel a loving pat as I drove to the discount store. Her body was dinged, and the tires were close to bald, but she got me where I needed to go and for that I was grateful.

The discount store wouldn't open for thirty minutes, so I forced myself to call Sue. She wasn't happy when I woke her but she did agree to cover my shifts. I dashed back to my apartment and stuffed everything from Emmett with a few odds I had into a small suitcase. I would hopefully find a jacket on my way to pick up Bailey.

My last chore was to pack up my kitty, Bugsy, and drop him at my neighbor Arlene's apartment. Arlene and I had an arrangement where she and I shared my cat. When my apartment got burglarized, she discovered him wandering the neighborhood, and now they're inseparable. It worked for me because he had company when I worked long shifts or was out with Jonas.

It worked for her because she had been lonely since her husband passed away. She spoiled Bugsy rotten and was to blame for the way his tummy drooped closer to the ground. Sometimes I was a little jealous of how happy he was with the split custody deal but mostly I was glad he had so much love in his life.

Suitcase packed, it was time to pick up Bailey and start our fun-filled trip. I had never been to Colorado and I didn't particularly care for the cold but, I would fill up on hot chocolate and spend days with my best friend. What could be better than that?

A short time later Bailey and I were seated in first class with glasses of Champagne in hand.

"This is the only way to travel," I said as I helped myself to another bubbly mimosa the flight attendant offered.

"Seems like a waste to sit in first class for such a short flight but this trip is all about spoiling ourselves."

"I'm glad the weather in Colorado is cooperating. I was afraid the blizzard that's predicted might delay our flight." I shuddered at the thought of heavy snow.

"I say let it snow. There is nothing like fresh powder."

I cleared my throat. "Is now a good time to tell you I've never skied before?"

Bailey's eyebrows raised and she took a gulp of her drink. "You know I love you like a sister but please do not break any bones or cause an avalanche."

"I'll have you know, despite my lack of grace, I have never broken a bone in my life."

She let out a sigh. "You know they say there's a first time for everything, right?"

"Ha, ha. You're too funny. I'll be careful and I'll take a lesson."

"Jonas will have my head if anything happens to you. Too bad Bugsy and Jonas's dog Molly can't get along better."

"I guess."

"Hmm. Still not ready to commit to that gorgeous hunk of a man, Jonas?"

"You know he's amazing. He's my dream cowboy. He's smart, funny, and hardworking. He's tall, dark, and handsome but he's so perfect."

"Too perfect?"

"He never has a dirty dish in the sink. His frig has healthy food. He washes his clothes and puts them away *immediately*. There aren't even any candy wrappers on the floor of his truck. It's hard to live up to that standard."

Earlier this year, when things were still in the initial stages with my boyfriend Jonas and me, I stayed at his house after an un-expected encounter with a killer. Fortunately, both the killer and accomplice were safely behind bars and would remain there for the rest of their lives.

After two weeks under Jonas's watchful eyes, Bugsy was climbing the walls to stay away from his dog's playfulness, and I was losing sleep and stressed over whether I had left my shoes in the living room. Admittedly, the loss of sleep had less to do with how messy I was and more with how gorgeous Jonas looked without his shirt on.

Still, I was ready to move back to my apartment where I could toss my clothes on the floor, eat cupcakes for breakfast, and leave the potato chip crumbs where they fell. I was falling in love with Jonas and someday I would be ready for a full commitment, but we had to find a compromise between "Hurricane Jayne" and "Hygienic Jonas."

"It's possible for you to be a bit neater."

"Bailey! Whose side are you on? "

"Yours, but Jonas is a great guy, and I would hate for you to let his ex-wife get her claws into him again because you don't like to make the bed."

I gritted my teeth. Bailey referred to Caroline who had relocated from the slightly bigger town of Prescott, Arizona on the pretext of finding work. When she was an hour away, she was like a distant cousin everyone dislikes but tolerates at the annual family reunion. Now, living practically in my backyard, she popped up like a blister on my heel on a busy night at the restaurant—unwanted and annoying.

If Jonas and I went to my favorite country bar, One Eyed Jack's Saloon, her presence buzzed around me like a cloud of gnats. The only thing worse than the smell of her overly ripe apple perfume was that she made sure to point out Jonas bought it for her when they were married. She used every opportunity to talk about the good old days while flipping her bleached blonde hair and squishing her chest against his arm.

She always conveniently left out the fact that she cheated on him with his brother. I felt conflicted about his ability to forgive - on the one hand, I resented it, but on the other hand, I was relieved since I am prone to making mistakes.

After an hour, in Caroline's presence, my jaw would hurt from the effort to smile. A migraine would be starting at the base of my neck and what minuscule fingernails I had would be ripped to the quick. I didn't want Jonas to think I was the jealous type, but her agenda was clear to everyone but him.

"If Jonas wants her because she's a neat freak then he can have her." I banged my fist hard enough on my tray to dump my drink all over it. "Darn it. She spoils everything."

Bailey laughed. "Let's not ruin our fun worrying about her. We'll land around 10:30 and the rental car place is nearby. We should be on the road by eleven and Tabernash is under two hours northwest. I'm hoping to drop the bags in our room and hit the slopes in Smokey Park for a couple of hours. The place we're staying at has a shuttle service to the ski slopes. That lets us choose to stay on-site and cross-country ski or go off-site and downhill ski." She bounced on her seat in anticipation.

I was so excited about the trip I didn't tell Bailey about my clothing concerns. I jammed everything from Emmett and the few items I found at the re-sale store into my suitcase without trying anything on. Between my natural lack of grace and my clothing situation, the potential existed for disaster.

We barely had time to enjoy our omelets and mimosa before the plane taxied to the gate.

Choosing first class had its advantages, including priority luggage handling and, as Bailey had accurately predicted, we were soon in our rented sedan and on the road.

Unaccustomed to driving in such a big city I got us lost twice, despite Bailey's phone GPS shouting at me in a British accent to make a U-turn at the next street. When we finally took the exit for

Interstate 70, I relaxed and risked a glance in her direction. Her long red hair had tumbled from the clasp and there were imprints in the armrest from her fingers.

"Would you feel better in the back seat?" I joked.

"I would feel better in the trunk or, at a minimum, blindfolded."

"Is my driving that bad?"

"It's not you. I'm like this with everyone."

"We haven't known each other that long but I've never understood why you don't drive. Do you have amaxophobia?" I was proud of myself for searching the internet to find out if being afraid of driving was a thing after a prior drive with Bailey in freak-out mode.

Bailey sighed and I could see from the corner of my eye the internal struggle that showed on her face. "I'm impressed you know that term. I don't think I have a diagnosable phobia, but I don't want to spoil our trip dredging up ancient history."

I shrugged. If she wasn't ready, I wouldn't push her. At the moment I had more important things to focus on such as the never-ending mountain switchbacks and slippery road conditions. The road was constricted by huge snow piles against the mountain and a thirty-foot precipice on the other side. Both of which were enough to keep my hands tightly on the steering wheel.

I risked a glance at her for a fraction of a second at the same time fifteen hundred pounds of belligerent moose ambled into the road. He turned to face my car, lifted his mighty head, and bellowed. I could see the whites of his eyes as he licked his snout in a dare. I hit the brakes and skidded to a stop so close the breath from his nostrils could have fogged my windshield. He might not have the same idea of fun that we did.

CHAPTER TWO

Bailey and I looked at each other in stunned silence.

"That is the biggest, take-no-prisoners animal I have ever seen outside of the movie theater."

Bailey, always the animal lover, powered down the passenger window and leaned out with her cell phone. "I've got to get a picture of this guy. This is incredible!"

The moose snorted and lowered his head so that the tip of his antlers prodded the hood. He backed up and butted the car's grill with six feet of armor on his head.

"Maybe I should back up?"

"Let me see what you're supposed to do in a situation like this. Darn, there's no signal here. Maybe if I get out, I can shoo him away."

I grabbed her arm before she could get her door open. "No way are you going out there. I'm backing up. If I have to go all the way down this mountain in reverse, I'm not waiting for him to push us over the cliff."

I glanced in my rearview mirror. I could see a car approaching quickly and for a moment I tensed, wondering if it would rear-end us. At least another car improved the odds. Two against one evened out the weight ratio.

The horn from the black sedan, as it slid to a stop inches behind my bumper, seemed to anger the cantankerous moose. His bulbous snout dripped a gob of snot on the car hood, or maybe it was drool. I bit my lip trying to remember if moose were vegetarians and if moose was singular or plural. Was mooses even a word?

For an instant, I felt as if the mammoth beast was staring into my soul with his deep brown eyes. If it's possible to have a connection with something so wild, we had it. I exhaled and relaxed my grip on the steering wheel as he gave a final bellow and finished his journey across the road.

The car behind backed up and pulled beside us. The tinted window lowered as Bailey, and I lost all composure in a fit of giggles.

"Are you ladies, okay?"

I recognized the man behind the wheel as the smoker-gum-popper-space-invader from the rental car line in Denver, who had stood close enough behind me in line that I swore I could feel his breath on my neck.

I gave a thumbs up as Bailey hollered, "I'm going to pee my pants."

"Excuse me?"

I waved him on. "We're good now."

He raised his window and zoomed past us. I marveled at his ability to negotiate the wintry conditions.

"Did that really just happen to us?"

Bailey snorted and wiped her eyes with a tissue. "We just did the tango with a moose. Why did I not get a picture?"

"I don't know how I didn't hit him." I didn't want to admit that my hands shook as I put the car in gear.

"This trip is starting out to be more exciting than I expected. I can't wait to see what's next. But you should go a bit slower from here on."

"I'll be happy just to make it to Smokey Park before dinner. I'm starving."

"Let's get going or I may pee my pants for real."

I eased off the brake and we moved ahead, at a much slower pace than the pre-moose encounter. This wasn't the best time to find out why she didn't drive after all.

Neither of us spoke for several miles. We were on Interstate 40, climbing and weaving around switchbacks. Snow dirtied from vehicle exhaust made the road feel like we drove through a never-ending tunnel. It was easy to recognize that one slight miscalculation behind the wheel and our car could plunge down the side of the mountain.

When I reached the town of Smokey Park, I was desperate to stop. I had been driving for almost two hours and the stress had sapped my energy. Tiny flecks of snow swirled as I pulled into the parking lot of Doc's Roadhouse Restaurant.

With the engine running and my hands still clenched on the steering wheel, I turned to my best friend. "Let's take a break. It might do us both good to go for a walk."

Bailey released her grip and nodded. I turned off the car and we stepped out into the glacial air. A frigid wind whipped my black hair into a tangle and blinded my vision.

"Wow, it's colder here than I expected. Let's get our jackets."

I opened the trunk and we pulled on jackets and gloves. My quickly purchased coat was a size too small, and the sleeves ended above my wrists leaving a gap between it and my gloves. I was able to zip it and, if I didn't breathe much, I figured it wouldn't split up the back. Catching a glimpse of my reflection in a storefront confirmed that I resembled a foot-long hot dog stuffed into a regular-sized bun.

"Let's get some fresh air and then eat lunch," I suggested.

Bailey nodded. On impulse, I pulled her in for a hard hug.

"I'm so glad you invited me on this trip. We're going to have the best time ever. I will make you proud on the slopes."

Bailey smiled. "Let's not get carried away. No matter what's going on with you and Jonas. I don't think he would appreciate you tumbling down a black diamond slope. And I prefer not to visit a hospital while we're here."

"Don't even think that. You'll jinx us. Let's see if there are any cute shops before we eat."

My hidden agenda was to see if there was a secondhand store where I could pick up something that fit me better, but as we trudged through the slush all hopes were dashed. The town was pricier than Scottsdale, where the slogan was the West's Most Western Town. For the locals who worked in the service industry, it was known as the West's Most Expensive Town.

I hopped over the areas where the snow had started to accumulate since I was wearing sneakers. I prayed the snow boots I borrowed would fit me better than the jacket. Snowflakes danced around us and melted on our lashes like butter on a warm freshly baked slice of bread.

After meandering along and peeking in shop windows for twenty minutes, my fingers were getting numb, my hair was matted, and my feet were soaked through.

Bailey must have read my mind. "Let's grab something to eat and head to Tabernash before it gets too late in the day."

We backtracked to Doc's and I ordered a hot chocolate, a double bacon cheeseburger, and fries. Yummy, gooey goodness chased away the shivers and invigorated me. We gobbled down our lunch and within thirty minutes we were ready to get back on the road. We couldn't stop giggling about our moose encounter. I felt a mixture of excitement and fear at what the rest of our trip might bring.

As we walked to our rental car, I noticed a man standing on the far side of the parking lot. It was the man from the black sedan who scared off the moose. There was no doubt in my mind it was the same man who lurked behind me in line at the car rental place. Normally while waiting in line, I wouldn't have paid any attention to him, but I almost gagged on the smell of stale cigarettes which swirled around him like an Arizona dust devil.

Every time he popped his gum, I was sure it would get stuck in my hair. For every step I took forward, it felt like he took two until he was so close, I could feel the heat from his body. I remembered thinking about personal space and how some people weren't aware it existed. When he saw me staring from across the street, he pivoted so fast the fuzzy ear flaps on his hat flared straight out.

I nudged Bailey. "There's the guy who stopped in the black sedan and chased off the moose, and he was in the car rental place too."

She looked around but he had disappeared around a corner. "What guy?"

"I shook my head. "It's probably just a coincidence." My stomach did a cartwheel the way it did when I ate too much or when my instinct was trying to communicate something.

Bailey nudged me back, "Lots of people were renting a car."

"Maybe I shouldn't have eaten that gigantic burger and all those fries so fast."

"Don't worry You'll burn off the calories on the slope."

I removed my jacket to fit behind the steering wheel and unbuttoned the top of my jeans. Day one and already my pants felt tight. I exhaled. I changed tactics mentally and vowed I wouldn't care if my pants were tight until after I got back home. I planned to eat my way through the next few days and enjoy every morsel, especially dessert.

Back on the road, I forced Bailey to sing along to Roger Miller's King of the Road, including the finger-snapping parts. We had only a short ride from Smokey Park to the tiny town of Tabernash, but the snow was dumped on the road like sugar dusted on French toast, so it took me an hour to negotiate the slippery conditions.

My lack of experience driving in harsh weather combined with Bailey's nervousness laid tension on my shoulders like a fully loaded dinner tray. Cars passed me at every opportunity except for one dark sedan that kept just far enough behind to leave me breathing room.

We found the road to the High Mountain Ranch Resort and Spa and rolled to a slow stop at the main lodge, a massive structure built to impress. Greeted instantly by the parking attendant, we grabbed our bags and sprinted up the steps to the lobby.

While Bailey checked in, I wandered around and took in the ambiance. I trailed my fingers over the aged stone fireplace and warmed my hands by the crackling fire. The smell of pine, freshly brewed coffee, and nutmeg calmed my senses. Buttery soft leather sofas bordered the fireplace as an invitation for guests to relax after a day on the slopes. Energized, I bounced on my toes ready to take on the challenge of my first winter escapade.

"We're in the Last Rustler's Lodge," Bailey said, holding up two keys. There was some confusion about our booking. At first, they said we had no reservations for today. But they were able to find it. They offered to bring our bags up for us but it's a short walk and I'm anxious to start our adventure."

Bailey led the way down the hall from the main lobby, past a small café, and out a heavy door. We followed a snow-packed path up a steep hill which had us both gasping for breath and used our key to enter the upper lodge. Our room on the second floor had colorful quilts over wrought iron queen beds, rustic furnishings, and a wall of windows with a panorama of the surrounding snow-covered mountains.

Bailey tossed her suitcase on the bed closest to the windows as I bent over trying to catch my breath.

"I forgot about the elevation change here. I'm going to need a day to acclimate," she said as she unpacked her suitcase.

"I'm going to need a week to get used to this." Ignoring the pain in my chest I spun around the room, touching everything. "Look at the old-fashioned wagon wheel chandelier and these quilts. They look handmade!"

Bailey opened the window letting in a blast of bitter air and a flurry of snowflakes. "If the rest of the resort is this spectacular, I may have to consider spending my winters here."

"Brrr. If you keep that window open, I'm going to have to sleep in my coat."

She closed the window with a happy sigh and carefully unpacked her suitcase while I tossed everything from mine into a pile on my bed.

"It looks like this is a working vacation for you and not just a meeting," I said pointing to a stack of file folders next to her laptop.

"I'm on the cusp of putting the final pieces of a puzzle in place. I have a suspicion that dishonest practices are happening at a company I'm writing the security for. I considered leaving this until we get back because sometimes taking a break gives me a fresh perspective. Then I decided that if the answer comes to me while enjoying fresh, crisp air, I'll have everything I need at hand to move forward."

"At least you only brought one computer. I'm used to seeing you surrounded by three or four at a time."

She plopped into the soft leather chair by the window, "I guess I've gotten into a bit of a slump and the only things I do are clean up after rescue animals or work."

"You don't give yourself enough credit. You take care of an entire menagerie of animals whose lives you've saved. You took in Jenny after her mom was murdered and are helping her get into college. You are always helping me out of one predicament or another."

Jenny was Bailey's foster daughter whose mother, Kiki had been killed when she tried to help me out of a murder rap. I would carry that guilt on my shoulders forever even though Jenny didn't hold me responsible. Despite Kiki's profession as an escort, Jenny was proud that her mother had tried to save me, even though the price was her life.

"I admire you, Jayne. You have such a bold, take-no-prisoners way of going through life and I'm scared of so many things I don't even try. It's hard for me to meet new people unless we are talking about work and even then, I prefer to do it over the phone."

I felt my face flush from her praise. "You do work more hours than anyone I've ever met deciphering computer gibberish to help keep a company's data safe. If I had half of your brain, I wouldn't know what to do with myself. I could barely get through my college courses, let alone have several master's degrees like you do."

"I'm not that smart. I just loved learning and the logic of computers makes more sense to me than people do."

"Just know that I'm happy and grateful to be on a free vacation so if you need to do a little work, don't mind me."

"I have to call Jenny to let her know we arrived safe and sound and give her a heads-up about the new donkey I picked up from the slaughter auction. He's jumpy around people so she'll have to move slowly. As soon as I make the call, I have a surprise for you. The front desk told me about a place close by that would be a perfect way to kick off the fun. Wrap up in your warmest clothes and we can head out as soon as I get off the phone."

I dug through the pile and stuffed myself into long johns, a turtleneck, a wool sweater that hung down to my knees, sweatpants, and ski pants and topped it off with a ski cap and scarf wrapped around my face.

Bailey looked at me and laughed. "Where do you think we are, the South Pole?" She proceeded to pick through her meager belongings to gear up for our first adventure.

"I get cold easily," I mumbled through the scarf.

"I hope you went to the bathroom before you put all that on."

19

"Dang it!" I undressed down to my long johns and used the bathroom before repeating the process again in reverse.

While I suffered under multiple layers, Bailey's outfit consisted of a simple tie-dyed t-shirt and a pair of leggings, which might have fit a twelve-year-old. I was amazed that she planned to tackle the sub-zero temperature in only a lightweight t-shirt under her hot pink faux fur-trimmed ski jacket. With a swipe of Chapstick, she was ready to tackle any weather conditions. I wished I had the confidence she did to wear such vibrant colors and make it look effortless.

Bailey slid her feet into a size six insulated boots and waltzed across the room. Her precise fingers flashed as she braided her hair tightly and let it drop down the length of her back.

I bent over and tried to reach my feet. "I can't reach my feet. Can you help me get my boots on?"

She laughed, "You're on your own. Try wearing only two layers." She ignored my pained expression and called down to the front desk to let them know we were on our way.

"Where are we going?" I struggled to keep up with Bailey's fast footsteps as she scampered down the hallway.

"You'll see. It's just a little way from the resort but, we have to get going because the resort shuttle only runs every hour."

We hustled back down to the main lodge and Bailey hopped on the shuttle. With a bit of assistance from the driver pulling on my arms and a man behind me pushing, I managed to get on and wedge myself into a seat. My arms stuck out at forty-five-degree angles, and I was sweating underneath the layers. I prayed the trip was a short one or I would have to start removing my clothes. As we drove away from the resort, I swore I saw the gum-popping man lighting a cigarette at the corner of the lodge. I felt the hairs on the back of my neck rise and, despite the heat, shuddered.

Ten sweaty minutes later we arrived at a blue and orange house-like structure where adults and kids alike were piling onto tractor tire size tubes and being pulled up to the top of a snow-packed hill. I barely waited for the shuttle to stop before I was out of my seat and ready to go.

"Oh Bailey, this is perfect."

We signed waivers, fitted helmets on our heads, and attached our tubes to the lift. Wedged into my tube, I had a view of the hill as the lift carried us up backward. Bailey might have the right idea about this place. Summers in Arizona are too hot for tourists and the restaurants struggle to survive, as do the servers. I guessed that even in summer, this place would have tourists galore, all geared up for fun and ready to spend their dollars.

I mentally calculated what I might earn in tips at one of the local restaurants. A shadow of guilt about Jonas flickered through my mind. How could I have a relationship with him and not live in the same state for months at a time? I rationalized that if he loved me, he would be supportive. Besides, this was only an impulsive dream.

We bumped, bounced, and blasted down the hill for an hour until sunset and, despite the layers of clothing, I was chilled to the bone. I shouted to Bailey that I was heading inside to thaw and sip hot chocolate from the concessions. She waved and hooked her tube up to the lift for another run.

I waddled up the rickety wooden steps, purchased a steamy cup of chocolately goodness from the concessions stand, and found a corner where I could lean and sip my drink. The warmth slid down my throat and the thaw started from my stomach and extended to my red fingertips. As soon as my insides felt toasty, I knew I would need to use the bathroom.

My immediate problem was how to undress in the tiny bathroom stall without dropping anything into the toilet. I managed to get the jacket off. The rest of the process took me another fifteen minutes of struggling. I began to worry that if she finished her run, Bailey would wonder what happened to me. Loyal friend that she was, she always had my back.

True to my prediction, I heard the door open and her voice calling my name.

"I'm in here."

"I wondered where you wandered off to. The shuttle is here if you are ready to head back to the resort."

"It may take me some time to get back into these clothes," I called.

She chuckled. "I'll be waiting in the van."

Working my way into the clothes took longer than I expected and when I reached the van, it was full. I didn't mind standing for the short drive. Wedging myself into the aisle was easier than trying to wedge myself into a seat.

Back at the resort, I waddled up the hill behind Bailey to the lodge. As we climbed the stairs to our room, I was anxious to shower and dress in fewer clothes. My stomach growled in protest over the length of time elapsed since lunch. I wondered if the thinner air made a person more or less hungry and if the effort to breathe burned calories when you weren't even trying. If I happened to go home lighter than when I left, that would be a bonus for the trip. I would show Jonas that his ex-wife, Caroline, wasn't the only one who could squeeze into tight jeans.

Bailey stood at her bed, hands on her hips a quizzical expression on her face.

"What's wrong?"

She looked around the room. "My things have been moved."

"Maybe it was housekeeping," I suggested. I looked at the mound of clothes strewn over my bed, unable to see anything different from when we left.

"It's too early for turn-down service and the room was ready when we checked in."

"Is anything missing?"

"No, everything is here, but I know I put my laptop on the desk and my phone was face down. Now the phone is face up and the laptop is open. I never leave it open." She opened the closet. "My case was zipped up and now it's not. And these folders aren't in the same order."

"Why would someone touch your stuff? Isn't everything you have triple password protected?"

"It would take someone knowledgeable about computers to gain access to my PC. Someone who is a better hacker than me and had a reason to dig around in my files."

"What's in the folders?"

"It's mostly just my notes and probably wouldn't make sense to anyone besides me."

My stomach gurgled another reminder that it was past my regular dinner hour. When I worked at the restaurant, I generally sampled whatever nightly special was offered during the pre-shift tasting at four p.m. If I was particularly hungry, I would snatch a roll between tables. I calculated the hours since lunch and the calories burned to maintain my body heat on the tubing hill. Dessert would be on the menu tonight.

"I can't remember the last time I went anywhere that wasn't work-related. I'm probably simply paranoid. Besides, we're both hungry. Let's get ready and go down to the main lodge for dinner."

"It's been a long day, and we were in a hurry to go tubing, so maybe you simply forgot how you left things," I suggested while thinking again of the odd man I kept seeing everywhere we went. I wondered silently to myself if this was just Bailey's imagination or something else.

CHAPTER THREE

I hadn't considered that we would need to schlepp from our toasty room back outside and down the walkway to the main lodge. The barely worn suede ankle boots I picked up from the secondhand shop were cute but not water-resistant, and the three-inch stiletto heel sunk into the packed snow with each step.

Snow that mounded on either side of the path formed a tunnel illuminated by twinkling lights like a scene from a holiday movie. The wind twirled snowflakes like butterflies, and then, as if to remind me of its strength, periodically slapped my face full force. My eyes watered and my nose started a downhill race any Olympian skier would envy. My black hair's curls so carefully gelled into submission, sprang out in every direction.

When we got to the Lodge, all the tables were taken so we squeezed into the bar to wait. I wiggled my toes to restore sensation and hoped my hair wouldn't dry into a frizzy tangled glob. Seated at the bar beside Bailey was an older gentleman whose strands of gray hair were combed over to hide his bald head. He was dressed simply but elegantly in a long-sleeved white shirt, tan slacks, and loafers with no socks. I suppressed a chuckle at the thought that his feet must be as frozen as my own.

Bailey ordered a bottle of sparkling wine and, to my stomach's relief, a starter of local cheeses. We toasted our girlfriend's getaway and her generous client. As we munched, the gentleman, who introduced himself as Arnie, struck up a conversation with

24

Bailey. My mind wandered as they chatted about boring computer jibber-jabber. I drifted back to my earlier thoughts of spending a season or two in Tabernash.

I hadn't called Jonas, nor had he called me. Before I left, we argued about his ex and why I was so anxious to dart off on a long weekend with Bailey but not as willing to go with him up to Prescott to meet his family. I didn't want to admit the feelings that hovered on the edge of my consciousness. If I were to be honest with myself, which I hated to do, I would admit I was worried his family would realize I wasn't good enough for him.

I could imagine spending a weekend constantly checking to make sure I hadn't dribbled food on my shirt or spilled red wine on their white carpet. Even worse, what if I had one of those toilet paper stuck to my shoe incidents. I wasn't petite, cute, or bubbly like Caroline. I tended to speak without a pause button and trip over my feet and my tongue simultaneously.

A bite of hard cheese wedged in my throat and the resulting coughing fit sent me dashing to the restroom. Once composed, I made my way back to the bar where Bailey was still deeply engrossed in a discussion with Arnie about hijackers and something called Secure Socket Layers which may as well have been Martian to my ears.

The seat next to me was occupied by a couple who were either honeymooners or cheating spouses based on the level of activity going on below the bar top. At a dark corner table in the bar area sat a stocky fellow with a full beard nursing a beer. I could tell by the wedge of lemon on the glass that he was drinking a wheat beer, probably even a locally brewed specialty.

He wore a long-sleeved shirt buttoned up to the neck with a polka dot bow tie. I tried not to stare, but I was mesmerized by the number of times he tugged at the collar. I wondered if he was waiting for an internet date by the way his gaze constantly darted around the room.

Whenever our eyes met, he would look down and I, caught amusing myself with ideas of what his blind date might look like, would look away self-consciously.

When the host called us to our table, Arnie said goodbye and Bailey waved off my questioning glance when he promised to call her tomorrow.

As we walked to our table, Bailey whispered, "You'll never believe who I was talking to at the bar."

I frowned, "Is this another riddle I have to figure out?"

"Arnie is the owner of the company I'm meeting with tomorrow. He likes to come in early and make sure his employees are settled before their team builder starts."

"You two seemed to hit it off."

"We did. It was odd because he seemed surprised that I was here to meet with him. I told him his assistant called and arranged it."

"That is odd."

"He shrugged it off and said he must have forgotten with everything they have happening this weekend."

"Sounds as if it all worked out perfectly."

We ordered our meal, but Bailey was unusually quiet, and I noticed her looking away as if she was lost in thought.

She rested her cheek on her hand and gazed at the fireplace wistfully. It was as if a shadow passed over her face and I sensed there was something not related to her good news on her mind.

She pushed her half-eaten vegetarian entrée away. "I guess I'm not as hungry as I thought."

"Wasn't it good? Mine was delicious," I patted my very full belly. I grabbed the dessert menu and wondered if I could squeeze in a dessert.

After a few minutes, Bailey said, "I had another reason for wanting to get away from Cave Creek. Today is the anniversary of my sister's passing."

I couldn't stop the gasp that escaped. "I didn't know you had a sister."

"It was a horrific period in my life. I never told you. I've never told anyone. I'm so ashamed. I killed her."

"What?" I spluttered.

I would swear I could hear our two hearts pounding as if the entire restaurant had hushed at her confession. An industrial-size mixer spun thoughts through my head. Bailey was my friend. She had saved my life more than once. I refused to believe she could have killed anyone.

"I'm sorry I blurted that out. We shouldn't have this conversation here." She waved to the server and signed the bill. "Let's go outside by the fire and I'll tell you a secret that I've carried with me for many years."

I followed her outside to the massive firepit in a daze. We each took a seat on the far side so we could talk privately and wrapped ourselves in the heavy wool blankets provided.

Bailey spoke in a voice so soft that I had to strain to hear her over the crackling sound of the fire.

"I've never told anyone this story before now. I'm afraid you may think differently about me when you hear it."

"You're one of the best people I've ever met. I can't get my head around what you said."

Bailey inhaled deeply before she spoke. "When I was in high school, I was involved in a bad accident. Remember I told you I completed my education early because I skipped grades?"

"Yes, you were like twelve years old or something."

"I started high school at twelve and was in my first year at college at fifteen. Anyway, my parents bought me a red convertible as a high school graduation present. I was supposed to wait to get behind the wheel until I got my driver's license. I thought that car was the best thing that ever happened to me. In my little girl's mind, I dreamed of becoming a popular girl. I wanted to fit in and believed the car would change everything. I could not have guessed just how much that was true."

My heart pounded but still, I tried to downplay what I suspected was coming. "That was an amazing graduation present! Mine was dinner at the Chuck Wagon restaurant. Funds were limited at my house."

"My mother's family was in banking and my father wrote a software program that he sold for six million dollars. I'm a few years older than you so back then it was a lot of money."

"It's a lot of money now.

"As you know, I'm not comfortable in social situations. Going through high school and starting college so young was awkward. I was awkward. I prefer the company of animals rather than most people. It may be the reason I love what I do for a living. I can communicate through my computer and limit my interaction with humans. I knew I was a disappointment to my parents. They wanted me to excel outside of the classroom. But when my sister was born, they had the perfect child."

The silence dragged out so long that I thought she changed her mind about confiding to me, but when I glanced in her direction, I could see the tears trailing down her face.

"Hey, it's okay if it's too hard to talk about it," I offered. Privately, I was desperate to hear what she had to say. I wouldn't be able to look at Bailey the same way until I heard the full story. I knew one version of Bailey. The person I knew was kind and generous. My Bailey was cautious and thoughtful. I couldn't reconcile what she said with the person I thought I knew.

"I can't explain just how amazing Lilly was. She was a bright light in our gloomy, serious family. When she laughed, it drew you to her like a magnet. I loved her so much that I felt my heart would burst from the first time I held her tiny hand. But as the years went on, I withdrew more and more from my family. I could never be as flawless as she was in every way."

"How old was she when she died?"

"She was seven. There were eight years between us. As soon as she could walk, she was my shadow. Everywhere I went and everything I did, there she was. Not only was she beautiful and talented, but she also had a brilliant mind. Everyone worshipped her, and I understood their feelings because I too loved her more than anything." Bailey paused.

I kept my eyes on the fire, allowing her to take all the time she needed.

"That stupid damned car was my trigger. I taught myself to drive and started sneaking out at night. First, I would cruise around the neighborhood. I felt so grown up behind the wheel, top-down and my hair blowing in the breeze. It wasn't long before I got braver and each time I would venture farther.

My parents had a busy social calendar, and the nanny was only there to care for Lilly. I was a teenager with too much money, a fast car, and no supervision. I became involved with an older crowd who hung out on the beach. They didn't care that I was smart or a little odd. It didn't take much convincing for me to supply the party favors from my house in the form of liquor. And the booze, and later the drugs they bought with my money, made me feel like I fit in. I was accepted."

I shook my head, "Most kids in my high school drank or experimented with drugs. I'm the only person I know that never tasted alcohol until I was twenty-one and I still haven't tried any drugs—I'm too afraid of the consequences."

"That's different from what I was involved in. Those people weren't kids. They were drug dealers and users. I may have been advanced mentally, but socially I was still a child and easily manipulated. I'm not making excuses. It was my choice to do the things I did. Hear me out and then if you don't want to be my friend, I will understand."

"I'll always be your friend." I hoped my voice sounded convincing. Based on the fact that she felt responsible for her sister's death, it was obvious this didn't have a happy ending.

"You say that now but let me finish before I lose my nerve." Bailey cleared her throat and when she spoke again, her voice cracked. "One day Lilly asked me if I would take her and her girlfriend, Melissa, to the beach. My parents were at a golf tournament and the housekeeper had gone to pick up groceries. I had been out the night before partying until 5 a.m. I was hungover, still under the influence of drugs, and sleep deprived. I'm not justifying what I did, only stating the facts."

"So, you drove her to the beach?" I tried to keep the judgment out of my voice but she winced as if slapped before she continued. I couldn't stop myself from chewing a fingernail.

"My car was a two-seater, not designed to hold three passengers. It was summer in California and everyone drove with the top down. Lilly sat in the passenger seat, and her best friend, Melissa, sat on the back of the car with her feet wedged between the seats."

Bailey paused and took a deep breath before she continued, "None of us wore seatbelts. I showed off, drove too fast, and took the curves in the road too quickly. At the last moment, I decided to turn off to Monastery Beach where I thought my so-called friends might be. I turned the wheel fast and hit my brakes. Melissa flew over the hood and landed in the street. She was run over by a car coming in the other direction and killed instantly. The sound of her scream haunts me."

I sucked in air so hard I choked. "Oh my God! That's horrible."

My overactive imagination played out the scene she described and blasted images through my head. I took a sip from my water bottle and tried to slow my heartbeat. I couldn't match the mild-mannered animal rescuer friend I had come to love with someone who could be so careless and destroy two children's lives. For once in my life, words evaded me.

Bailey took a deep breath and went on. "Lilly's neck was broken. She was in a coma for weeks and when she finally awoke, she was paralyzed. She had brain damage, but she was alive. I walked away from the accident with barely a scratch. Something inside all of us died that day."

I bit my lip. I never had any siblings but, if I had been that lucky, I couldn't imagine losing them, especially not because of my actions. It had taken me years to stop feeling guilty because I wasn't able to save my father from drowning when our boat capsized. I had been just a child myself at the time. But this kind of guilt was beyond my comprehension.

"Lilly lived for a year in a hospital bed. She never came home. She never got to finish school, go to college, get married, or have kids. I have never forgiven myself.

My parents couldn't stand to be around me and shipped me off to a new college across the country. I wasn't there when Lilly passed away. I didn't get to say goodbye. I never went home again." Bailey's voice had dropped to a whisper.

I bit my lip. My words came out as a squeak. "It was an accident. You didn't mean for any of that to happen."

Bailey moaned. "I tell myself that every morning when I wake up, but in my heart, I have to live with the fact that I killed two little girls because of my stupid, self-centered behavior. I can't stop myself from believing that it should have been me who died."

I glanced at her out of the corner of my eye. I wanted to un-know the story and have our friendship go back to when I was the only screw-up in our relationship.

"My parents were shattered. There was too much destruction to keep the marriage alive. My father left town and my mother drank. They tried not to blame me but there was no question that it was my fault.

Melissa's family wanted the county attorney to press charges but by the time I was tested, my blood didn't show any drugs or alcohol. Her older brother Mateo threatened to get even so many times we got a restraining order. I'm sure Melissa's family hates me to this day. It was ruled as an accident, and I didn't pay for the crimes I committed nor for the lives I took. I killed my sister and her best friend and then I went on with my life. I graduated from college and got two master's degrees and my doctorate. I see myself, the murderer, in the mirror every day and I wonder who she is. How can this person live and those girls not?"

We sat for minutes without speaking. I needed time to process, and I wanted to be sure I didn't say the wrong thing or condemn her more than she had herself for what happened years before.

The crackling fire sent flickering tongues of orange and gold dancing into the night, casting a warm glow over the surrounding area. Each snap and pop of the burning logs echoed softly, punctuating the quiet stillness with the comforting sounds of the firepit.

As the flames licked at the air, fragrant tendrils of smoke rose lazily toward the starry sky, carrying with them the unmistakable scent of woodsmoke and charred embers. The fire's gentle warmth enveloped everything in its vicinity, inviting all who gathered around it to bask in its cozy embrace and lose themselves in its mesmerizing dance. The other guests laughed unaware that our world had been shattered.

Finally, the words tumbled out of my mouth as if someone much cleverer than me put them there. "Bailey, the accident was horrendous and unspeakably heartbreaking for everyone. You made exceptionally bad choices and those girls paid for it, but you were a kid too. You made a mistake but that doesn't mean you have to suffer for the rest of your life." Tears blurred my vision. I could feel the intensity of her pain.

Bailey's hands covered her face, and I could barely understand her words. "I don't know how to live without that guilt. It's like a cancer that feeds off my soul. I can't eradicate it."

"It took a killer almost taking my life for me to realize I could start to let go of my past. I felt guilty about my father's drowning, and it wasn't my fault. You do so many good things for animals and Jenny. When a killer murdered Jenny's mom to prevent me from figuring out who murdered the mayor, you took her in. You're helping her get into a good college. You put your house up as collateral to bail me out of jail."

"I rescue animals, donate half my earnings to charities, and created a scholarship in Melissa's honor, but nothing I do will ever bring Lilly and Melissa back."

"No, it won't, but punishing yourself every day won't bring them back either."

"I know that in my head, but in my heart, I don't believe I deserve happiness. It's one of the reasons I never let anyone get too close to me. Except for you. Now you know I'm a horrible person."

I thought she and I were close, but this revelation was hard for me to accept. I bit my lip and tried to give her the comfort she needed.

"We can't change the past, but we can learn from it and do better. I know that's what you have been doing."

Bailey reached for my hand. "Thank you for coming on this trip with me. I didn't plan to ever share my secret, but now that I have, I realize I needed to tell you about Lilly. I hope I haven't ruined our getaway."

"I think you will always be sad and miss your sister. I think of my dad every day. But I've learned that instead of focusing on his death, I focus on his life. Lilly sounds like she was a beautiful girl who loved life. We can celebrate your love for her and treasure the happy memories you still have. It was a tragedy and both families suffered the loss. It sounds like your sister loved you. I bet she wouldn't have wanted you to spend your life being miserable and blaming yourself."

She sighed. "You're right. I'll do my best to only focus on the happy memories. Everything I try to do is to honor her. I suppose I've been punishing myself for a long time and I don't think she would have wanted that for me."

"Is that what that tattoo you have on your wrist represents?"

She held up her wrist. "LC7 is for her initials and how old she was when she died. It's my reminder to never take a chance with someone else's life like I did."

"You should add something to it. Something that makes you think of happier times."

"I like that idea. Maybe I will when we get home," she said wistfully.

So many emotions churned through me and I needed to let them simmer on a back burner for a bit until I could revisit them in a calmer moment. I needed to lighten our moods. "On that note, we should go over to the other side where they have the fixings for S'mores. Dessert always makes me feel better."

She smiled slightly, "It can't hurt. Let's eat our way into happiness."

We hugged and then waddled wrapped in our blankets to the S'mores station where couples were seated on the stone rim of the firepit with marshmallows that melted into gooey madness stabbed onto the end of long skewers.

I found a spot to stand, and in one quick move, stabbed a marshmallow and prepped my graham cracker and chocolate. In the shadows near where we stood, someone smoked a cigarette, its pungent odor overwhelmed the gentle pine of the wood. I crinkled my nose as the smell threatened to ruin the taste of my dessert.

I sipped the sensuous tawny port and licked the melted chocolate from my fingers. This was pure bliss. There was no doubt my current career path would not lead me to this lifestyle. I would have to step up my game or find another job that paid better—a lot better. Three S'mores down and Bailey stepped inside to use the restroom to freshen up after our heart-to-heart. My fingers twitched with the temptation to surreptitiously unbutton my jeans.

A couple wandered by and I recognized the bearded, uncomfortable man from the corner of the bar. It looked as if his companion had shown up. He walked with his hand possessively on the small of her back. A plain knitted scarf was wrapped around her face and head, revealing only a glimpse of her eyes as they passed. They didn't stop at the fire but walked on quickly as if headed to the rooms at the Rustler's Lodge.

"Nice evening for a fire."

I jumped at the sound of a man's voice over my shoulder. As I turned to the voice, I realized it was the man who kept popping up wherever I seemed to be. The smell of cigarette smoke lingered on his clothes, but it was the cheap bourbon on his breath that made me take a step back.

"Have we met before?"

"You should be careful." He waved at the fire. "Stand too close and you could get burned."

His voice had the gravel coarseness that comes from years of smoking, his eyes hooded and bloodshot. His threadbare coat strained to stay closed over his large belly.

"Um, okay." I wanted to turn away, but my mother's teachings about good manners kicked in. "I'm Jayne." I held out the hand without melted marshmallow stuck to my fingertips.

He gripped my hand too tightly and held it for a second too long.

It could have been the food coma my body felt or maybe it was the wine but, despite the smell and the closeness, something about him reminded me of my father. Not in the physical sense, but in a way I couldn't pinpoint. I shook my head to clear the image of my dad when he would come home after a long shift at the police station. He always carried an extra burden on his shoulders that lingered long after he removed his badge and gun. My mom said he was too sensitive for the job, but it wasn't the job that took his life. It was the sea and I'd always believed, to a degree, it was me.

He looked around at the people gathered by the fire. "Are you and your friend enjoying the resort?"

"We just got in today but so far it's been amazing."

"Will you be skiing in the morning?"

"I'm going to try. I've never been but my friend is excited to hit the slopes. How about you?"

He considered me for a moment. "My plans haven't been confirmed yet."

Minutes ticked by in awkward silence as he and I stared at the fire. I looked around for Bailey to come to my rescue. If this man had been a guest in Wild Bronco, I might have had an easier time making conversation. Here, far away from my comfort zone, his gaze drilled into me as if he were trying to discover my deepest secrets or as if I had something to hide. I shivered despite the proximity to the roaring blaze of the fire and my heavy coat.

"Would you care for a marshmallow?" I offered him the plate.

He patted his stomach, "My doctor says I need to lose a few pounds, but smoking may be the death of me unless something else gets to me first. I try to stay away from sugar these days other than its liquid form." He held up his glass of amber liquid.

"I guess I'm lucky that I could eat an entire box of Girl Scout cookies and never feel the side effects except for the tightness of my pants." There I went volunteering information that might be too personal.

Bailey popped up next to me and I handed her a freshly toasted marshmallow.

I waved my hand in the direction of my new acquaintance, "Bailey is this, ah, I've been so busy babbling, I didn't catch your name."

"Harry Schepp, at your service."

Bailey reached out to shake his hand, "Nice to meet you, Harry. Have you been to Devil's Mountain before?"

"No, it's my first time."

I wondered why Harry, whose fingers twitched with the urge to light another cigarette and who looked like he couldn't bend over to put on skis, would have picked this place.

"It's our first time too. I'm a server and Bailey fixes computer warts," I volunteered.

Bailey smiled, "Have I taught you nothing in all these months? Not warts, viruses."

"I'll bet you're pretty good at what you do to afford this place," Harry said, glancing around.

"I do okay." Bailey looked at him quizzically.

"Bailey invited me on this trip. My jobs as a restaurant server and at a senior living center don't pay me enough to come here on my own. I'm lucky to have such an amazing best friend who would bring me along."

"You are indeed lucky to have such a generous benefactor."

"Jayne, we should head back to our room. It's getting late and if you eat any more of those you will be bouncing off the walls." Bailey took my hand and steered me away from Harry.

"I'll see you around, Ladies."

"Nice meeting you, Harry," I called over my shoulder.

"Remember what I said, you ladies be careful."

As we headed back through the restaurant, Bailey whispered in my ear, "That man gave me the creeps."

Again, I thought of my dad. "He seems lonely."

"Maybe, but something about him makes me uncomfortable."

"I told you he pops up everywhere we go, but he said he's staying here so it makes sense to me that he would do some of the same things we do."

Bailey said nothing but glanced over her shoulder. She stopped so suddenly I ran into her back. I followed her gaze and saw Harry slip into the shadow as he lit another cigarette.

"Now he's starting to give me the creeps too," I said.

"It's not him that startled me. I thought I saw someone I used to know." She rubbed her eyes and shook her head, "I'm imagining things. It couldn't have been him. All this time spent reliving the past is making me feel haunted."

"Him, who?"

"Just someone I once knew. It's nothing. Let's get back to our room and get some sleep so we're ready for the morning bright and early."

"How early were you thinking?"

"I would like to be on the slopes when they open. We can get in a good four hours before lunch and then maybe take a soak in that outside hot tub."

Inwardly I groaned. As a restaurant worker on the dinner shift, I was not inclined to wake up early. Most nights, I didn't fall asleep until well after midnight. Nine a.m. was early for me, but I vowed to catch up on sleep when I got home.

"Okay, I'll do my best."

We snuggled into our beds, relishing the high-quality linens and fluffy pillows. I was convinced the drama of the day and the activities yet to come would keep me awake for hours, but my eyes closed while Bailey was still talking about which trail we should swoosh down first.

CHAPTER FOUR

I awoke to Bailey singing loudly in the shower. I had buried myself in an avalanche of blankets, even going as far as to steal the quilt off her bed. I peeked out from under my cocoon to see snow flurries swirling around the room. She was nuts. The temperature in our room felt below freezing.

I rolled the blankets around me, stood up feeling like a Popsicle, and waddled over to close the window.

"It's freezing in here," I yelled to the closed bathroom door.

"You better get used to it. It's significantly colder on the trails than here. Don't you feel invigorated?" She bounded out wrapped in a towel with her long hair piled on top of her head.

I grumbled under my breath about crazy redheads and shuffled into the bathroom praying for hot water to thaw me out.

Dressed in multiple layers, we walked, or waddled in my case, down the trail to the main lodge and had breakfast in the main dining room. Despite what I felt was an exceptionally early hour, the restaurant was busy. While we waited for a table, Bailey decided to go rent our equipment—beginner skis for me and expert for her.

I had just been seated and was trying to decide between cinnamon French toast, waffles, or both when Bailey returned.

"Bad news. I waited too long to rent skis and they are all booked. We can take the chance that there will be some at the ski slope or we can snowshoe."

"What's the difference?"

"Snowshoeing is like hiking. If we snowshoe, we stay on the resort property and wander around here. Plus, there's something else that came up that I need to run by you."

I considered her first question for a moment and figured it couldn't be that hard. "I vote for snowshoe."

"Perfect, because I already reserved them. While I was at the outfitters, I also reserved skis for tomorrow and set you up with a lesson. We have limited time, so we have to maximize every minute."

"What's the other thing that came up?"

"Arnie called with a time for us to meet which is sooner than I expected."

"That's great."

"His Vice President of Operations arrived and they want to meet for lunch. I feel bad leaving you alone."

"No problem. That was the reason for your trip and it's important. I'll be fine on my own. I can soak in that giant bathtub in our room or walk down to the stables. They have a movie theater so I could watch a movie or just take a nap." The nap idea struck me as a true luxury.

"Thanks. If I can finalize this account, I might be able to swing Jenny's first year of college without dipping into the money left by her mother."

"Go for it. I consider myself lucky to be on this trip, so you don't need to entertain me."

Bailey placed the call to Arnie and confirmed plans to meet with him for an early lunch. He promised to send his driver to pick her up at the resort. While we ate, she explained the concept of a snowshoe and how it was designed to allow a person to walk on top of snow rather than sink in. The shoe would clip onto our boots with bindings like a snow ski and used crampons which were little spikey things that dug into the snow. Crampons sounded too much like tampons, so I couldn't for the life of me figure out how that would make anything fun.

My idea of a good workout was when I had a busy night at the restaurant. Bailey constantly tried to get me to hike with her. As a rule of life, I avoided extended physical activity. Despite that, I promised myself I would try everything this trip offered since it was doubtful an opportunity like this would present itself again anytime soon.

Fortified with eggs, bacon, hash browns, and a biscuit or three, I squeezed into my ski pants, turtleneck, ski jacket, scarf, and gloves, and we shuffled over to get our gear. Actually, I shuffled and Bailey glided. I couldn't bend over to reach my feet so Bailey showed me how to step into the shoes so they clipped on. Hat pulled low on my head, trail map in hand, and we began our quest for fun.

After fifteen minutes, I was sweating, had fallen down three times, and uttered a few curse words even I didn't realize I knew.

"I can't move another step!" I shouted to Bailey's back.

She turned, hand on her hip, and laughed at me. "I told you to take off some of those clothes."

"I'm listening now." I took off my jacket and hung it over a trail sign that pointed right for Moosestomp and left for Redtail. Balanced on one leg at a time, I slid off my snowshoe, snow boot, ski pants, and jean leg so I stood in only my tights. I then repeated the entire process and repeated it with the other leg. I tied my jeans around my waist, along with my turtleneck, shook the snow off my jacket, and was ready to go. "That is so much better. I feel thirty pounds lighter."

"Come on lightweight. We've got miles to go."

"Miles?" I refused to admit that my legs were shaking from the effort, and we were still in sight of the lodge.

Her exuberance carried me for thirty minutes until I wheezed to the top of a hill, where I begged for a break on a snow-covered bench. We sat in companionable silence, absorbed in the beauty of the valley below us.

In the distance, I could see cattle in their heavy winter coats, following a trail of hay thrown from a wagon. There wasn't another human in sight. The air was so crisp it hurt to take a deep breath but also refreshingly clean. Bailey was right—it was invigorating.

I looked back on the crooked trail we blazed through the flawless snow and couldn't help but imagine early settlers. How was it possible they traveled this harsh country using horses and wagons? Every so often I could see where I had gotten my feet tangled and made an inadvertent snow angel. I chuckled to myself. Not so much an angel as a clumsy girl falling and windmilling her arms to try to retain balance.

Bailey spread out the trail map on her lap. "We got off the trail, but it looks like we can pick it up again over that way." She pointed to a wooded area on a higher ridge.

"Are you sure we shouldn't head back the way we came? We can follow our tracks."

"No, this should loop us around so we'll go by the stable before we head back to the lodge."

"Okay, but..."

"Don't worry, I never get lost. I have an odd sense of direction."

I was embarrassed to admit that I was worried. By the time we reached the woods, my toes were numb and my fingers frozen from removing my gloves to blow my nose every ten steps. The woods provided relief from the biting wind, but without the sun I felt the cold more intensely.

"See here's the trail." Bailey pointed excitedly. "And there's a yurt where we can take a short break if you want."

"I want." I didn't know what a yurt was, but I could see it was a shelter of sorts and I hoped for heat and a snack bar.

It was farther than it looked to reach the yurt and I was sure I wouldn't make it without frostbite. We unclipped from our snowshoes and walked up the three steps to the door. Inside stood a rusty wood stove, two scattered ladderback chairs, and plastic-covered windows that quivered with each gust of wind.

I plopped down in a chair and removed my boots, relieved to find that my socks remained dry even though my toes were as scarlet as a tomato.

"Any chance there's some wood for that stove?"

Bailey stepped outside to check for anything dry enough to start a blaze, but even if she had found something dry, we had no matches. She returned empty-handed.

"Are you okay?" She looked at me with concern etched on her face.

"I'll be fine in a minute. I just needed a break."

"We can stay here for a few minutes, but then we'll need to get going if I'm going to make my appointment."

I groaned. "How long did you say this loop is?"

She consulted the map again. "It looks like it's only three miles from here back to the resort."

"Maybe we should go back the way weame."

"Come on, where's your sense of adventure?"

"It must have fallen out of my pocket the last time I tripped over my snowshoes."

She laughed and whipped out her camera phone and took embarrassing photos of me. "Maybe we can take a shortcut."

"I'm all for that. I'm going to soak in that massive bathtub in our room while you're gone."

Too soon for my quaking legs, she was ready to move on. I gathered up my clothing and wrapped my scarf around my face so that only my eyes were visible. We exited the yurt and clipped our snowshoes on. Bailey held the map up again to decide the best course.

"Are those our footprints?"

"They couldn't be. We came from the other direction directly to the door. Those tracks circle the yurt. I don't remember seeing them when we came in."

"Me either, although I was more focused on getting inside than anything else." Despite my light tone, I trembled. "Do you get a cell phone signal here?"

Bailey dug out her phone and peered at the screen. "Nope. No way to know how far we might be from a cell phone tower. If you think you're going to call a ride you're mistaken."

"You're a funny girl. No, I got an urge to call Jonas. We sort of argued and I suddenly feel bad about it," I lied. The truth was that Jonas had come to my rescue on more than one occasion and a feeling *of deja vu* poked at me.

"You can call him when we get back to the resort. If we follow the trail through the woods, we'll come out near the stables. That will give us a chance to warm up before the final push. I'd like to book a sleigh ride while we're there."

I kept my head down and tried to step into Bailey's footprints. With each step, it became more difficult to lift the heavy shoes. We went up what she referred to as a hill and I called a mountain, and then, down the other side. The landscape was breathtaking but unchanging. Snow clung to every surface as the wind tossed mini flurries at us, which made my eyes water and my nose flow like a faucet.

Each time I paused I would glance over my shoulder and listen. A tremor passed through me at the thought of a hungry pack of wolves fighting over our bodies. In my case, it would take them an hour to rip off all the gear before getting to flesh. Beast or man, my over-active imagination made me hurry to catch up to my friend. Mother Nature was intimidating.

We hobbled through the snow in a circle for another hour and ended up back at the same yurt. The wind picked up and ripped the map from Bailey's grasp. Visions of my frozen body not discovered until the spring thaw flashed through my head. My fingers were completely numb, and the cold crept up my legs. I understood why people gave up and let the cold seep into their bones for blissful relief.

Her frustration and my fear made us lash out at each other for the first time in our friendship.

"I don't know how we got so far off course. You need to pick up the pace, so I don't miss the meeting."

"You said you knew which way to go," I whined.

She blew out her breath in frustration. "I told you we should have turned left back there but you insisted we go right. You need to move faster."

"Yes, boss," I mumbled under my breath knowing the wind would capture my complaints so that only the mountain would hear my voice over the creaking of the trees.

Our snowshoes crunched for another quarter of a mile before I called out to her.

"I'm out of breath. Can't we stop for a rest?"

Bailey slid her pink plastic sunglasses down on her nose and peered at me for a minute. "Remember how you told me at breakfast you wanted to work off those biscuits? Well, this is how you do it."

"My biscuits are frozen!"

"It's not that far now. I'm sure I remember passing this point and the tracks are going up that ridge. I'm sure the lodge is just over there a mile or two."

My lip quivered but I was determined not to cry. I couldn't believe the words as they slipped over my tongue. "Go ahead and I'll catch up. I have more time than you."

"Really? If you don't mind, I can get back and have time to change quickly before Arnie's driver comes. I'm going to cut through that tree line."

I seriously thought she would scoff and tell me she wouldn't leave me in the wilderness. Now having made the offer, my pride refused to allow me to beg her not to go. "S-Sure. I can follow your tracks back to the lodge."

Bailey gave me a quick wave and dashed off as fast as she could move her snowshoes. To me, she looked like a cartoon figure flying over the snow. The only difference was instead of finding the situation funny, I wanted to cry. What if I couldn't find my way back? Our tracks crisscrossed in every direction. Not to mention wondering about whatever it was that I was sure lurked just out of sight.

I had no choice but to head in the same direction that the blurred form of Bailey had gone. I took a deep breath and steeled myself to get back to the resort before I was a frizzy-headed icicle.

My hearty breakfast had long since burned off, and the more my stomach growled the weaker my muscles grew. I crested the hill and could see two people a short distance from each other both proceeding in the same direction. One of them was Bailey, so obvious to me from the florescent color of her outfit. I was relieved to know I was on the right track. I stopped to catch my breath and heard the crunching of footsteps in the snow continue for a second longer.

I looked over my shoulder and called out. "Hello?"

There was no response except the wind whispering *stupid girl* in my ears. I swallowed and bit my chapped bottom lip. I vowed that when, or if, I got back to the lodge I would call Jonas and apologize. I hoped he hadn't been filling his empty hours with Caroline.

I heard movement behind me and turned around to see a flash of gray fur as a creature darted behind a tree. A poor lost dog or a coyote, I hoped. Neither of which should frighten me, unless of course in the case of the coyote, if he was especially hungry. I felt the hair on the back of my neck rise and sweat trickled down my chest. I swallowed hard and picked up my pace again.

I focused on shrinking the distance between Bailey and myself. I put my head down and moved one heavy snowshoe-bound foot in front of the other. A wolf's long, desperate melancholy howl sounded so close I swore I could feel its breath on my face. Footfalls crunched in the snow closer to me. I changed direction and blindly stumbled through a thicket of bristlecone pine.

There was no time to waste. I needed to take the direct route down the hill rather than the zigzag Bailey took. The faster I pushed myself, the clumsier I became. I managed to maneuver around a boulder before I lost my footing and plummeted down the incline like a snowball, only to be stopped by a hard impact with a trail marker appropriately named Wolf Pass.

I lay still and stared up at the lapis blue sky, mesmerized by the puffs my frozen breath made like a miniature steam train. If I was about to be eaten, then at least my view was stunning. Tears left frozen tracks on my cheeks. I heard the howl of the wolf again, but this time it came from farther away. I caught my breath and rolled over on my side. One snowshoe had remained firmly clipped to my boot. The other protruded from the snow as if planted there.

I stood up on shaky legs. I staggered over to the snowshoe and tugged at it. It didn't budge. I yanked harder and up came the snowshoe with a size eleven man's boot attached. Connected to the boot was a leg, a frozen leg, connected to a body. A very dead body.

CHAPTER FIVE

For a heartbeat, there was only silence. The birds didn't sing, and the wolf had ceased his howl. My chapped skin didn't feel the touch of the wind that fought my forward progress all day. Despite the heavy clothes I wore, my body shivered uncontrollably. I tasted a trickle of blood coming from where I had bitten my lower lip. I closed my eyes tightly to block out the image I knew was just below the surface of the snow. Behind my lids, I could envision a face with the lips frozen in a grimace as death set in.

My screams echoed through the mountain, sending a flock of Rosy Finches, who must have watched my discovery from a safe distance, into the sky with a desperate whoosh of wings. I backed away from the corpse and turned to run, but with only one snowshoe, I tripped and landed in a deep drift.

"Help! Can anyone hear me?" I screeched and clawed my way out of the snow.

My heart hammered against my ribcage. My head pounded as blood slammed into my brain. I yanked off my remaining snowshoe. Wolf or no wolf I would get back to the lodge if I had to crawl on my hands and knees. I lumbered in the direction I thought the lodge would be but turned around after only a short distance. I couldn't leave that person alone for the animals to find.

My legs felt like mush and my fingers and toes were numb. Slowly I retraced my steps to where the body lay encrusted in a glittering grave. I used my discarded snowshoe to gently scrape away the snow. Even though my experience with dead people was

48

limited, I knew there was zero chance of resuscitation. I couldn't make myself rush the task.

As I dusted the last snow from the face, I recognized the fuzzy ear flaps. Here he was again, the same man who I had been running into since this trip began - Harry. It was then that I saw what might have been the cause of his death. The snow beneath his head was stained red.

I glanced back at the trampled snow where my fall ended, thinking this could have been me. If he slipped and hit his head, he might have lost consciousness and then froze to death. This was no place to die -- alone on the side of a mountain.

I cautiously reached into his pockets to see if he had a cell phone. I didn't know if 911 could find us out here but, it was worth a try.

In his jacket, I found matches, a crushed pack of cigarettes, dried-out-looking mints, and crumpled pieces of paper. I stuffed it all in my pockets without thinking and tried to reach into the pockets of his pants. No cell phone turned up but, I did find a small flask with the initials HS and a year. I left that with Harry.

I removed my scarf and wrapped it around a tree to mark the spot. I made a mental note of the trail marker. More determined than when my own life felt at risk, I was a girl on a mission. I would get to the lodge and find help. I couldn't save his life, but at least I could make sure he had a proper burial so that his family, if he had one, would be able to say goodbye. I hitched up my ski pants and sans snowshoes, I slogged through the pines.

It took me an hour to travel a half mile, but finally, I found a packed trail that appeared recently traveled. I sat on a boulder to catch my breath and imagined I heard the soft jingle jangle of bells. I wondered if a person hallucinates before frostbite sets in. Is this what it feels like to be dying? I closed my eyes and said a prayer to my father.

"Hi, Dad, it's me Jayne again. If you are watching over me, now would be a good time to send me a sign."

I felt a gust of wind on my back seconds before I heard the ear-shattering bellow. I jumped up and whirled around. Suddenly I was standing almost nose to nose with a giant bull moose. His deep brown eyes gazed into mine. His nostrils flared as he inhaled my scent. His strong musky odor threatened to overwhelm me.

I wasn't sure if I was supposed to stand still, run, or cry. I opted for the second two. I turned and ran with everything I had away from the moose, praying as I went that he wouldn't follow me. Tears blurred my vision causing me to veer off the path and into a dense cluster of young fir trees. Branches scratched my face and I stumbled. On my hands and knees, I crawled through the underbrush.

I heard jingling again and swore I smelled horse. I moved toward the sound until I reached the trail. Exhausted and shaking, I gave up and collapsed to the ground. Regardless of what happened, I rationalized that my body would be found, hopefully before a predator decided to have me for lunch. Deep in my thoughts, I ignored the sounds around me and imagined myself back at home with my kitty Bugsy snuggled beside me.

"Miss, are you okay? Can I help you?"

I opened my eyes and stared up into the bearded face of a young version of Clint Eastwood, his stained cowboy hat tilted back off his head at a jaunty angle. He sat on the seat of a wagon pulled by a team of four black draft horses who stomped their hooves and shook their manes in impatience at the unplanned stop. He jumped down and held out a gloved hand in my direction.

"Can you stand up?"

I moaned, "I don't know." I struggled to stand on my frozen feet.

"Are you hurt?"

I started to cry. "He's d-dead. There was a wolf and a moose. I rolled down the mountain and the snowshoe was sticking up. I thought it was mine, but it wasn't." I hiccupped.

"Whoa now. Backup a bit. Who's dead?"

"It was the guy from the rental car place and the marshmallows. H-H-Harry. I found him back there somewhere." I waved my hand towards my crooked path from the woods.

He took my arm. "You aren't making sense. Let's get you back to the lodge and warmed up. I'm Travis. I run the sleigh rides and manage the barn."

He pulled me to a shaky stand before my legs gave out. He heaved me up onto the seat. Despite his slender build, he was strong and capable. There is a reason women are swept off their feet by a man in a cowboy hat, even if they do smell like horses. Who hasn't dreamed of a man riding up on a white horse to her rescue? In this case, it was a man with pieces of hay stuck to his coat and a team of draft horses but everything else was white.

"What's your name, Miss? You're shaking. Take a drink of this to warm you up." He handed me a silver flask and clucked to the horses.

My teeth chattered and I could see two of Travis "I saw him. I know I did."

"Do you remember where you were? I haven't heard that anyone is missing from the lodge."

"I was lost but I tied my scarf around a tree so he could be found."

"We're close to the lodge. I'll take you there and get the manager."

"Hurry. A gigantic wolf was chasing me and..." The thought that the wolf might find him before the authorities did sent shivers through me.

The horses made quick time back to the lodge, and Travis drew them up to the fire pit where I had only the night before enjoyed the delectable taste of toasted marshmallows. So much had changed in one afternoon. I took another swallow from the flask to settle my nerves. Travis applied the brake and jumped down. He patted the horses as he walked around to my side of the sleigh. He missed the urgency of the situation, so without waiting for him to help me I jumped down and rushed through the restaurant to the front desk.

I stepped in front of a young couple who stood with their arms around each other. "I need to see the manager right away."

"Excuse me, is there a problem?"

"Yes, I found a body!"

"You found a what?"

"A dead person -- you know a body. You need to call the police."

The front desk clerk stepped back, looked from me to the couple, and promptly passed out.

Except for my dad, my previous dealings with the police hadn't gone well. I was falsely accused of murdering the lecherous mayor of Cave Creek. The next time I had dealings with the police, I was almost toasted in a shack in the desert before escaping from a killer with no help from the authorities. My confidence wasn't high that this time would go any better, especially since I found the body.

Twelve minutes and twenty-nine seconds after we revived the clerk, three cop cars slid to a stop in front of the hotel with sirens blaring and lights flashing. Despite waiting in the lobby by the warmth of a crackling fire, I couldn't stop my body from trembling. I wondered how long it would take someone to freeze to death or if he was dead first and then covered with snow. I had left three messages on Bailey's cell phone to call me but still hadn't heard from her.

"Excuse me, Miss. Are you the one who reported the body?"

I looked up to see a Grizzly bear-sized man with a jagged scar trailing down his cheek. His dark eyes seemed to pierce my skin with their intensity and his badge shown brighter than the Northern Star.

"Yes. I found him."

"I'm Sheriff Dale Cox. I would like you to show me where you found him and then we can talk about everything that led up to it."

I stood slowly and swallowed the bile that came up my throat. "I was hoping I could just tell you where he is."

"Well miss, that would be okay if we had street signs out there but, in this case, we'll need you to take us there."

"Travis found me. Maybe he could show you the way back."

"Mr. Kincaid will be present. However, your cooperation is necessary since you were the one to find this person."

I let out the breath I had been holding and glanced around the room. I wished Bailey was there for backup. The churning of my stomach had nothing to do with hunger. I stuffed my arms into my jacket which felt more like a strait jacket with every wearing and followed behind the Sheriff.

"You and I will be on this snowmobile and Mr. Kincaid will ride with Deputy Carson." He handed me a helmet and pointed to the back of the seat. "Don't worry. I drive carefully."

I climbed on and clung to the bar behind my seat. "This is one time I wouldn't complain if you got a speeding ticket."

The sheriff gave me a long look, placed his cowboy hat in the pack on the side, and pulled on a helmet.

It didn't take long for Travis to point out where he found me and then the Sheriff to find Harry's body. I sat on the back of the snowmobile while the area was taped off and the Sheriff's team began their work. I was thankful he hadn't parked me with a view when they uncovered his body and moved him to a sled for transport to the hospital. The area was a bustle of activity but all I wanted to do was hide my face and pretend none of it was happening.

Two hours later, I straggled into the restaurant and plopped down on a sofa adjacent to a blazing fire. I ordered a hot chocolate and a shot of whiskey and drained them both in two gulps. As my frozen limbs thawed from the drink and the fire, I moaned at the thought of peeling off my layers of clothes. Part of me wanted nothing more than to crawl into bed and pull the covers over my head, but the growls emanating from my stomach and lightheadedness convinced me that despite all that I had experienced, I still had to eat or risk passing out.

I'd had no call from Bailey, which worried me, but could have meant any number of things, good or bad. I didn't want to overreact based on what happened in her absence. There wasn't anything she could do about poor Harry, and I knew that if she thought I was in trouble, she would rush to my aid. I hadn't told her about finding a body in my multiple messages. That was a bit of news better told in person. I had simply asked her to call me when she had time.

I glanced around the room. There were only three tables of guests as it was past the lunch rush and too early for dinner. I surreptitiously removed an article of clothing one piece at a time until I was down to my tights and turtleneck. A mound of clothes occupied the remaining half of the sofa. My stomach growled in an order for food. I knew I needed to feed the beast. Nonetheless, the thought of eating made me feel queasy.

After I forced down a cup of soup, I felt strong enough to gather up my clothes and stagger back to the room. There was a bathtub large enough to accommodate two people calling my name and I planned to soak my weary limbs until my skin was more wrinkled than a centenarian. I hoped Bailey's meeting had simply run longer than expected and she would be back in the room by the time I finished my bath.

I filled the tub, poured in a healthy dose of bath salts, and slid down until the water touched my chin. I hurt in places I didn't know I had muscles to ache. I couldn't get my head around what had happened out there on the trail.

Based on what I overheard the sheriff say, Harry had been dead hours before I found him. My roll down the hill had negated any evidence that might have been left in the form of footprints – at least from that direction. The Sheriff didn't confirm my suspicions that Harry's death wasn't an accident, but he didn't deny them either. Although it seemed he was found far from the lodge, it was a short walk if you took the direct route along a path that I missed. Why would Harry have been wandering around? My exhausted mind wondered if he was meeting someone he knew. More importantly, why would someone hit him on the head hard enough to kill him?

Questions scrambled my brain until my head hurt. Then I cried. Not the pretty one tear down the cheek kind of cry. The all-out sobbing until my throat burned and my eyes were swollen. I cried for that poor man who seemed out of place and lonely. I cried for any family he may have had who would learn he passed away alone. I cried for the poor desk clerk who had a knot on his head from when he hit it going down like a felled tree. I cried for the little animals in the forest who may have been the only witnesses to the crime. I cried for myself because once again I somehow managed to sandwich myself into a huge mess.

Finally, wrung out and prune-like from my bath, I reached for my cell phone. It was time to call Jonas. I hoped he would be proud of me for surviving without needing him to rescue me. Then again, he might be mad that I managed to find trouble wherever I went.

His phone went directly to voice mail, so I left him a lengthy message about how much I missed him and how much fun we were having. I hoped he wouldn't notice the lack of enthusiasm in my voice. I left out the part about the dead body. I decided it was better to tell him in person when I got home—when the thoughts didn't make me lose my breath.

After a second, I hit redial and left him another message giving a few details about what I would do to prove exactly how much I missed him. Snapping my outdated flip phone closed I sighed, confident he would have something to contemplate until I returned and which might keep Caroline at arm's length a little longer.

My bath water was chilly, I crawled into bed and buried myself under a heap of blankets. As stressed as I felt, the food in my stomach, my clean body, and my warm cozy bed gave me peace. An image of Jonas with his muscular chest and soft lips danced through my head before I nodded off.

"Jayne, are you under there?"

I pulled the quilt off my face and peered into Bailey's eyes. "Is it morning?"

"No, but it's time to get ready for dinner. I made reservations at the fine dining restaurant for seven-thirty. The main lodge has a movie theater so I thought we could either play pool in the game room or catch a show afterward."

I stretched and forced myself to shake off the fogginess in my head. Had I dreamed about finding Harry dead? Bailey looked so happy I hesitated to ruin the trip for her. I forced excitement I didn't have into my voice, "Is there no end to the surprises here?"

"We're only getting started. We have a full day coming up. First, we'll ski in the morning and then we'll have massages in the afternoon at the spa."

"Your meeting ran long, I was worried."

"I should have called, but the CFO's flight came in late and then we got so busy going over the details. I'll tell you about it over dinner."

"About today, I wanted to tell you…"

Bailey held up her hand to stop me, "I'm sorry I left you to fend for yourself. I felt guilty leaving you behind, but see, it all turned out fine. You made it back to the resort in one piece."

She was so happy about her meeting that I bit my tongue and changed the subject. "About skiing, is now a good time to remind you that I've never skied before?"

She laughed, "I booked a lesson for you so you can stay on the bunny slope while I hit the advanced black diamond trails."

I pictured a fluffy little bunny hopping along a flat trail, stopping to nibble a carrot along the way, and figured I could handle that. A lesson meant there would be other people around so there would be no chance I could get lost or find another body. I resolved to grit my teeth and go for it. After all, I sort of conquered snowshoeing so everything else had to be as easy as making a cake from a box mix—simple and delicious.

We dressed and ambled over to the building which housed the upscale Moose Head restaurant. My mouth watered, but the prices made me hesitate. Bailey sensed my apprehension and patted my hand.

"Order what you want. Tonight, we're celebrating me winning Arnie's account."

"Sounds like your meeting went very well." I raised my wine glass to toast.

"Nothing is finalized, but he wants my newest software, and I may be able to include maintenance in the contract. It would require travel, which would leave Jenny on her own, but she's so responsible, I don't worry. Well, I do worry but I trust her. Besides, I know you'll keep an eye on her and my animals."

"Of course. I'm so happy for you.

"Here's the best part. He invited us to a party at his house. His top staff is in town, so I accepted because it's good business. I won't go if you don't want to."

"I'm on a free vacation at a first-class resort with a spa appointment scheduled and now you want me to also go to a party? Who would say no to that?" Secretly I looked forward to a diversion of any sort.

"Yes, I know these first-world problems are tough."

She prattled on throughout our dinner of vegetarian pappardelle for her and chicken coq au vin for me. Her eyes sparkled as she rattled on about the party and our plans for the next day. I pretended to listen and nod at all the right places, but everything was blurred by the memory of Harry's face in the snow.

I managed to choke down each bite. As delicious as it probably was, I couldn't taste anything. Thankfully, she suggested we watch a movie which allowed me to sit quietly with the thoughts that raged in my head.

I promised myself I would tell Bailey all about it in the morning after I had time to digest the day's events. I didn't think waiting another hour or two would make a difference to poor Harry now. If only I had remembered how dominoes work – when one falls, they all go.

CHAPTER SIX

Bailey woke me early the next day, anxious to whoosh down the slopes. We gobbled breakfast and despite all the calories I was sure I had burned the day before, my pants felt a notch tighter. Every time I started to tell her about Harry, I choked. The words wouldn't come out and I felt like someone would have to give me the Heimlich maneuver. She was so happy that I convinced myself to tell her later. I rationalized that whether she knew now or later, Harry was still dead and nothing I could say or do would change it.

Rather than take the shuttle, I drove the rental car the short distance to Smokey Park. Thankfully, no snow was falling, and by nine we had our rental gear. With a quick wave, Bailey jumped on the ski lift and she was soon a tiny blur against the mountain backdrop.

I aimed my skis in the direction of a group of kids ready for my first lesson. I fell twice before I made it ten feet. I could barely look down without picturing the snowshoe sticking out of the ground when I found Harry.

Falling was easy as usual for me but getting back up and untangling my skis proved to be an unexpected hurdle. Bad Jayne suggested I leave the skis and head to the lodge to do some window shopping far, far away from the slopes. Good Jayne insisted I needed to step outside of my comfort zone and stop being a baby.

Through sheer determination and a push from a ten-year-old, I managed to line up for class. The instructor, Henri Bouchard, told us he was originally from Montreal but recently moved to Colorado from Saskatchewan. His heavy French accent and dark hair with a streak of white down the middle made it hard for me to think of him as anyone other than the cartoon skunk, Pepi Le Pew, my mother's favorite animal character of all time.

Henri demonstrated how to push off, snowplow to a stop, bend at the knees, and how to get up from the ground. I'm sure the last lesson was directed at me since I fell four more times, once taking the kid to my left down with me.

The beginner slope didn't look as high as the mountain I had trekked up the day before, so I felt cocky when I grabbed the tow rope. I pictured what my group must have looked like with me towering over twelve grade-schoolers—the lone adult beside the instructor. Despite the cold, I couldn't remove the smile from my face as I glided to the top hanging on to the tow rope, listening to the sound of my skis as they skimmed over the lightly packed powder.

When I reached the top, I let go of the rope as instructed and skied like a seasoned pro over to my group. It was when I turned around to get a look at where the hill ended that I gasped. Where were the bunnies when I needed them? The three-story lodge now resembled a doll house and the people no bigger than bunny droppings. I looked at Henri and shook my head.

"There is no way I'm going down that hill. Is there another way down?"

"Come, you go with me now!" He yelled as he pointed at me.

The rest of the class was already at the halfway point, weaving back and forth in a perfect line. A little girl I thought adorable earlier fell but jumped up immediately. Giggling, she stuck her tongue out at me. I made a childish face back at her. Show off! She didn't look as cute to me now. Tension worked its way up from my toes to my jaw. No way was I going down that hill.

I sized the instructor up. He was an inch shorter than me and weighed less too. I thought I could take him if it came down to it. But I didn't have the opportunity to resist because Henri gave me a shove down the hill which made me feel as if I'd been shot out of a cannon.

I dropped the right ski pole and almost took out someone's grandmother with my left. My arms windmilled to remain upright, and my screams were loud enough to break the sound barrier. I picked up speed midway down until everything was a blur. I had to decide to plow down a couple of kids or throw myself to the ground. Fortunately, for them, I opted for the second choice. I landed face down in a heap.

"You must listen to your instructor. This will not do." Henri yanked me up from the back of my jacket. He righted my skis and handed me the poles. "We will do this again."

"I'm not cut out for this. I'll just watch from the lodge."

"Je n'abandonne pas. Henri does not quit. You will continue until you are flawless. Come." He grabbed my pole and dragged me to the tow rope. "You will point your skis this way. You will float down the slope, not wave your arms like a clumsy oaf."

I tried to explain to him that clumsy oaf came naturally to me. Float and feet were two words that did not blend in my head. To his credit, he didn't give up on me and after two hours, much of which I spent on my butt sliding down the hill, I was able to do several runs where I remained upright for the entire trip down. My legs were shaky and my hands numb, but by the time I met Bailey at the lodge, I was impressed with myself. All that effort pushed Harry's death onto the back burner of my brain for a moment before random questions popped into my head. Who was Harry and why did he come here?

With a whirlwind of questions swirling around me, I had to face the next item on Bailey's agenda. As lovely as a spa treatment would be, I couldn't bring myself to tell her about the dead body I found. I was sure I wouldn't be able to spend the afternoon luxuriating in the spa, but the strong hands of the massage therapist helped work out all the tension I'd built up and the sore spots I created over the last two days. I tried to focus on relaxation and drain all thoughts from my mind but felt as if I couldn't breathe. The same questions kept rotating like a lazy Susan in my head. Sadly, death has a way of shadowing me and this time wasn't an exception at all.

I forced a smile on my face as we soaked in the outdoor hot tub. For the adventurous, you could swim from the outside pool into the indoor section without getting out. Polar bears had nothing on me now. I dunked into the icy water, and with teeth chattering, moved directly into the steamy sauna. By the time we finished our relaxation, we needed to dress for dinner.

After two full days of activity and one dead body, I was hoping for a quiet night. Bailey was excited to try an Italian restaurant recommended by the resort a short drive away. I vowed to tell Bailey about Harry over dinner, mainly because I knew she had to sense something was off with me.

After we ordered a salad for her and fried mozzarella for me, I took a deep breath and told her all the details about finding Harry.

"I can't believe you didn't tell me this yesterday!"

"Honestly, by the time you got back, I was exhausted from telling it one hundred times to the sheriff. Besides, you were so happy about the new account, I didn't have the heart."

"Jayne, this is shocking. I don't know what to say. Have you heard anything more from the sheriff?"

"No, he said he would call me if he had more questions. I told him we would be here until Thursday, and he has my contact information."

"That poor man. I wonder what happened."

"I don't know but if there is a killer on the loose, I would prefer not to be the next person he or she comes across."

"It had to be someone who knew him. Someone who followed him on the trail and then hoped he wouldn't be found. Or..."

"Or what?"

"Well, you did say he seemed to turn up everywhere we were. You don't think it could be someone you know, do you?"

"What are you saying? Do you think someone wants to kill me?" I winced at the thought.

"As you know, the mayor's killer is still on the loose. What if you're the target and Harry got in the way?"

Silence hung in the air between us as thick as caramel. I struggled to swallow and felt my chest constrict. If the mayor's killer wanted the money I found, it was too late. That money wasn't in my account or anywhere I could get my hands on it.

"If someone was after me, why kill Harry? He didn't know me."

"Good point. I'm being paranoid. Just the same, did you tell the Sheriff about what's been going on in your life this year?"

"No way! The last thing I wanted was for him to think death follows me everywhere I go."

"Lately, it seems as if it does."

My hands trembled as I pushed my plate away. I didn't want to dredge up my experience with murderers. If someone was after me, I would have to tell the police. On the other hand, it wasn't as if I carried a get-out-of-jail-free card with me everywhere I went, and a killer could just show up and I could serve up redemption. I have nothing to my name except my old kitty, Bugsy.

"I don't think this has anything to do with me. I only found Harry by accident."

"Nevertheless, please be extra cautious and call the Sheriff in the morning."

My heart was heavy with thoughts about someone I had only just met, murdered at the hands of a crazed person. I prayed it didn't have anything to do with me. I couldn't bear the responsibility of another homicide on my shoulders.

When we arrived at our room, the light on our phone was flashing. Bailey called down to the desk and was told there was an envelope left at reception for her. We were too exhausted to claim it then, so we quietly undressed and fell into our beds.

Despite the exercise, we both slept fitfully. I rolled around under the heavy pile of blankets until I was as tangled as day-old spaghetti. I could hear Bailey's sighs and wondered if she was as worried as me about who killed Harry, and whether his death had anything to do with me.

When the sun's rays peeked through the drapes, I was up and showered. The first thing on my agenda was to call the sheriff. Bailey was right that I should have told him about a killer on the loose who might or might not be after me.

While she showered, I called but had to leave a message with a Deputy. Then I checked my phone for a response from Jonas. The activities of the last couple of days were overshadowed by the tragedy, but I couldn't believe there was no message from him. Was he finally done with my drama? Part of me wanted to call him again but the other part, the one with too much pride, said to heck with him. It left a knot in my stomach the size of a cantaloupe.

We plodded down to breakfast, the snow on our shoes feeling heavier with each step. I swore I had no appetite, but ordered an omelet with feta cheese, a side of bacon, hash browns, and more biscuits. A girl has to maintain her strength.

Bailey finished her breakfast first. "We only have two more days to enjoy this place. We don't know if what happened to Harry had anything to do with you, so we need to regroup."

"But what if it did?"

"What if it didn't? I say we let the Sheriff do his job and we do our best to enjoy the time we have. There is still more to do here and if we mope around, we'll miss out."

I grudgingly agreed. I could sit in the room watching a movie in my head about Harry in the snow, his face blue and frozen into a grimace, or I could make my best effort to appreciate this opportunity Bailey set up. Besides my dilemma, I was here to help make Bailey remember her sister and maybe relieve some of her guilt on the anniversary of her sister's passing. I wasn't doing a particularly great job of it so far.

"You're right. I have to put Harry's fate in the back cabinet of my mind and do something out of my comfort zone. Well, something else out of my comfort zone."

"Great. We could rent snowmobiles and drive out beyond the resort where the nature trails start."

My mind flashed to my snowmobile ride with the Sheriff. My face was hidden behind his burly back as we buzzed through the snow to greet death.

Seeing my hesitation, Bailey continued, "We could go on a sleigh ride."

I bit my lip thinking about Travis rescuing me.

"We could go ice skating. Or they have fat bikes here where you can ride a bike through the snow. We could also cross-country ski."

I knew Bailey loved to ski, so I opted for cross-country skiing. Since we were early today, skis were available and a lesson was scheduled to start in one hour. With a better attitude, we stopped off at the front desk to pick up the envelope for Bailey, which she assumed was from Arnie and hurried back to our room to change into warm clothes. I was emboldened by the idea of skiing on a flat surface. It was hard to admit but the thought of another day going up and down mountains wasn't appealing to me. The added advantage was that the cross-country ski trails stayed within eyesight of the resort. No opportunity to stray across a wolf, a moose, or a dead person.

The sky looked ominous as we walked to our room, so as a precautionary measure, I buried myself in three layers of clothes. We only had a brief time to dress and return to the lodge before the lesson started. I prayed this went better than my downhill experience.

Ten other people were attaching their cross-country skis to their boots as we joined the group. None were children, so I felt emboldened.

"It is my most challenging pupil come back to me."

"Hi, Henri. I didn't know you also taught lessons here."

"Henri is in very high demand," he beamed.

I motioned to Bailey beside me. "This is my friend Bailey."

He gave Bailey a cursory glance. "Her, I do not concern myself with. I can see how she stands with her weight evenly distributed. She will not make my day interesting. But you are a student worthy of my talents."

I grimaced. My muscles hadn't recovered from the last time I made his day and it was at least ten degrees colder today with snow flurries swirling around my head.

"Line up everyone and we will start."

Bailey nudged me to the front of the line, chuckling to herself. She was enjoying my discomfort way too much.

Henri demonstrated how to swing our arms in sync with the opposite leg. He showed how to slightly bend at the knees and glide through the tracks. It looked ridiculous, but I was surprised to find that I was a natural at it.

For the first time, I felt graceful, and it made me want to go farther and faster. Henri beamed at me as I whooshed by him and he shouted, "Très bien!"

Then I saw the hill. I had gathered enough momentum to pass everyone and now, in the lead, I had to decide if I should check my speed or barrel down the hill. The only problem was that I didn't remember how to stop. For a split second, I pondered whether I should simply fall to the side and hope no one ran me over or go for it. I went for it. My remaining active brain cells remembered to bend at the knees and sit back slightly. Trees flew by in a blur and my eyes watered from the cold. I sensed, more than saw, when I reached the bottom. Henri slid to a quick stop beside me, cheering.

"That was perfection!"

"It was scary but fun. I looked over my shoulder to see that the enormous mountain I thought I zoomed down was just a slight rise in the track, barely enough to be noticeable had I not been on skis.

Bailey shouted as she flew past me on the track, "Great job. I have a video." She waved her phone at me and kept going.

We skied with the class for a period and then had time on our own for another hour. The snow continued to dance with soft flakes that landed on our faces and quickly melted.

Just as we returned to the ski rental lodge, and I was feeling overly confident about my supreme mastery of the sport, I fell. Ten more steps and I would have had a perfect record. I lay in the snow while Bailey laughed and took more pictures.

"I'm done. I cannot take one more step. Please come pull these skis off my feet and send me out a burger."

She laughed, popped out of her skis, and pulled me to my feet. "Come on. Let's return our equipment and have lunch."

"I'm starving."

"When are you not?"

"I admit that sometimes I eat my feelings. Right now, I have a whirlwind going on."

We quickly dropped off our extra clothes in the room and lumbered to the restaurant. I gorged myself on a chicken barbeque sandwich, crispy shoestring fries, a side salad, and dessert. I was ready for a nap. Bailey wanted to open her envelope and catch up on emails.

Back in the room, we were surprised to find that not only hadn't the housekeeper cleaned, but the room was in worse condition than when we left before lunch.

"What's going on here?" Bailey asked.

"I swear you made your bed before we left and look my stuff is a mess."

"Jayne, someone's been in our room. My laptop and files are all gone. Someone even took the envelope."

"My stuff's a mess!"

"That part is hard to tell since your suitcase exploded as soon as we got here. Hard to tell the difference now. We need to call hotel security and the sheriff as well."

Bailey dialed down to the front desk while I tried to reorganize my clothes. In minutes there was a brisk knock on the door. Bailey stepped around me and opened it.

"Miss Chauncey, I'm Patrick Young with hotel security. What is the problem?"

"We haven't been in our room for most of the day, but it was all right when we got back from skiing. But when we came back after lunch, someone had been inside and important things are missing."

He strolled around the room, checked the windows, and looked at the door lock. He kept eyeing me with a suspicious look on his face.

"Was your door open when you returned?"

"No, we used my key."

"And you both have possession of your keys?"

"Yes."

Bailey showed him her key and I dug through my pockets to find mine was missing.

"I know I had my key when we left the room this morning. I had it in my coat pocket the entire day."

"Was there ever a time when it could have dropped out?"

I shook my head, but I couldn't be sure. I had taken my coat off several times in the rental lodge and the restaurant. When I fell on the slopes, it could have fallen out.

"Regardless of how someone entered, my laptop and cell phone are missing and possibly other items. What can be done about it?"

"I will write up a report and you can file with your insurance."

"How would someone even know which room the key opened?"

"Perhaps you were followed." He looked directly at me. His eyes narrowed. "What is your name?"

"Jayne Stanford."

He rested his chin in his hand as if to stroke a non-existent beard. "I knew I recognized you. You're the person who reported the dead body."

"Yes." I squirmed under the intensity of his inspection.

"Do you think this is related?" Bailey asked.

"Highly unlikely. I would guess someone saw Miss Stanford drop her key and since she has developed a bit of notoriety, a thrill seeker might have wanted to know if you had the scoop on what happened."

Bailey and I exchanged glances, our discomfort as intense as the Arizona sun in July. I wrung my hands, wondering again if this was all my fault.

"We should call the sheriff to let him know about this break-in," Bailey interrupted. "I had highly confidential data on my laptop."

"I don't think we need to drag the sheriff back here and upset the guests further. We've never had such a thing occur in this establishment before now." He looked pointedly at me. "I'll ask the housekeeping staff if they saw anything suspicious. In the meantime, we will issue new keys and you can make a list of anything else that is missing."

He left after another extended stare at me and with the parting comment, "Miss Stanford, I get the impression that trouble follows you. Please try to stay away from it while you're here. Oh, and do enjoy your stay."

Bailey practically slammed the door behind him. I gave up folding my clothes and laid face down on my bed.

"I'm calling the sheriff. I want to find out what he knows about the murder and if it involves you. We may need to change our flight and go home."

"I might do my share of stupid stuff, but I've never been a quitter. I don't want to give up our girl's trip. I know things haven't turned out the way we expected, but we only have two more days. What else can happen?" I mumbled into the pillow, instantly regretting my words in case I jinxed us.

Bailey found the sheriff's card and dialed the number on the hotel phone. While she was on hold, I went into the bathroom.

"Bailey, the shower's wet. It almost looks as if someone took a shower while we were gone. All the towels are hung up but one is wet."

I carried the wet towel into the bedroom with my fingertips.

She put the phone on speaker and we listened to the music on hold. "That is very odd."

"Ewwww! I wiped my face with this towel! Someone I don't know could have used it to dry off whatever body parts I can't think about. I may have to throw up."

I didn't know where to put the wet towel, so I unlocked the room door and dropped it in the hallway. Let the housekeeper think we were slobs, but I couldn't leave it in the room as a reminder of what might have gone on in our absence.

While still on hold, Bailey went through her suitcase and drawers methodically to see if anything else was missing. My clothes, which lived on every surface of my side of the room, made it hard to tell if someone had gone through them or if that was how I left them. Regardless I was determined to set everything to right.

Finally, the sheriff came on the line and it was obvious he had researched my name. He asked a few questions and informed me he wanted me to go to the station with the clothes I wore so forensics could gather sample threads. He didn't say, but I suspected he hoped to obtain a sample of my DNA as well. If the killer left anything behind, the police would find it. Bailey promised him we would be there first thing in the morning. That meant we wouldn't be leaving early, even if we wanted to.

In my father's day, they had to determine means, motive, and opportunity the old-fashioned way—by witnesses, fingerprints, and what could be seen by the naked eye. Investigations had come a long way since then and now a miniscule hair could lead the police to a suspect. I just hoped it didn't lead them wrongly in my direction.

The sheriff also inadvertently gave us a little information about Harry when he asked if we knew why Harry had a folder on Bailey in his room. It turns out Harry was a private investigator. Who hired him, and why, remained a mystery.

Bailey paced the room deep in thought. I made another attempt to fold my clothes but gave up and threw them in a ball in the corner. The room felt oppressive and the joy we felt when we first arrived had morphed into a gray cloud of fear. Everything I touched felt dirtied by the violation of a stranger's hands.

"I need to get another laptop right away."

"Someone broke into our room and all you can think of is work?"

"I need to find out who hired Harry, and if he had a computer, I could hack into his cloud account. But to do that I need a special program."

"My phone! I just realized I haven't checked my phone." I leaped up and dug through all my clothes, and my jacket pockets, checked under the bed and in the bed, where I finally found it under my pillow.

Bailey smirked at me. "Do you think someone would steal a flip phone? Do you even have pictures on it?"

"It has one redeeming quality. It's cheap."

She took it from my hand and opened it. "A flip phone is better than no phone. I can call my cell to see if someone answers." Bailey dialed herself and listened to her voicemail.

I checked my messages to find that Jonas had finally called me back. His message was brief, saying only that he couldn't wait for me to get home because we had things to discuss.

I picked at my cuticles, wondering if he was going to break up with me. There was no way I would call him back and tell him about finding a dead person. I imagined that would be the final storm that would push him over the edge. I sighed and flopped on the bed.

Bailey stood with her hands on her hips. "There is little else we can do about the situation and we don't have much time before the party at Arnie's, so I suggest we rest and then get ready. If we leave early, maybe we can find a place where I can pick up a new laptop and phone." Bailey opened a book she brought and settled on her bed.

"Sounds like a plan to me. I'm beat, and a few minutes of shut down would be..." I drifted off to sleep before I finished my sentence, secure in my belief that whatever else happened, it couldn't be worse than what we'd already experienced.

CHAPTER SEVEN

My brief nap ended when Bailey shook me awake. "We need to get ready for the party. The front desk told me about a place where I could pick up a laptop and phone that would work well enough until I got home. I want to leave early."

I dragged myself out of my cozy nest of a bed and showered. I hadn't brought party clothes, so I made do with a pair of black pants and a sweater. I hoped this event wasn't all business or too dressy, as in either situation I would be as unwelcome as a moldy piece of cheese.

Without the option of changing my clothes multiple times to find the perfect outfit, I was ready in record time. I suggested we swing by the stable on the way out to make a sleigh ride reservation for the following day. The rides only ran once a day, and so far, had been booked. Even though I already rode on the sleigh with Travis, I hoped I could replace that memory with a happier one.

Bailey decided to wait in the car rather than traipse through the snow-packed parking lot by the barn. Nearby a sleigh and wagon were parked as if waiting for their next passengers. As I entered the barn, the smells of horses and hay filled my nostrils. The munching sound of the horses eating dinner made me smile. Chickens pecked and squawked at each other as they wandered down the neatly swept center aisle. Bridles with brass buckles polished to a mirrored shine hung on the wall.

I didn't find Travis, but the office was occupied by an older gentleman with a name tag that read: John Whiteskunk. Two long braids of silver hair hung on either side of his wrinkled face. His shirt was denim, as faded as the early morning sky, and around his neck, he wore a necklace of agate stone. On his gnarled fingers, he wore rings of silver and turquoise.

"Hi, John. That's an interesting name, Whiteskunk."

"I am Ute, a descendant of the great peacemaker Ouray."

If Bailey hadn't been waiting in the car for me, I would have sat down on the worn leather sofa to hear more of his story. Instead, I introduced myself as a guest of the resort and told him I wanted to book two for a sleigh ride the next day.

He took my hand in his and held it a moment longer than was comfortable. He stared into my eyes, "My people believe in the healing powers of the earth. I see you have something weighing on you," he said.

I bit my bottom lip and squirmed under his gaze. "How can you tell?"

He shrugged his shoulders and winked at me. I laughed nervously and glanced around the room.

On the wall opposite the desk, my eyes were drawn to shelves bulging with dusty trophies and faded photos of a dark-haired man dressed in traditional garb and a horse with a glistening black coat and snow-white mane that fell down his shoulder. If I looked carefully, I could see a resemblance between the man before me and the one in the photos. Despite the grime that settled on the glass, I could tell the man and the horse shared a special bond.

I stepped closer to examine the photos. "Is this you, John?"

"Might have been once."

"Such a handsome fellow."

"I was a looker in my day. Had all the ladies chasing me, but only let one catch me."

I giggled at his assumption that I meant him when I referred to the horse.

"John, do you still ride?"

A male voice, singing loudly and way off-key, approached the office. Suddenly, all business, John stepped around the desk and handed me a clipboard. "The next ride is tomorrow at ten unless the weather is too warm or too cold. Fill out all the information and sign on the bottom."

I sat on the worn leather couch and entered our names, addresses, room information, and weight, which I may have lied about slightly. Intent on my task, I didn't notice he had slipped out of the room until Travis sauntered in still singing something about a cowboy and his pickup truck.

He looked at me nervously, "If you're here to talk about that dead guy, I told the police everything I know."

"No, I'm here to book a sleigh ride, for me and my friend."

"Sorry, I've been on edge since that happened."

"I know. I keep seeing his face."

"Yeah, that was the first time I'd seen a dead person."

Part of me almost said that I'd been involved with more than my share of dead bodies lately but thought better of it. Instead, I offered a weak smile and handed him the clipboard.

"Looks like your paperwork is in order. Be here thirty minutes before."

I thanked him and left the office. I couldn't resist a moment to stroke the silken nose of a beautiful bay draft horse who stood with his enormous head hung over his stall door. I inhaled the smell of horse and hay which gave me a happy fluttery feeling. He nuzzled me in search of a treat but only got a scratch under his chin. I promised him I would bring him an apple when I returned to take the sleigh ride.

As I turned to leave the barn, John called out to me where he stood near the entrance to the paddock on the other side of the barn, his face in the shadows.

"Every morning, I have seen a Moose on the hillside. He is waiting for you."

"Um, okay."

"He will guide you. Don't be afraid."

"He will guide me where?"

I turned as Bailey tapped the horn as a reminder for me to get a move on. When I turned back to ask John what he meant, he was gone.

I climbed into the car and looked at Bailey, who scribbled on a scrap of paper furiously.

"I just had the strangest experience. There was a man at the barn who said something to me. Did you see him?"

"What man?"

"The old guy that was just talking to me right there at the doorway to the barn."

"I didn't see anyone."

I peered out the windows but didn't see any sign of him. The hairs on the back of my neck stood up and my stomach did a flip-flop. I started the engine and Bailey gave me directions to the town so we could pick up a new laptop for her.

On our way, minuscule snowflakes swirled around in the air, so light they were barely visible. As the roads were clear from the resort into the town, I wasn't worried. This area could handle a flurry or two and I didn't predict any trouble. We had an hour before we were expected at the party which meant I could take my time driving.

My mistake was in not anticipating that Bailey would take forty minutes to decide on a laptop and another twenty in a checkout line that had only one cashier and twelve people in line ahead of us. I hated to be late, but Bailey didn't seem concerned.

"Stop fidgeting. If I remember the directions Arnie gave me, his place should only be a couple of miles outside of town. We have time."

"What if it's a sit-down dinner and we're the last people there? What if they pass appetizers and we don't get any?"

"It's fine. No one serves dinner as soon as you walk in the door."

"Hold that thought," I said as I slipped out of line and rushed toward the candy aisle. I figured it wouldn't hurt to have a candy bar to hold me over in case we missed the appetizers. I was back in line before it moved more than three steps with M&M's, a chocolate bar, and mints. Mints were an afterthought since I didn't want to have chocolate on my breath when we walked in the door. Bailey checked out my backup food and shook her head.

If I were being truthful, chocolate was more a way of self-medicating when I felt uneasy or stressed. Since the encounter with John at the stable, I had the "I need to keep eating" anxious feeling. There was something about his demeanor that reminded me of being in church. Even though my family attended services every Sunday when I was young, I was never able to sit still long enough to read the Bible. That might explain why I couldn't follow along when the minister quoted passages. I admit I was more focused on the possibility of going for a pony ride afterward than I was on paying attention during the service.

Now, I had that feeling again of not paying enough attention, of not having the answers to an exam when I should have studied, but instead spent my time daydreaming or being on the edge of knowing the name of a song but never quite remembering. Despite my memory of odd details, that talent was useless when I couldn't get my mind to slow down long enough to figure something out.

My attention was diverted by a couple who hurried into the store, shaking snow off their clothes. I nudged Bailey but didn't voice my concerns over the sudden change in weather. She was enough of a paranoid passenger without me adding fuel to her anxiety.

The sun set in a hurry while we dilly-dallied. From inside the store, I could see only a fog of white swirling flakes as big as my hand. The idea of skipping the party and ordering room service flickered across my mind. I imagined snuggling under the quilts in my fluffy bed with a grilled cheese sandwich and a mound of crispy fries on a room service tray. My stomach growled in agreement.

Finally, Bailey's purchase was made. We tromped to the car through an accumulation of several inches of snow. I could feel the tension running from the base of my skull down to my toes which were curled tightly in my boots.

I kept a tight hold on my candy stash as we slip-slided across the parking lot to our car. I turned the heater on high and swished the snow off the windshield with the wipers. The parking lot cleared out as quickly as the flakes fell. Everyone's sense of urgency had been amplified. Bailey directed me to head out of town, reading from the directions she had scribbled on the scrap of paper.

"So um, I should tell you the directions to Arnie's house were on my phone. I remember them, for the most part." She turned her handmade map around and then around again. "We need to get back on the main road and then go north on Route 171 and then take the left fork in the road by the old mill. Or maybe it was by the old barn. We'll figure it out."

I drove with more focus than I knew was possible, hands clutched the steering wheel and teeth gritted.

Ten minutes later, I glanced at Bailey, "I've already gone more than two miles, but I haven't seen a fork, a mill, or a barn. Are you sure this is the right way?"

"Pretty sure."

"Like about seventy-five percent sure or more like twenty percent sure?"

Bailey turned on the interior light and studied her map again. "Somewhere between thirty and fifty percent sure."

We drove another two miles in silence as my wipers lost the battle against Mother Nature. We were the only car on the road and the farther we drove, the more nervous I became. I had the heat on high and the defroster blowing a gale inside the car, but outside the temperature dropped steadily.

"We must have missed the turnoff. Turn around as soon as you can," Bailey instructed. She flipped open my phone. "If I could get a signal, maybe I could call the resort for directions."

I rolled my shoulders to release the tension and dropped my speed to a crawl. I couldn't tell where the road ended and the shoulder began. Sweat rolled down the back of my sweater.

"I'll have to keep going until I find a driveway or a place wide enough to turn around."

Bailey remained silent. The only sound was the pounding of my heart. After what felt like ten miles, although the odometer indicated only one, I saw a rusty mailbox at the edge of a road.

"It's snowing harder so maybe we should see if there's a house we can stop at. I don't know if I can make it back to town."

Bailey looked at the driveway and held my phone up. "When we get home, I'm buying you a decent phone. This one doesn't get a signal here. What if there's no one home?"

"If there's a house, we'll knock and if no one is home, we can wait in the car until they return." I didn't say that if there was a house that matched the mailbox it might not have been occupied during my lifetime. If it was no more than a hunting cabin, then no one would be there until the season started. Worse if it wasn't used often, it could be without power which meant we might be stuck there until someone came to clear the road.

"Wait! I got a signal. It's only one bar but it should be enough to call someone and find out where we are."

She dialed the main number for High Mountain Ranch Resort. Someone answered but the voice was muffled and crackled with static. Before we could understand him, the signal dropped entirely. Bailey punched redial three times before tossing my phone on the dash.

"Want me to try?" I suggested halfheartedly. "Should we take a chance at the house or try to make it back to town?"

"Let's check out the house. If someone is there, they may have a landline. If not, the signal could be stronger there."

I turned down the drive moving at a snail's pace. The road wound to the right at a sharp angle and I almost slid off into the blue Spruce which stood sentry along the sides. Bailey had a grip on the dashboard with one hand and the phone in the other, periodically waving it around to find a signal. After creeping along for fifteen minutes we spotted a ramshackle building. It leaned like a domino, ready to topple at the slightest gust of wind. The roof buckled under the weight of previous snowfalls. The broken windowpanes stared back at us like empty eye sockets.

"It's abandoned. We'll have to turn around." I struggled to keep the quaver out of my voice. I couldn't see anything behind me except for the indentation of our tracks.

"I'd suggest we go inside but it doesn't look safe," she said.

I carefully made a three-point turn to retrace our path. We were now in a complete white out and I could only see a few feet in front of the headlights. I blinked my eyes as the heavy flakes mesmerized me.

I gently pressed the gas enough to move the car forward foot by foot. I was able to follow my tracks enough that we didn't wind up in a ditch or against a tree. The drive out was uphill, so I had to be sure to get sufficient speed to not slide backward. I took a deep breath; Bailey dropped the phone on the floor and used both hands to cling to the dashboard as I pressed harder on the accelerator.

The snow weighed down on everything around us, even inside the car. The heater coughed, gave a final blast of warm air, and then ceased its struggle.

Neither of us said a word. I was focused on keeping us safe and it felt as if Bailey believed my driving improved with silence. I doubted whether quiet or a marching band mattered at this point. My limited experience driving in snow flurries wouldn't hold up against this blizzard.

I made it to the top of the drive and immediately turned onto the road. I didn't want to risk stopping and besides, the likelihood of another car coming along was low.

Once back on the road, our situation didn't improve. In fact, it was worse. I couldn't see my previous tire tracks at all. I did my best to stay in the middle of what I guessed was the pavement. I managed to get around the first two curves in the road without a problem, but we had miles to go until the town was in sight. I had been so focused on the road I didn't remember if we passed any houses on the way out of town.

I tasted blood in my mouth from where I bit my lip until it bled. My knuckles were white and the muscles in my neck knotted. I could hear Bailey's rapid breathing beside me and, although she desperately wanted to, she didn't make any suggestions about how to better manage the weather conditions.

I accelerated enough to make it almost to the top of the next steep hill, but then we started a fast slide backwards.

"Holy heck. We're going to die!

"Jayne, steer in the direction of the skid."

"I'm trying but we're going backwards. I don't know how to steer into a backward skid."

The rental car blasted across the slippery surface of the snow-covered road, unable to find any traction. Pain stabbed my shoulder as I wrenched the steering wheel to the left and back to the right in a futile attempt to avoid kissing the side of the mountain.

Despite pumping the brakes as I thought I had been taught in driver's education, we continued to slide. It occurred to me too late that it was pump the brakes when you were moving forward.

"If I can just make it to the bottom, we'll be...ah." My words changed into a scream as the rear wheels gave up the battle and shot off the shoulder of the road. We hovered for a second before plunging backward down the mountain at Indy car speed.

I looked at Bailey. Her red hair stood straight up like when you shoot down a roller coaster from the highest point, and time is suspended for a fraction of a second. Instinctively I grabbed her hand. She was my best friend and if I was going to die, it might as well be with her. No point in steering into the skid now.

We roller-coastered over natural moguls, hung on two wheels and, when we were sure we would never stop, slammed into a behemoth pine tree, which ended all backward progress and dumped an iceberg-sized mound of snow over the top of the car.

The engine ticked in the silence as Bailey and I took in our surroundings. The headlights illuminated the zigzag path of destruction left by the car on its journey down the hill. Snow swirled around inside like a fairy dance before I realized the driver-side window was shattered. I could feel blood run down the side of my face and drip off my chin.

Unexpectedly we heard an explosion as Bailey's air bag deployed. Her head was slammed backward before the air whooshed out and deflated. A gunpowder smelling cloud mixed with the snowflakes and stuck to our faces like wet ash.

Blood gushed out of her nose. Neither of us moved.

"You're bleeding."

Bailey pointed at me, "So are you."

I realized I still had my foot pressed on the brake with the car in gear. I put it in park and then also set the parking brake. It was an unnecessary precaution since the tree prevented us from going any farther rearward.

Bailey held her hands to her nose. "We can't stop here."

"Duh," I snapped.

"Sorry, I guess it wasn't crucial to state the obvious." Her voice sounded muffled.

"I'm sorry. I didn't mean to be snippy." I looked around for my purse to find tissues. "We have to stop your nosebleed."

Bailey tilted her head back. "Ouch, that really hurts. It might be broken."

I turned the ignition off and on again. The car groaned, sputtered, and decided it wasn't worth the effort,

"We're stuck." I swallowed the lump in my throat. All my tears wouldn't help this situation.

She dug around her side of the car until she found my flip phone. "There's no signal here, but I could walk back to the house and try there."

"The car is still warm. How are you going to climb that hill with a bloody face? Besides, if you walk all the way back to the house and you don't get a signal, you could freeze. It's a bad idea to leave the vehicle and wander off."

"It's not far and that's the last place I was able to make a call. If no one comes down this road, we could be here all night."

"What do you think the odds are the car will miraculously start and we can drive up that hill?"

"Zero, but you get points for wishful thinking. The best we can do is hike up to the top and flag down someone on the road."

She climbed out of the warm car into the heavy wet blanket of snow. I unhooked my seat belt and struggled to open my door. I pushed and heaved but it was wedged shut. I climbed over the center console and out the passenger door to stand beside Bailey. Together we surveyed the situation.

The canopy of pines prevented an accumulation of snow in our location. It looked like a ninety-degree climb back to the road, one which I wouldn't have been comfortable attempting without the blizzard conditions. We carefully peered around the tree to determine if there was a way to go downward rather than up.

"I don't see any other way. We have to climb out."

I grabbed her arm. "We should stay in the car. It's freezing out here. Let's at least try to drive up."

Bailey shook her head. "You and I both know that isn't going to happen."

"Stranger things have happened."

"I'll give you one minute and then I'm going to climb up. If you make it out before me, wait for me at the top."

I crawled back in the car from her side and over the console to the driver's seat. I shivered so hard from fear and cold that I could barely hold my hand steady enough to turn the key. To my shock, the car started on the first try. The heater, however, refused to cooperate and would only send out bursts of freezing air and the wipers could only carve out a small opening in the center of the window. I hopped out, scraped the window clear of snow with my hands, and unstuck the wipers. Once again, I climbed in and gently pressed the pedal. The tires spun and dug in deeper.

Bailey and I looked at each other through the windshield. This was going to be a long night unless help came to rescue us soon. I wanted to cry, but I was quite sure my tears would simply freeze on their way down my cheeks.

She watched me struggle for another few minutes before she climbed back into the car.

"We have two choices. We can sit in the car until someone comes by to help us. Or we can walk back to the cabin to see if I can get a cell signal strong enough to call a tow truck."

"I vote for staying in the car. It's still snowing, and that cabin didn't look like anyone had lived there for years, except maybe rats." I shuddered.

Neither option was appealing. Eventually, the car would run out of gas and what little heat we managed to store would dissipate causing it to be as cold inside as out, especially with the broken driver's window. But then again, walking in a blizzard to a rickety cabin in the dark was crazy talk. I wasn't confident that I could make it up to the road before I became a frozen sculpture.

"If I can get a cell signal, then we could be back to the hotel enjoying a nice dinner."

The thought of dinner made my stomach growl, despite my nerves. My feet were only starting to thaw, and my light boots were made for cuteness, not for trudging through snow up to my knees.

"We need to stay in the car. Don't you watch those shows where people abandon their cars, walk for miles in circles, and then freeze to death? I'm the one who usually comes up with the crazy plans, not you."

"I can't just sit here waiting. I have to do something. I'll walk back toward the cabin where I last had a signal. If a car goes by before I get to the cabin, we'll be rescued. Besides, I'm wearing winter clothes and my feet are dry. If you get help before I come back, you know where I'll be. Regardless of whether or not I get a signal, I promise to walk back to the car in twenty minutes."

"I don't like it. It's dark out. It will take twenty minutes to get to the top of the hill."

"I hike worse in the heat of the summer in Arizona and I grew up spending winters in the snow. My body is accustomed to weather extremes. This doesn't bother me at all."

I heard her words but there was no weight behind them. My heart told me she was as frightened inside as me but putting up a brave front. Someone had to rescue us, and this was one time when

I wished Jonas was nearby. He was always calm in a Jayne emergency.

I gave Bailey my borrowed fake fur-lined gloves and my scarf because it was neon orange and could be seen more easily on the road. Before she stepped out, I grabbed her for a hug.

"Promise me you will be careful, and you'll be back here in twenty minutes."

She hugged me back hard. "Don't worry. I'll get a signal and have a tow truck here before you can miss me."

"I'm going to blow the horn every five minutes, so you know which direction to find me."

"I won't get lost."

"I'm blowing the horn." I pressed the M&M's into her hand. "Take these in case you need some energy."

She gave me a halfhearted smile. "Stay in the car. I'll come back for you. I promise." She clambered out and I watched her slow progress up the snow-covered hillside.

My chest hurt and I had a sick feeling in my stomach. Every five minutes I blew the horn in the hope that she could hear it and would return quickly. Even if she couldn't, it made me feel like I was helping.

I berated myself for not going with her but part of me knew I wouldn't make it ten steps without rushing back to the semi-warmth and safety of the car. I was sure someone would eventually drive down the road and either see her walking or see our tracks off the edge. With every tick of my watch, I regretted the decision to let her go alone. Was it a mistake that could cost one or both of us our lives? I berated myself for allowing fear to keep me immobile. I realized that it wasn't only this situation but in my life in general. I blew the horn in frustration and fear.

I continued to blow the horn for forty-five minutes. Bailey didn't return and the snow fell in smaller flakes. I moved into the back seat to stay dry. The driver's seat was buried under a thick blanket of white as if nature wanted to devour both it and me.

The first verse from an old Simon and Garfunkel song kept running through my head, *The Sounds of Silence*. My father used to play their music until it was embedded in my memory. Darkness didn't feel like my old friend. It felt like my enemy and I hated snow with as much love as I felt for cupcakes, my cat Bugsy, my family, and my friends all smushed in together.

I had waited long enough. It was time to act. I couldn't leave Bailey out there wandering alone. I had to go for help myself. How I would accomplish that goal was the million-dollar question for which I needed an answer.

CHAPTER EIGHT

An hour after Bailey left, I made up my mind to do something other than be buried under a white blanket. My imagination ran wild with thoughts of what could have happened to her. We needed help. Despite my advice to her not to leave the car, I felt compelled to do so myself. I didn't have any fingernails left to pick at and my neck hurt from swiveling it around in the hope I would see her return.

I wrote a note on our rental contract that said I was heading toward the town because I felt my odds of finding help were better. I left the keys in the car but turned off the headlights. No point in running down the battery. If Bailey returned, she could start it and hope the heater worked. If someone else found the car they would know which way we headed—in opposite directions.

The snow had petered out to sporadic light flakes. I didn't have the advantage of a cell phone flashlight, but the sky showed clear in patches and the moon glittered off the fresh snow as if lighting a path. I stepped out of the car in my bad decision boots and sunk up to mid-calf. This wouldn't be easy, but it was now my mission.

Without my gloves and scarf, the cold was a shock to my system, especially after the partial comfort of the car. I was hungry, tired, and cold but determined. I would not let my friend freeze trying to save us. Maybe that meant we would both freeze, but I would do what I could to prevent it.

I rationalized that I was young and healthy, even if I rarely exercised. I looked up to where I knew the road lay. I focused on placing one foot in front of the other. I stopped sporadically to catch my breath and risk a look back to make sure I was making progress.

My lungs burned from the cold and my breath came out in crystallized puffs. The blood caked on my cheek and a steady drip ran from my nose. The night was silent except for the crunching of my feet through the snow, which made me wonder if there might be a creature who watched and listened for such sounds to find his prey.

Once I swore I heard the sound of a vehicle on the road above me and saw what appeared to be headlights. I yelled but the sound disappeared into the night.

I grasped branches and scrabbled over rocks. I slipped but kept my forward momentum until, with my final effort, I fell face-first into a soft knoll. I rolled over to face the mute black sky. The flurries ceased and I could see moonlight through patches of clouds. I was on the road and not a moment too soon.

I stood on quivering legs and leaned against a tree to catch my breath. I was thankful that I could define the general area of the road and at least had a path to follow. To the right was the direction Bailey would have headed to the cabin. There were no visible footprints from where I stood.

The path to the left would head to the town. I debated which course would be the best. Follow the route Bailey took or go toward where I might get help. The options waged a war in my mind. I called out for Bailey in case she could hear me. My calls flew off into the night with no response. I turned left toward the town. If help were found, it was more likely to be closer to civilization than away from it. There was no time to waste.

The going was hazardous, but I managed to maneuver to places where the wind blew the snow in patterns that allowed me to walk more easily. Occasionally, I could feel the hardness of the road under my boots which made me hopeful and propelled me forward faster. Around a bend, I came to a fork in the road. I didn't remember which way was correct. Would the right take me to town? Or was it the left?

Before I could decide, I heard a crashing sound in the trees beside me. I stopped and looked around for a place to hide. My choices were limited to either the road or the woods. There was no way I could shimmy up a tree if a bear came after me. I searched my memories to remember what the wilderness experts advised if someone encountered a wild beast. The last time I encountered the moose, I ran and that didn't work out too well for me. What if it was a mountain lion? Should I freeze, make a loud noise, or be quiet? Which was it? I opted for freeze since I was too cold to outrun even a sloth at this point.

I held my breath and waited to see what type of beast would approach. I prayed this was my imagination run amok while I tried to stop the shaking of my legs. I knew that given the chance, animals take the path of least resistance, and the road was easier going than tromping through the trees and undergrowth.

A colossal bull moose stepped gingerly out of the woods and stared at me. He was intimidating, but in some odd way, I also found him calming. His deep brown eyes looked into mine and I swore he wanted to communicate. He watched me for a moment, unblinking, and then he turned and ambled down the fork to the left. He stopped, gazed over his shoulder at me, and grunted. I remained as still as a statue. He snorted, backed up, eyed me, and then looked in the direction he was headed. He repeated this process three times.

Sweat ran down my back. He smelled vaguely like Bugsy's cat box. I swallowed the lump in my throat.

Although I was sure that I left what little common sense I had in the car when I decided to walk for help, my mind believed that the moose wanted me to follow him. My numb toes and frozen face likely added to my confused state. I remembered moose crossing signs in town. If they frequented populated areas, I guessed he was guiding me. I tried to remember what the man at the stable told me. It was getting harder and harder to focus. I closed my eyes to clear the fog from my mind. Everything moved in slow motion.

Mr. Moose walked and I stumbled for thirty minutes until we reached a driveway. The house was close to the road and there was a pickup truck parked in front with a snowblade attached. The moose gave me one more grunt and then gracefully picked his way back into the woods beside the road.

I staggered up to the front door and banged with all my might. At this point I didn't care if a serial killer lived there. I needed help! When the door opened, I saw a man dressed in only his long underwear. My jaw dropped.

He looked me up and down. A smile turned up one side of his mouth and he nodded before waving me inside.

"Henri, thank heaven. I've been walking for what feels like hours. Bailey's lost and our car slid over a cliff. I need help. Maybe an ambulance," I yammered while my teeth chattered uncontrollably.

"Please let me take your coat. Would you like a drink? Perhaps some brandy?"

For a second, I wondered if I was hallucinating. Then again, if that was the case, I would imagine someone like Blake Shelton or Ryan Reynolds in his underwear and not my ski instructor.

"No, I don't want a drink. Is that your truck out front? I need the keys."

"You're here to borrow my truck?"

"No, I'm here because my car flew over a cliff and my friend Bailey is out there probably lost and freezing to death. Why do you think I would be banging on your door at this time of night?"

"Everyone loves me. I'm told I'm the sexiest man on the slopes." He flexed for effect. "It wouldn't be the first time someone came to my door for extra, shall we say, lessons."

I suppressed my gag reflex. "I hate to break the news to you, but you aren't my type, and this isn't the time to play games. Do you have a phone I can use? I'll call the sheriff to see if he can start a search and rescue. I'm sure something bad has happened to her."

Henri finally realized that I wasn't playing a game where I was the damsel in distress but was truly in distress. He grabbed his landline, called the sheriff's office, and told them the general area the car went off the road so they could send a deputy out.

Seeing me shivering in my wet shoes and pants, he insisted on loaning me a fresh pair of long underwear, a sweater, and way too big ski pants and jacket. Even though nothing fit, and I was a little wary of putting on his long underwear, I attached his suspenders to keep the pants up and for the first time in hours, I was warm. He didn't have any shoes that would fit me, so I changed into dry socks, which were an improvement.

He poured brandy into a flask and grabbed an emergency kit that he kept packed for this type of situation. Despite the first impression he gave when answering the door, his efficiency in an emergency was impressive. He hustled me out the door and gave me a boost into the passenger side of his lifted four-by-four truck.

"Give me a description of your friend. What was she wearing?"

"She was in the cross-country ski class with me. She's got red hair, she's not as tall as me, and she's the nicest person I know." I started to cry. "We were going to a party at a new business associate's house and got lost. I should have paid better attention when we left town. I was focused on dinner," I wailed.

He patted my arm as he backed out of the driveway and turned toward the way I had come. "We will find your friend. When I was

92

in Saskatchewan, I was a member of the rescue team. Henri knows how to find someone in the snow."

As much as it irritated me when he referred to himself in the third person, I prayed he told the truth. And I prayed that it wasn't too late.

"Maybe she found help and she's on her way to find me."

Henri didn't say anything but lowered the blade on this truck so he could clear the road as we went. At first, I thought he was wasting precious time, but then I considered that if we did find Bailey and she needed medical care, the road would need to be passable.

Even going slowly, we reached the place where Bailey and I slid off the road in less than ten minutes. He climbed down the hill and reported the car remained as I left it—empty. Bailey hadn't returned to the car. My note remained wedged in the heat vent, exactly where I stuffed it.

He brought my purse and Bailey's but left the keys in the ignition at my insistence. I imagined that if she somehow returned to the car, she could start it to warm up. I could sense that Henri didn't share my belief.

"Do you remember how far you went before you turned around?"

"I'm not sure of the distance we drove, but we turned around at a cabin. She was able to get a bar of cell service there. The cabin looked ready to collapse so we didn't go inside. I hope we'll find her there."

"The dispatcher didn't say anyone had called for assistance. You should always remain in your car. It's the first rule when driving in dangerous weather."

"I tried to convince her to wait but she was sure she would be able to get help faster."

He patted my hand again. "We will find her. Don't worry."

His words carried no conviction and my worries piled up higher than the snow pushed aside by the truck's blade. I shouldn't have let her leave the car. If she had stayed, we would both be safe now. My chest hurt and I swallowed to keep the anxiety from sending me into panic mode. One question kept forcing its way to the tip of my tongue, but fear kept me from voicing it aloud. What if we didn't find her?

We proceeded deliberately. Henri stopped if we thought we saw any sign of Bailey, like tracks in the snow or anything to suggest that she stayed on the road. We found a set of tire tracks which could have been from the rental car, but it was difficult to tell for sure.

"Look over there!" I bounced up and down on the seat and hurriedly powered down my window. "That's my scarf. Bailey was here."

The headlights captured a tree on the edge of the road with my unmistakable orange scarf dangling from its branches. If we hadn't been going around a turn, we would have missed it. Henri stopped the truck and we both jumped out. I yelled Bailey's name while he shined his flashlight around the area.

"These are human tracks." He pointed the light to the area leading up to the scarf. "But these over here are animal, probably wolf."

I continued calling for Bailey to no avail. The only response was the wind whispering through the trees. I untangled the scarf and held it close to me. So many questions swirled through my thoughts. I couldn't hold back my fears.

I turned to see that Henri had wandered down the road a short way. He kneeled in the snow and stared at something I couldn't see.

Thinking he found something else Bailey may have dropped, I called him. "Did you find something?"

"I need to radio the sheriff from my truck."

I felt as if my heart would explode and rushed over. "What is it?"

He pointed to tracks in the snow and something else. "Those are tire marks which could have come from your car. These tracks are human. I can't be sure if it's all the same person or not. Over here the tracks are animal. Mountain lion to be exact." He pointed to another spot in front of us. "And that looks to me like blood."

I drew in a breath sharply and it came out as a sob. This trip was supposed to be about fun and food. Sadly, it had been one catastrophe layered on top of another. If something happened to Bailey, I didn't know what I would do. She was the best friend I had and like a sister to me. What started as a happy girlfriend getaway already ended for one person in a snow-covered grave. I wondered if Bailey had reached the same fate. My legs gave out and I crashed to the ground.

I wasn't sure how much time had passed when I woke up to see the sheriff's face hovering over mine. I wasn't sure if I had been unconscious for two minutes or two days. I felt lightheaded and nauseous. I sat up slowly. The back of my head throbbed and my vision was blurry.

"Take it easy." He laid his huge hand on my shoulder and waved to someone behind me.

A woman of about my age in hospital scrubs and a heavy parka rushed to my side. She looked too young to be a doctor, but right now I didn't care if she was a dental assistant. All I wanted to know was had Bailey been found.

I tried to stand but she held me down and shone a light in my eyes. "Try to follow this light."

I did as she instructed but white dots danced in my eyes. "Sheriff, have you found my friend Bailey?"

"We're looking into it. You should know better than to leave a car when you're stranded."

"I tried to get her to wait for help. She was sure she could get cell service. She went for help and now she's lost." My voice faltered, and I fought back tears, struggling to maintain composure.

"We found a cell phone that might have been hers." He held up a flip phone.

"That's my phone. She took it with her to try to get a signal."

"Were you arguing before she left?"

"What?" I didn't understand where he was going with his question. "No, we didn't fight. Well, maybe we argued a little about how we got lost, but that happens, right?"

"Were you angry?"

"No, I..." I couldn't finish my sentence because a deputy summoned the sheriff to the other side of the road. They stood with their heads together in deep conversation. I strained my ears to hear what they said, but all I could hear was the pounding in my ears from my heartbeat.

The emergency medical person finished checking my vital signs and helped me stand up.

"You may have a concussion. We should send you to the hospital in Waverly and get a CT scan." She dabbed my forehead with something that stung. "You've got a cut on the side here that didn't come from your fall."

"I think the window cut it when we crashed into the tree at the bottom of the hill. I'm fine. I need to find out what happened to my friend."

"I can't force you to go but you have a good-sized bump on the back of your head from hitting the ground when you fainted. That's going to hurt. Pay attention for the next few hours to how you feel. If you are dizzy or nauseous or if the headache gets worse go immediately to urgent care."

I promised I would monitor my symptoms. I knew I lied. I couldn't focus on myself when my best friend was missing. Had she been dragged into the woods by a mountain lion? Had someone come along and given her a ride? What if she was wandering alone in the darkness, freezing and afraid? I needed answers and I was prepared to do whatever it took to get them.

CHAPTER NINE

It was well past midnight, and the sheriff was determined to get me out of his way. I had a choice of going to the hospital for an exam or going back to the resort. I opted for the resort, and rather than have his deputy drive me I coerced Henri into doing the job. A wrecker would come once it was daylight to pull my rental car up the hill and determine the damage. That was the least of my worries. A rental car can be replaced, but a best friend doesn't come along every day.

I was in a trance as Henri drove to my hotel with my phone clutched in my hand. As he pulled up at the lobby entrance, I shook myself to focus.

"Does the sheriff have any clues as to where Bailey might have gone?"

Henri shook his head. "I suspect he has an idea. Of course, he wouldn't share it with me."

"Bailey's missing, why didn't he call the National Guard or round up a posse or whatever it is that you do when someone is missing here?"

Henri heaved a sigh. Tapping his fingers on the steering wheel he paused while he contemplated his words. "I'll tell you what I suppose happened."

"Please don't tell me a mountain lion got Bailey. I honestly couldn't survive that thought." I shivered so hard that my teeth chattered despite the heat blasting through the truck vents.

"The tire tracks were not from your car. They were made by a larger, heavier vehicle. Someone picked her up and she's safe and warm."

"If that happened, she would have made the driver come back for me. She expected me to wait in the car for her to return. Bailey would never leave me there all night."

"I don't have an answer for that."

"You don't know Bailey. She is the kindest person I've ever met. She takes in every stray animal and even a teenager. You think something happened, don't you?"

Henri put his truck in park and looked over at me for a long minute. He patted my hand gently. "You should get some rest. The sheriff will find your friend."

"What if he doesn't? I need someone to find her before it's too late."

I gave up and let the tears stream down my cheeks. I would find another car and go looking for Bailey myself. If I couldn't rent a car, I would take a snowmobile and keep going until she was safe.

"The sheriff is good at his job. He'll find her. He doesn't need you wandering around making it two people who need to be rescued."

"I'm not convinced of that." I started to climb out of the truck, but a thought stopped me. "Henri, you said you ran search and rescue operations. Will you help me?"

He shook his head but then reconsidered. "Here's what I will do. If the sheriff has not found your friend by morning, call me. I will help you as much as I can. I am sure she'll be found before then." He dug in his console for a scrap of paper and scribbled on it. "Here's my cell phone number. Call me either way." He handed me the bag with my wet clothes.

I took both with trembling fingers. "I'll call. I hope you're right and she is okay. I can't stop thinking about the alternative."

"Good night, Mon Cher. Try to rest. Tomorrow could be a long day."

I stumbled on deadened feet up the steps to the lobby. My head throbbed and my stomach growled in protest from the lack of food. Despite that, the thought of eating even a cracker made me want to gag.

The clerk at the front desk eyed me warily as I filled a cup with hot chocolate to take back to my room. I hoped it would stop the tremors running through me, but I shook so violently that most of it spilled before I made it halfway.

I held my breath as I opened the door to our room and made a wish that I would find Bailey in her bed. The silence of the empty room crashed in my ears and trashed my hope. All was as we left it when we dashed out for dinner. I lay down on Bailey's bed, pulled her ski jacket over me, and let the tears cascade down my cheeks. I was too tired to undress and sure I wouldn't sleep but exhaustion won, and eventually I dozed.

I woke at daybreak to the sound of a chainsaw ripping through my head. Eyes closed; I reached over to nudge Jonas to stop snoring. I opened my eyes to see an empty bed. Then I remembered I was in Colorado with Bailey—only she was lost in a blizzard and not here either. I had snored myself awake, which would have been embarrassing except it made me choke up. Bleary-eyed, I stumbled out of bed to splash water on my face. I still wore Henri's clothes and my hair was a matted beehive. My face was chapped from the cold and my salty tears.

Where was Bailey? I stared at my reflection in the mirror. *You have to find her, no matter what it takes.*

Easier said than done. I would need a plan. The priority was a change of clothes, and then I would start making phone calls. If the Sheriff wasn't available, I would park myself in front of his desk until he told me what they had done to find her. I would search for her alone if that's what it took. Henri agreed to help me, and I could possibly round up more people from the resort staff.

I would call Jonas. I needed to call Jonas. If there was anyone, I could count on in a time of trouble it was him. After the shortest shower in history, I dressed in layers. I needed to be prepared to sit in an overheated hard chair at the Sheriff's office, trudge through snow, or climb mountains at a moment's notice. I wasn't going to return to the resort until I had my friend with me, or at least knew she was safe.

I placed a call to the Sheriff's Office. He, of course, wasn't available, so while I waited, I double-checked the room for any clues. She wasn't wearing her warmest clothes, but she did have good boots, a jacket, and my gloves. She had no food and no water.

I remembered that you should not eat snow for moisture because it dehydrates you. Your body must heat the ice to melt it. All those late nights after I got home from working my restaurant shift might be paying off if only I could remember more tips from any one of the dozen survival shows I watched. Of course, it didn't matter what I knew. It was all on Bailey to stay alive until I could find her.

It was too early to call Henri, but my pacing created a path in the carpet, so I dialed his number with my fingers crossed. After five rings it went to voice mail.

I needed to get out of the room or I would lose my mind. I gathered up everything I thought I might need for my version of a search and rescue mission and headed down to the lobby. I figured if, --*no when* -- I found Bailey she would be hungry and thirsty.

The snow was falling heavily enough that my footprints were covered as soon as I made them. The gift shop wasn't open, so I went into the restaurant. I wanted supplies I could carry in my pockets like water or cookies. Those weren't options at the restaurant. Instead, I ordered takeout for Bailey and something for myself as well. I rationalized that it made no sense for me to wander the countryside without ample fortification.

I explained my predicament to the server, Faye, and asked her to keep an eye out for Bailey or anyone strange lurking about the resort. I have no idea what would qualify as strange or lurking, but at least I felt like I was doing something.

I wolfed down a bowl of oatmeal, which I despised but it was the fastest option and fortifying. It stuck in my throat like sludge. Faye brought me an egg and cheese sandwich wrapped in foil and two bottles of water. She hugged me as I left the restaurant and wished me luck. As I walked out the door, I had a thought and rushed back to her.

"There was a guest here that Bailey met. His first name is Arnie. I don't know his last name. He has property around here not far from town. That's where we were headed when we got stuck in the snowstorm. Do you know who he is?"

She tapped her pen against her chin and thought for a minute. "The name doesn't ring a bell. What does he look like?"

I closed my eyes to focus on our first night at the resort. I recalled he was sitting at the bar and wasn't wearing socks under his alligator loafers. What hair he had was dyed a dark black, probably five feet six inches, with a slight paunch. He had a glass of red wine, likely a Cabernet Franc due to the rich color, and he was eating the Oysters Rockefeller. He didn't eat the bread the bartender brought which surprised me because most people like to have bread to soak up any juices left from the oysters and butter. He touched his mouth with his napkin after every bite and his nails were nicely manicured.

I repeated all of this to Faye, who looked at me with a strange expression on her face. I shrugged my shoulders. It was a quirk of mine that I could remember odd details but not where I left my car keys.

"I'll ask around. Maybe the bartender knows him. He comes on shift around three today so you should stop by and talk to him then."

I promised I would but hoped Bailey would be found long before then. We could be sitting at the same bar laughing over how she stayed the night in the ramshackle cabin and pried open a can of cold beans for her dinner. Or maybe a gorgeous wealthy computer nerd, like herself, found her, took her to his mountainside cabin, and served her foie gras and champagne. Well, not foie gras because she's a vegetarian and it's disgusting to force-feed a duck more food than it would ever eat to make its liver fatty. I shivered at the thought of it.

I headed out to the parking lot to drive over to the Sheriff's office before I remembered that I had no car. I stomped back inside and asked the front desk clerk how I could rent another one. I needed a sturdy four-wheel drive vehicle that could scale a snow-covered mountain, if necessary. There were no cars available at the only leasing place in town, so I used my fallback plan and called Henri again. Still no answer, so I knew it was time to call Jonas.

I missed him more than I thought was possible. In the brief time we had been dating, he had become my sounding board, my voice of reason, and a calming presence. He was my confidant and my hero. and I realized that I might be in love with him.

It should have been a love at first sight experience as he was everything that I ever wanted. He was the total package in the looks department, loved animals, and was a hard worker, but those alarm bells kept ringing in my head. Was he too good for me? Did I deserve that kind of happiness? Would he figure out what a mess I am and leave me when I finally let him in my heart?

I considered that since we met, there had been several murders in which I was involved, inadvertently of course. Was I unconsciously pushing him away so he would prove to me how much he wanted me or was I trying to keep him safe? My head throbbed with the questions I didn't want to face and the answers that might break my heart.

Ultimately, I had to admit to myself that it was my hesitation that pushed Jonas away from me and maybe into the arms of his ex-wife. How could I call him and tell him I found another dead body and that now Bailey was missing too? Would he stick by me through more chaos? Death has a way of making its face known whether you want to see it or not. Now was the time to find out who my real friends were.

I took a seat off to the side of the lobby not far from the fireplace, listened to the crackle of the logs, and stared at my flip phone. I jumped as a log splintered and split into a dozen pieces, sending the smell of pine and cedar swirling around me. I bit my lip and dialed Jonas. This could go great or it could go so wrong, but I had to make the call.

When he answered on the second ring, I was so startled I dropped my phone and disconnected. He called back as I struggled to locate my phone under the chair.

"Hi, darlin.' Been missing you."

My heart swelled. I swallowed and took a deep breath to compose myself, but it didn't work.

"Oh Jonas, I miss you too."

"What's wrong?"

I blurted out the entire story without stopping to breathe, "Bailey is missing. We were driving last night. I couldn't keep the car on the road. We slid backward down a mountain and hit a tree. She left to find help. No one knows where she is. I begged her not to go but she was determined. I waited, but she didn't come back. I followed a moose to get help. We found my scarf but there was blood on it and no Bailey. I don't know what to do," I wailed.

Jonas cleared his throat. "Hang on. Say that again. Did you say Bailey is missing? You slid off a mountain? Are you okay?"

"I'm okay but I'm not okay at all." I softened the volume of my voice as people walking through the lobby were staring.

"Slow down. You aren't making any sense."

"Bailey and I were headed to a party at the house of her new client. The snow was blinding and we slid off the road over a ravine. I've never been so afraid in my life, except for when that killer was holding me with a gun pointed at my head. And the moose was gigantic. I didn't know if I was supposed to follow him or run away. Ultimately, I followed him and he led me to safety."

I considered the part about the moose didn't make sense even to myself. I took a deep breath and tried again.

"I waited for Bailey to come back to the car, but she never did. That's when I knew I had to go by myself for help. Once I got help, we went back down the road the way I'd come to try to find her. Beyond where the rental car went off the road, we saw the scarf I loaned her caught on a tree branch. She wasn't anywhere to be found. The sheriff is involved, but he won't tell me what he's doing. There were animal tracks. She's out there somewhere alone. She could be hurt or, or, worse!"

Jonas was silent for a minute, which felt like an hour. "Do you want me to come?"

I really wanted him to come and make it all better, but the reality was I didn't think he could. Jonas didn't know the area. As far as I knew, he had never driven a snowmobile. I didn't know if he even owned snow boots. As much as I knew I wanted him to save me again, I wanted, just this once, to fix it myself. I was tired of being a helpless girl who was constantly rescued by a guy.

CHAPTER TEN

"I don't know what to do. I'm afraid something bad has happened."

Jonas spoke slowly, "Take a deep breath. Bailey is one of the smartest people I've ever met. She wouldn't just wander around in the snow aimlessly. I'll bet she got a ride and just doesn't have a cell phone signal to call you. Or maybe she is holed up in a cabin waiting for the weather to break." His words sounded convincing but the tone in his voice said he didn't believe himself either.

"She didn't have a cell phone with her. Hers was stolen and she didn't have time to activate a new one. She took mine, but the Sheriff found it on the road."

"When did you last talk to the sheriff?"

"I left a message this morning. The dispatcher said he wasn't in."

"So maybe he's out looking for Bailey right now. There's a ski resort there and I'll bet they have search and rescue teams for lost skiers. They might be following her footprints right now."

"The only prints we saw last night were animal ones." Then I remembered a set of tire tracks. "Wait, I did see tire tracks. I thought it was from our rental car."

"I'll bet someone gave her a ride to the next town. I can cancel my appointments and catch the next flight up if you want."

Even though Jonas had a good business doing remodel work, he was a one-man operation for the most part and if he didn't work, he wouldn't get paid. Asking him to come just to hold my hand seemed wrong. I squirmed in the chair and debated with myself.

"No, you're probably right. I'm sure the sheriff has it under control and I'm overreacting. It's not been the trip we imagined, and I'm so anxious about Bailey."

"Are you sure? I could be up there by tonight at the latest. I'm worried about you."

I sighed. It was hard doing the right thing. "I'm sure."

"You won't go off looking for her alone, will you? Promise me."

I didn't want to lie to him. At the same time, I couldn't say I wouldn't do that exact thing as soon as we hung up. I hadn't figured out how I was going to find Bailey; only that I would.

"I promise to call the sheriff and get an update. If he has a search party, I will be part of it."

"I guess that's as much as I can ask for."

"I'm sorry I haven't even asked how you are. I got the message that said you wanted to talk to me when I get back. Is everything okay there?" I figured now was as good a time as any to rip off the bandage if he was going to break up with me. What could be worse than one dead body and Bailey missing?

"It's nothing that can't wait. You have enough on your mind with Bailey missing. You'll be home soon, and we'll talk then."

"I do miss you and not just because everything is crazy here."

"I miss you too. Call me as soon as you know something."

"I will."

"And darlin' try to stay safe."

With that, Jonas hung up. I sat staring at my phone, willing it to ring again and this time to be Bailey. My stomach was on the verge of rejecting the food I had hastily crammed down. Her sandwich sat squished in my pocket, congealing into a glob. It was time for action.

Henri hadn't returned my call, so I decided to head down to the stable. I may not know how to drive a snowmobile, but thanks to lessons as a girl and time in the saddle on Jonas's horse, I did know how to ride a horse, and I knew exactly where to find one.

I was grateful that the walk to the stables was cleared of snow and only a short distance from our room. Every cell of my body ached from exertion and stress. A cold had settled into my bones that I felt wouldn't dissipate until the Arizona summer. I promised myself that when this ordeal ended, I would stay in my tiny town of Cave Creek and not venture farther than downtown Scottsdale. If I didn't see snow again in my lifetime, it wouldn't be a loss.

I trudged to the barn, planning as I walked how I might convince Travis to hook up the team for an impromptu sleigh ride. If that wasn't an option, I hoped there was a saddle large enough to fit a draft horse. I may not have been a confident server, nor a confident girlfriend, but I was sassy enough to believe I could manage two thousand pounds of horse, even if I had to ride bareback. On second thought, I decided bareback wasn't a clever idea. I had no way to get on and off a horse that stood eighteen hands.

Translated into non-horse person language, that puts a Clydesdale's height at approximately six feet at the withers, which is the highest point of the back by the neck. It would be the equivalent of vaulting onto the top of a man's head. Even at my height of five feet nine inches, it was an impossible task. I needed a smaller horse and a saddle.

The odor of horse manure blended with the sweet smell of hay. I could hear the chomp, chomp sound of equine breakfast. I paused to absorb the scene and wrapped my mind in the cocoon of security it gave me. Many of my best childhood memories involved horses. From the time I could walk, I dreamed of owning my own horse. It wasn't possible on my dad's policeman's budget, but my parents ensured I was able to take lessons and ride as often as possible.

I heard someone whistling off-tune. "Hello. Is anyone here?"

There was no answer, so I continued down the center aisle of the barn checking each stall as I went. Each horse had his name engraved on a plaque above the stall door. There was Titan, Simba, Midas, and Matilda. I reached over and stroked Matilda's soft nose, sorry that I didn't think to bring treats. When I reached the last stall, I found Travis focused on grooming a chestnut gelding with a mane that reached down to his shoulders. Travis spoke to the horse in a soothing tone and was rewarded with a head butt which almost knocked him off his feet.

"Whoa there, buddy," he said with a laugh.

"Hi, Travis."

He jumped at the sound of my voice. "Sleigh rides were canceled today because the snow is too deep. You can reschedule for another day if you want."

"I'm not here for the sleigh ride, but I was hoping for something else."

He gave the horse a final brush before leaving the stall. "I'm not sure I want to know why you're here."

"My friend and I went off the road last night in the snowstorm. Our car was abandoned halfway down an embankment and Bailey is missing. She left the car to go for help and she hasn't been seen or heard from since. I need your help."

"Did you call the sheriff?"

"Yes, and he came out last night, but I haven't heard back from him today." I checked my phone on the off chance someone had called. No luck.

"What do you think I can do?"

"I need to borrow a horse. I want to search for Bailey on my own. I know which direction she headed."

"You want to take one of *these* horses on a search and rescue mission?"

"Ideally a smaller version if you have one."

Travis shook his head and walked down the aisle away from me. I heard him mumble something that sounded like crazy girl. He opened the office door and closed it in my face. He didn't know I wouldn't give up that easily.

I shoved the door open so hard it slammed into the wall and bounced back in my face.

"These aren't riding horses. They are specially trained priceless animals, and I don't lend them out to anyone."

"I know how to ride, and I would be incredibly careful. I have to find my friend. This might be the only way I have to do it."

"Why don't you call the sheriff again? He's well respected and he knows his job. You can't go riding off into the mountains with no idea of where to go. You'd get lost and take my horse with you. I can't allow that."

"Why don't you go with me? I'll pay you. We can think of it as a trail ride but with the added benefit of rescuing someone in need. You'd be a hero."

I decided to try a different tactic. "Bailey's my best friend. She brought me on this trip so we could spend girlfriend time together. I've never known a person who cared more about others than she does. She's the first person to volunteer when someone needs a hand or if there's an animal that needs a home. She would give you the shirt off her back or put her house up to raise your bail. She needs me right now and I have to come through."

He looked down and I could see the wheels turning. "I suppose we could take two horses out for a trail ride. Not those horses, mind you. I do have trail-riding horses and mules who know the area well."

My knees wobbled. "Thank you! Can we leave now?"

"It will take me an hour to get the animals brought up from the pasture, groomed, and saddled. Come back then."

"I'll help. I can groom and saddle my horse. We can't waste another minute."

"Something tells me I'm going to regret this but come on. Grab those two halters and follow me."

Travis poured grain into a bucket and headed out the gate behind the barn. He whistled and in minutes three horses and two mules headed in our direction. He singled out a sturdy mule named Candy for me and one for himself. We led them up to the barn and attached the halters to rings on the wall. I grabbed a curry comb and worked in a frenzy to clean my mule's coat so I could saddle her up as fast as possible.

In only fifteen minutes, we had western saddles on both mules. Travis disappeared into the office and returned with a revolver strapped to his hip like a gunslinger. I looked at him with a question in my eyes.

He put a canister into my saddlebag. "Where we're going there are mountain lions and wolves. I'm giving you bear spray. Hopefully, you won't get close enough to use it, but better safe than sorry."

He gave me a leg up on my mule and mounted his. He reined away from the barn, and we started down the path. It was the same one I traveled with Travis on the day I found poor Harry's body.

Travis assured me he knew the mountains better than anyone. He was a native of the area and he led rides in the warmer months in addition to driving the sleigh in the winter. I described the route Bailey, and I took the prior evening. Travis was sure he knew a shortcut that would take us through a pass that wound down to the road on the other side of town. What would be a six-mile journey from the resort by car would be only two miles by mule.

The beginning of the ride traversed a path cleared earlier that morning. We rode in silence, side by side. My mule sensed my

111

anxiety and tossed her head, flickering her ears back and forward. I tried to slow my heartbeat. Please let Bailey be okay and please let us find her soon I prayed.

The pine-scented air was clear and crisp, the sky cloudless. Sun glistened off the fresh snow like white sapphires. I listened to the sound of Candy's hooves tromping along the path. Travis's hat was pulled low over his face and his mouth was set in a determined line.

"We'll be leaving the packed trail soon and heading through that pass. Follow me and pay attention. There's no telling what we might come across out there. We're going to keep to the trail the wildlife uses. That will help us stay out of the deeper drifts."

I needed to fill the void with chatter, so I asked Travis about himself. It was like fishing without any bait. At first, he answered in single syllables. Gradually he warmed up to me and told me about his childhood in Colorado, his love of horses, and his dream of becoming a rodeo cowboy. As we slogged on, he described the colors of fall and the first buds of spring on the mountain. He told me about the lore of High Mountain and how the First American people lived here before white settlers arrived.

It was an effort for the mules to trek through the snow to the top of the pass, so we took a break and dismounted. While we rested, I asked the question, even though I knew I might not like his answer.

"Do you think Bailey's out here somewhere?"

He stroked his mule's ear and cleared his throat. "It's pretty cold out here for a woman to be wandering around. We got about five inches of snow last night on top of what we already had."

"I hope you're going to say, but..."

"It's possible if she's here, she survived. She might have found a place to shelter."

"She needs to be okay."

We mounted and continued our plodding pace. I wanted to gallop, but progress, even slow, was better than sitting in the hotel room waiting. I pulled my phone out of my pocket and checked for a signal. There was one bar and no missed calls. Where was the sheriff and why hadn't he called me back yet?

Travis led me through a wooded area which opened into a pasture. At the far end, I could see the back of the cabin with the sagging roof where Bailey and I had turned around. I felt hope surge through me as we neared, only to have it dashed when there was no sign of activity. We rode around to the front and Travis handed me his reins.

"Wait here with the mules. I'll look inside. It's only one room so if she's in there I can tell quickly."

I sensed from the expression on his face he dreaded what he might find. The shattered windowpanes wouldn't have protected her from the cold. If Bailey had managed to walk here, I knew she would have called out when she heard us ride up. My shoulders sagged with the expectation that she wasn't there, or worse.

He stepped gingerly on the rickety porch and peered in the window. I held my breath until he shook his head in the negative and mounted.

"Should we try going down the road?"

"There's a different way back to the stables that takes us by a stream. I want to water the mules and give them a break there. The old elk trail crosses closer to where you say your car went off the road. We can look for footprints as we go."

I heard a helicopter overhead. Travis and I followed its path with our eyes across the sky as it hovered and moved on.

He pointed. "That'll be the sheriff's posse looking for your friend. He's probably got a team on horseback and one on snowmobile. We may intersect them." He clicked to his mule and gave her a nudge with his legs.

113

Candy and I followed behind, both of our heads lowered with effort. Travis was right, the mules were tiring. I felt disappointment through to my bones.

When I was arrested and charged with the murder of the mayor of Cave Creek, Bailey was the one to bail me out of jail. When I battled for my life against a killer, it was Bailey who used her skills to track my car's GPS and find me just in time. When Jenny's mother was murdered and she had nowhere to go, Bailey stepped up and gave her a safe place. She was my shoulder to cry on when I argued with Jonas. She was the sister I never had. How could I fail her the one time she needed me?

After another thirty minutes of riding through fresh snow, we came to a rapid stream. Ice crusted the shore. We dismounted and watered the mules. I hadn't ridden in months and my legs threatened to give out when I tried to stand. Travis attached feedbags from his saddlebag to their bridles and let the mules eat while we all rested.

"We'll head downstream where there's a natural bridge and cross there. It's a short ride down an old mining road, and we'll be at the bottom of the crest where you say you ran off the road."

I nodded. I had nothing but determination to contribute. My energy was too sapped to talk. After a short break, we mounted up, ready to finish our mission.

Deep in thought, I was almost unseated when Candy's head flew up and she leaped to the side. Travis whirled around in the saddle just in time to see a yearling bear cub crash onto the path steps in front of me. I scrambled to reach the bear spray in my saddle bag and still hang on.

The cub seemed more curious than afraid. Candy and I weren't waiting around for his mom to come to his rescue. Travis shouted. Candy spun around on her hindquarters and bolted in the direction we came from. For a calm mule, she was able to go zero to sixty in five seconds flat. I lost both stirrups and grabbed onto the horn of the saddle for my life.

We galloped faster than I thought possible for a mule back the way we came. I ducked as Candy whirled around a bend and almost beheaded me with a low branch. I heard a gunshot behind me and prayed no one was hurt, including the bear.

It was minutes before I was able to pull Candy up to a stop. We both panted from the effort and her neck was lathered in sweat. My heart threatened to explode in my chest. With a quivering hand, I gently stroked her neck to calm us both, certain the threat was well behind us based on the distance we covered.

Travis caught up to us, his gun still drawn.

"Are you okay?"

I swallowed and nodded, unable to formulate words.

"He's gone. I only fired a warning shot to make the baby run back to his momma. Black bears aren't mean unless they are threatened, but a yearling cub won't be far from his mother, and she can get riled up." He motioned for me to follow him, and we rode back over the same trail.

I kept a watchful eye on my surroundings, a tight rein on my mule, and stayed that way for the remainder of the ride. My spirits sunk more as each stride brought us closer to the barn and farther from finding Bailey. We didn't encounter any searchers, but we crisscrossed hoof prints and snowmobile tracks. Periodically I checked my phone with the same result. No messages, no calls.

I could tell by the hunch of Travis's shoulders that he felt frustrated. I was grateful we didn't have a use for either the bear spray or the pistol again. The barn was quiet except for whinnies greeting from the draft horses. Candy whinnied in return and picked up her pace. I knew she was anxious to return to the warmth of the barn. I slipped down from the saddle and pulled it off her. Her back was damp from the exertion, so I brushed her down before I put her in an empty stall. I gave her fresh water and a leaf of hay.

I felt as limp as a ragdoll. Travis steered me to the office and pushed me to sit on the worn leather sofa. He microwaved a cup of hot chocolate and placed it in my hand. I slumped in the seat and put my face in my hands. We failed.

"Hey, don't be upset. We saw the effort the sheriff's department is making. He's got everyone looking for your friend. The people around here are like family, and they won't quit until they find her."

"What if they find her too late?"

Travis rubbed his chin. "You don't have a choice but to believe it won't be too late."

"I'm trying but every minute that passes makes it harder."

My imagination flew in every direction. There were dangerous animals, ones which Travis felt he needed to carry a pistol to protect us from. There were dangerous people out there too. I knew that firsthand. "Where could she be?"

Before he could figure out a plausible answer, my phone rang. I dug it out of my pocket and flipped it open. It was the sheriff with an update of sorts. They hadn't found Bailey -- a fact I didn't need him to confirm. He promised me the team would remain on patrol and extend the search area. Strangely, he asked me to be at the station within the hour to answer questions. He reminded me to bring the clothes I wore when I found Harry and to bring something that had Bailey's scent.

I thanked Travis for taking a chance with me and for spending hours of his day on my quest. He patted my shoulder awkwardly and told me to call him as soon as I heard anything. As I left the barn, he called out to me.

"I'll keep looking. If she isn't found by tomorrow, I'll join the recovery, er I mean, search team. Don't give up hope."

Travis's slip of the tongue made my heart stop for a breath. I prayed it was still a search and not the recovery of a body.

CHAPTER ELEVEN

After my excursion with Travis, I walked back to my room as quickly as my legs would carry me. I remembered the sandwich I had packed in case we found Bailey. It was squished into a flat splotch of greasy bread with egg and cheese oozing out the sides. I tossed it in the trash can and stood over Bailey's open suitcase.

I needed to bring an item that belonged to Bailey, preferably one that had her scent embedded. Underwear was absolutely out of the question. She would be mortified if I gave the sheriff her granny panties. Then again, if it helped them find her, I would bring her entire suitcase, clean or dirty.

I opted for the t-shirt she wore the first day we cross-country skied. I could smell her light jasmine perfume on it, so I rationalized it was worn but not overly embarrassing. I wrapped it in the dry cleaning bag from the closet and stuffed my clothes in my laundry bag.

I changed into my only clean jeans and sweater to smell less like a mule and headed to the lobby to catch a cab into town. I had limited freezing-weather clothing choices left if the sheriff kept my clothes.

A brief time later, I sat in the hard-backed vinyl chair in front of a metal desk large enough to sleep on while the sheriff shuffled papers. The room had a strong smell of cleaning fluid and traces of cigar smoke. The fluorescent lights hummed overhead and made my eyes blink from the glare.

"Miss Stanford, thank you for coming in."

"Please call me Jayne. I'm happy to do anything I can to help find my friend."

"Would you care for coffee? Water? As you know we haven't found your friend. I do have some questions for you which might shed some light on what's happening."

"Water, please. I'll do my best."

He set a bottle of water on the desk in front of me and steepled his fingers. "Let me start with the reason you were driving in that area during a snowstorm. Why did you ignore the warnings?"

"We never heard any warnings. We were invited to a party at the house of a new client of Bailey's. His name is Arnie, and he lives in the area. Do you know him?"

"I'm not familiar with everyone who lives here. What is his last name and his address?"

"That's the problem. I don't know. Bailey was going to do some work for his company, and she had his address on her phone. As you know, her phone was stolen from our room, along with her laptop and some files."

He reached behind him onto a desk overflowing with stacks of manilla folders and picked up a large clear plastic bag with a laptop inside. "Do you recognize this?"

I picked up the bag with two fingers and stared at it. "This looks like Bailey's laptop. She had similar decals on the top but, I can't be sure."

"Do you know her password?"

I closed my eyes and rubbed my temples. Bailey accessed her PC in front of me all the time. Did I remember what combination of keys she entered?

"I don't remember the password. She might have used her face or her fingerprint. Where did you find it?"

"I'll ask the questions, Miss." He took the laptop from my hands. "What was Miss Chauncey's relationship with Mr. Harry Schepp."

"I don't understand. She didn't have a relationship with Harry. We only met him at the resort the first night we were here. I remember seeing him behind me in the rental car line and then a few times here and there."

"Did Miss Chauncey discuss her work? Specifically, did she mention any contact with Schepp Investigations?"

"No, we didn't talk about her work. Well, sometimes she would make general comments like when she signed a new client, or she was installing a new security program. Most of what she did sounded like gibberish to me."

"If you want to help us find your friend you need to cooperate."

"I am cooperating! What does any of this have to do with Bailey trying to find help when we run off the road?"

Then the lightbulb went on in my sleep-deprived, frozen brain. "Do you think Bailey's disappearance is connected to Harry's murder? You do, oh my God!" I slapped my hand over my mouth.

"We suspect there is a connection between your friend and Harry Schepp. Although we couldn't access Miss Chauncey's laptop, we did find evidence in Mr. Schepp's room that he was following her."

"Why would he do that? Bailey hasn't done anything wrong. I don't understand all she does, but I know she helps companies protect confidential information. Why do you think Harry was tracking her?"

"Only he could have answered that, so we'll never know the truth. The files we confiscated show he tracked her for several months. He knew where she lived, who came and went from her house, who she met with, what she did for a living, how much money she made, even down to what she bought at the grocery store. You must know a reason he would assemble all those details."

I shook my head. "I honestly can't think of a reason." It occurred to me that Bailey's foster daughter, Jenny, was alone at her home. "I haven't called her foster daughter to tell her Bailey is missing. If someone hired Harry to follow Bailey, could Jenny be in danger?"

"I'll place a call to the sheriff in Maricopa and ask him to check on her. How old is her daughter? Do we need Social Services?"

"She's eighteen. Bailey would be devastated if anything happened to her."
Sheriff Cox picked up his phone and gave orders for someone to contact the sheriff in Arizona.

While he talked, I examined his office. There were photos of him taken with celebrities, awards, and even his college diploma. I was most impressed by a framed note on the wall. It was written in a child's hand with what appeared to be crayon. The note read, "Thank you for saving my life and rescuing my puppy too. Love, Annie" I looked at the sheriff with raised eyebrows and a new respect.

He shrugged at me and hung up the phone. "Someone will stop by and check on the girl. It might be a good idea for her to stay with friends until this is resolved."

"I'll call her as soon as we're done. I don't want her to find out from the police that Bailey is missing."

"Let's get back to business. Do any of these names look familiar to you? Perhaps Miss Chauncey mentioned them in passing. You might have overheard a conversation she had."

"I'll try to remember."

He passed me a piece of paper with four typewritten names: Core Logistics, Walter Caldwell, Walter Caldwell, Jr., and Lauren Davis. I studied them carefully. Come on Jayne, I told myself, think. Bailey must have mentioned one of these names for the sheriff to feel they were significant enough to mention.

There was something significant about Core Logistics. I couldn't quite get it into focus. I shut my eyes, pressed my fingers to my temples, and ran through my memory like the pages of a calendar. Where had I heard that name? There was a blank space. I repeated it aloud to see if that provoked an image. Nothing.

Sheriff Cox cleared his throat. "Anything?"

I shook my head. "I don't think Bailey ever mentioned any of these names."

He plucked the sheet from my hands and inserted it back into a folder.

My attention was riveted on the folder, so I didn't hear his next question.

"Excuse me, Miss Stanford. I said, did you bring the clothes as I asked?"

"Sorry, yes." I snapped out of my trance and reached down to the bags of clothing. "The laundry bag is a shirt of Bailey's she wore snowshoeing. This other bag has my clothes from the day I found Harry. I don't have much else to wear so I hope you don't have to keep these." I handed him the bags.

"I doubt there is much information to be gleaned from your clothing, nevertheless we'll take a look."

"Can you tell me what you're doing to find Bailey?"

"We're doing everything in our power. I have limited resources, but we've mobilized volunteers from all over the county. No one hates a missing person in my county more than me."

"Can I join in the search somehow? I need to be doing something useful to find her."

"Check with the dispatcher at the front on your way out and he'll give you information on the search parties. We can use every available person to help."

I stood thinking our time was up. The sheriff gestured for me to be seated. "A few more items I would like to go over with you."

"Who's paying for your hotel room? I know you work in a restaurant, which unless you are doing more than serving meals, wouldn't put you in the income bracket to afford the High Mountain Lodge. We accessed Miss Chauncey's credit cards and there are no charges for the hotel room. There is one charge for dinner two nights ago and nothing else."

I was proud that I was a restaurant worker. I did the best job I could to make my guest's dining experience a good one. Never until this moment had I felt ashamed of my profession. I gulped the water which sent me into a coughing fit.

"Bailey planned this trip last minute to meet with the client, Arnie, I told you about. I can't explain why the charges weren't on her credit card. She invited me because she wanted a girlfriend getaway. This was the anniversary of her sister's passing and she was dreading being alone. That's why she decided to invite me."

"So, you're saying you never saw a name or a credit card receipt?"

"Bailey signed for everything at the resort."

A heavy feeling settled over me. I mentally kicked myself for not asking more questions. Why didn't I ask Bailey about Arnie? Why had I never paid attention when she rambled on about how important data security was for everyone in the internet world? I sucked as a friend. Hang on Jayne, you aren't done here yet, I told myself.

"Just one more question. Since you arrived here, who have you met with or spoken to?"

I considered everyone whose paths we'd crossed.

"First there was the rental car lady. She was nice and upgraded us without extra charge. Then the server at the restaurant where we stopped for lunch. He gave me extra fries. Oh wait, there were two flight attendants, I don't remember their names. They didn't seem upset when I spilled my drink right after takeoff. The bellman who opened the door, the first clerk who registered us, and the housekeeper we saw in the hallway a few times. There was the bartender, James. I've talked to him a couple of times. Arnie, who Bailey had a meeting with and a potential job. The server at the resort restaurant. Her name was Marie. Poor Harry, who I spoke to only once by the s'mores on our first night here. Henri my ski instructor. He pronounces that the French way, so it sounds sort of like ornery."

The sheriff tapped his pen and cleared his throat. "That's a good start but maybe you could narrow the list down to those people you had a conversation with who weren't just doing a job which required them to speak to you."

I sighed. On television, the detectives always told the witnesses to try to remember everything because they couldn't know what was or wasn't important. Reality was different.

"That would be Arnie and Harry. Everyone else we spoke to was working."

Sensing my frustration, he added, "When you go back to your hotel, I want you to write down everyone. You can drop it back here or have the hotel fax it to me."

"Did Harry have any family?"

"Why do you ask?"

"I was worried that there was no one to see that he received a proper burial. I only met him one time but he seemed lonely to me."

"We were able to track down a family member. Now, if there isn't anything else."

"I have one more question for you Sheriff."

He folded his arms across his broad chest and leaned back in his chair. "Shoot."

"What do you think happened to Bailey? Do you think whoever killed Harry had a reason to go after Bailey?"

"I'll be honest with you. There was blood, which appeared to be human, on the road where she disappeared. There was also another set of tire tracks. Ones which I don't believe to be from your rental car. I suspect whoever hired, and maybe killed Harry Schepp, has endangered your friend."

I sucked in a breath. This wasn't the news I hoped to hear from him. "Do you think someone killed Bailey and left her body in the woods, just like Harry?"

"I won't say that. I will say we are doing everything in our power to find her."

My legs jiggled uncontrollably, and I bit my fingernail. Bailey wasn't wandering alone on the snow-covered mountain. Even if the Sheriff wouldn't say the words, someone had come along with no plan to rescue us. That someone might have been after Bailey all along and this was a setup to hurt her. She must have known information important enough to kill for. How could I find out what it was in time to save her? If it wasn't already too late.

I left the Sheriff's Office and took a rideshare back to the hotel. I had a plan of my own outside of what the Sheriff was doing. Rather than beat the bushes to find her I wanted to do my research. I needed to remember why Core Logistics' name was somehow familiar to me. I also needed to find out what connection Arnie might have had to her disappearance.

It was close to dinner time, and I hadn't eaten anything since the oatmeal that morning. More importantly, I knew the night bartender would be on, and I could quiz him about the other guests at the hotel and the mysterious Arnie.

I went directly to the restaurant and squeezed into the last seat at the bar. I recognized the bartender from our first night when Bailey met Arnie. He acknowledged me with a smile and set drinks in front of guests at the opposite end.

"Good evening. I'm James. Would you care for a drink? The specialty cocktail is a Devil's Margarita which is tequila, red wine, lime juice, and simple syrup."

I made a face. The last time I drank tequila I slept half on, half off my sofa with my face in a trash can. It wasn't my best look.

"Hi, James. I'll take a diet soda and a menu please."

"Sure thing." He placed a menu in front of me and laid out a napkin, placemat, and silverware rollup. "Would you like to hear the specials?"

I let him go through the menu. I was at the point of barely functional. I needed energy food before I threw twenty questions at him. Besides, I figured it would be better to wait until the bar wasn't as crowded. At Wild Bronco we had a policy about not gossiping about guests to each other or other guests. I suspected the same rule applied here. I had to be careful if I wanted to get as much information as possible without alerting him as to my objective.

I ordered soup and nibbled on the edge of a piece of sourdough bread while I waited for the best opportunity to talk to James. When it didn't come, I ordered a small salad. By the time the bar cleared out enough for me to start a conversation with James, I had consumed five diet sodas with enough caffeine to keep me charged until the next afternoon. I'd crumbled the bread into so many tiny pieces I could have fed a flock of seagulls and pushed more salad around the plate than I ate.

James stood nearby polishing glassware, ready to fill my glass again should I need it. I grabbed my chance.

"I was in here the other night and met a nice older gentleman. His name was Arnie. I haven't seen him since. He's a local. Do you know him?" I prayed James didn't think I was trying to pick Arnie up.

"Oh yeah, Arnie's an interesting fellow. I think he invented that super popular space game. He's in here once or twice a week when he's in town. Haven't seen him in days though."

"He and my friend were chatting like crazy about computer stuff. He must be in the same business as she is."

"What does your friend do?"

Argh, wrong tactic I thought. "We were invited to a party at his house. Well, my friend was invited, and I was her plus one. Have you ever been?"

"Who me? No chance unless I'm working it."

"Does he have lots of parties?"

"I wouldn't know. He doesn't exactly run his social calendar by me." He laughed at his humor.

"We never made it to the party. Had a bit of, er, car trouble. I was going to call him to thank him for the invitation. Unfortunately, my friend had the number and her phone died. Would you happen to know his last name?"

"Sure, it's Arnie Miller. He's got that gated place down off Route 171 just outside of town. Hey, put in a good word for me. I'd love to pick up extra work bartending a private party."

"Sure thing." I dug out my credit card to pay. Without Bailey, it felt wrong to charge anything to the room. Fifty-two dollars plus tip later I wished I had eaten the bread rather than shred it.

I stopped by the front desk to ask about the use of a computer. They had one available for guest use but it only had limited internet capability. I couldn't search on my flip phone so I had to hope that I could look up Arnie Miller and find his address. Bailey's new laptop and phone had been left in the trunk of the rental car so using either of them wasn't an option.

I powered up the computer which was almost as ancient as the one I had at home. As a self-proclaimed professional online shopper, one thing I could do well was search. No matter how obscure or odd the merchandise, I could find it.

I searched for all the Arnie or Arnold Millers in Colorado. There were seven hundred and fifty-two. I narrowed my search down to include those who lived in Tabernash. Zero results. I tried those who had something to do with gaming or game apps. Zero results. I cleared the search history and started over. I looked for the most popular games online. Once I found out what company developed them, I searched for company executives. Bingo and duh! Miller Communications' chief executive officer was Arnold P. Miller. Miller Communications owned a property outside of Tabernash. Taa daa.

I gave myself a pat on the back and wrote down the address on a scrap of paper. I was thankful the evening was still relatively early. Arnie and I had a date tonight. He just didn't know about it. I dashed up to my room and changed into the only pants I had that were clean -- my tight black jeans. I dug through Bailey's clothes and pulled on a gray sweater with a cowl neck. I stepped into my only pair of boots, much worse for the wear, but it was those or sneakers.

I swiped on lipstick and fluffed my hair. I didn't have time to succeed at glamorous. I had to hope or pray that when I knocked on his door, he wouldn't slam it shut in my face. If he had anything to do with Bailey's disappearance, I would find out no matter what it took.

On the way out an idea hit me, and I swung by the gift shop and purchased a black stocking cap and a set of warm gloves. The purchases were a *just in case I needed to be stealth* contingency. They went on my credit card. I would worry about paying for the charges later after Bailey was safe. I stuffed the cap in my purse and hurried to get in the waiting cab.

On the way, I remembered to call Jenny. A deputy had already been by, and she was frantic. I missed the three phone messages she left. Dang flip phone.

I tried to reassure her, but my words lacked punch. I didn't believe everything would turn out fine. Jenny never met her father, and her mother had been murdered. For her to lose Bailey would be more devastating than either of us could withstand.

I promised her I was doing everything I could to find Bailey, and she knew I wouldn't stop until I did. She wanted to jump on a plane and come to help with the search, but I convinced her everything that could be done was happening and she was needed to care for the animals.

The cab pulled up to the massive iron gate which, to his surprise and mine, stood open like a giant with arms outstretched to welcome me into its warm embrace or gobble me up like an appetizer. We proceeded slowly down the immaculate tree-lined drive which glittered with lights every ten feet.

We passed a five-car garage and then arrived at a two-story main house lit up like Times Square on New Year's Eve. Behind the house, a snow-covered mountain stretched as high as the sky. I wondered if this was part of the same mountain Travis and I had negotiated by mule, albeit from the other side.

I paid the driver and stepped out onto the stone veranda. I could hear music and laughter. Hopeful that I wouldn't need to imitate super spy 007 and slide in the back, I held my head high and knocked on the heavy mahogany door.

A moment later the door was opened by a man dressed in a suit and tie holding a tray of sparkling wine. I froze in the entryway like a rabbit caught in the clutches of a bobcat. A party was in full swing and I no reservations about joining in.

The foyer, if it could be classified as such, was all stone and mahogany with a staircase that negotiated around a boulder the size of my apartment to the second floor. The ceiling was framed with what appeared to be hand-painted panels of the surrounding mountains. My boots clomped like horseshoes on the marble tiles as I took a few hesitant steps inside.

People dressed casually in jeans and boots held glasses of wine and mingled. A server ambled with a tray of appetizers in hand. Easy listening music blended with conversation. I decided to follow the sound and try to blend in. I rationalized that Bailey and I were invited to a party here, so it was entirely possible we mixed up the date.

I snatched a glass of red wine from a passing server. It was a nice burgundy with a hint of pepper and dark cherry. Cautiously I inched my way to the periphery of a group discussing the merits of iPhone versus Android. Oh boy, I said a silent prayer no one asked my opinion. I imagined myself saying, *I use a flip phone because it's easier than trying to learn how to navigate a smartphone. Who needs all those applications when all you want to do is call a person? Yes, I'm a throwback but it's cheaper.* I suppressed a chuckle and turned off my inner monologue.

"It's always the same argument. IOS versus Android."

I started at the sound of a voice close to my ear and spun around. "Um, yes. It never ends, does it?"

He was dressed like the first time I saw him at High Mountain Resort in the bar. Same too tight blue bowtie and, the same hipster beard. Tonight, he wore dark blue jeans, and brown loafers, with a striped button-down shirt. His beard was neatly trimmed, his eyes a captivating blue. His cologne made my eyes water.

"I don't think we've met. I'm Matthew." He held out his hand.

"Jayne. Nice to meet you."

"What department are you in?"

"Um." What department did I work in? I blurted the first thing that came to mind and prayed it wasn't the department he was in. "Accounting."

"That explains why we haven't met. I'm in game development."

I wondered if he remembered seeing me at the resort. It didn't take an astrophysicist to figure out this was a company event. I wondered if Arnie put everyone from out of town up at the lodge. I couldn't imagine locals staying there. I thought back to my internet search on Arnie Miller. If the company owned this estate, it might have had more than one location, but in my haste, I didn't dig deep enough. I bit my cheek wishing I had researched further before rushing headlong. I recalled that Bailey said Arnie's top brass was due here this week. I guessed this party was a team building work event happening at the same time.

I grabbed a napkin off the tray from a server as she passed by with smoked salmon canapes and dabbed my eyes. "I'm new. Have you been here before?"

"I've been with Miller for three years. I haven't seen you at any of the other events this week. Have you been hiding out?"

I tried to think up an excuse. "I haven't been feeling well."

He narrowed his eyes at me. "Sorry to hear that. You're looking very well tonight."

"Thanks, it was a twenty-four or forty-eight-hour type of thing."

"Twenty-four or forty-eight, which was it?" His smile sent a shiver down my back. I took a step closer to the edge of the group.

This guy paid attention. I would have to be craftier or sidestep to another group. Chatting with him wasted precious time. I needed to find Arnie and figure out if he was involved in Bailey's disappearance. Then again, perhaps a bit more information wouldn't hurt.

"What have I missed?"

"A lot. You missed the axe throwing, the two-legged races in the snow, and the snowman-making competition."

My mouth dropped. "Wow."

"I'm kidding. It's been meetings all day long. I've taken pages of notes on what the company expects for the next fiscal year."

I breathed a sigh of relief. The other staff, at least one hundred people strong, were milling around. With that many, they probably had not all met. I figured I could circulate and pick up some intel on whether Arnie was present last night for the entire time. If he wasn't, my theory was that he might have been the unidentified person who hired Harry and then ultimately snatched Bailey. How he would have managed to do it all while being present at his company event remained a mystery. Even more curious would be his motive. If he wanted to kidnap Bailey, he could have done it during their meeting.

I scanned the room. "I don't see the boss around."

"I saw him on the patio earlier talking to Courtney." He made a face.

"I don't think I've met her. Is she in your department too?"

He snorted. "You're lucky you haven't met her." He stepped closer as if to share a secret. I leaned in and held my breath.

"Why is that?"

"She's not a good person." His soft voice tickled my ear.

"Um, why do you say that?"

"She didn't have to climb the corporate ladder to get ahead. She had other ways to get where she is."

I suppressed a chuckle. "And what would that be?"

"Er, well you know."

I was tempted to say I didn't know what he meant. As much as I wanted to delve into what she did to get ahead, I doubted this Courtney person was relevant to my investigation. I moved the conversation in a different direction.

"Wasn't there a company event here last night too? I thought I heard something about a party."

He stroked his beard for a moment. "There was an early meeting of the board members. That might have been before the employee awards dinner which started at seven on the top of the mountain. We all rode up in the tram for a buffet with a view. I was surprised at how nice it was. My wife, Audrey would have loved this place." He gazed off with a wistful look in his eyes. "It's a shame we weren't allowed to bring our families. I live only thirty minutes away."

I guess I had been wrong about his meeting an online date the first night I saw him. I was temporarily sidetracked with the thought of an employee award ceremony. I pictured what it would be like to stand before my co-workers and receive an award. The closest I'd come was the night when I sold more dessert specials than any other server. My prize was a gift card at a coffee chain. I passed it on to Emmett since I didn't drink coffee. That was before I realized the chain also had yummy coffee cake. I sighed at the memory before I continued. I was always so easily distracted by the thought of food. "Did Arnie give out the awards?"

"Arnie? Do you mean Mr. Miller? Is everyone in accounting on a first name basis with the boss?"

I took a sip of wine. "I wouldn't call him Arnie to his face, of course. But was he there for the entire award ceremony?"

"If you attended the company events, you would know. Why do you ask?"

Fortunately for me, I didn't have to make up a reason as another employee staggered up. His tie hung loosely around his neck, his button-down shirt had splotches across the front and his hair was sticking out in all directions. I felt he was a kindred spirit as that's how I finished every night at the restaurant, only I was always sober.

He slapped Matthew on the back so hard he fell into me and splashed my wine into my face and down the front of my sweater. "Hey Mattie. How's it hanging? Finally coerced someone to talk to you?"

"You idiot! Look what you made me do," Matthew shouted and shoved him away.

"Whoa, buddy. Take it easy. I was just having a little fun with you."

"You're drunk and I'm not your buddy. Get away from me," he hissed.

"It's okay." I looked around for a towel. "I'll just go to the bathroom and try to clean up. Um, can you tell me which way it is?"

Matthew offered to escort me, but I declined. I needed time to regroup. I headed in the direction he pointed which took me under the crystal chandelier and down a long hallway that felt something like what I imagined the Queen's palace would resemble. I opened ten doors before I found a bathroom. That also served as a chance for me to look for anyone held hostage.

Inside the guest bath, the granite vanity looked to be five inches thick. I fingered the softness of the brilliant white guest towels monogrammed with the letter M. So, this is what luxury felt like.

Red wine dripped from my hair. The stain on the sweater was the color of dried blood. I dabbed it with toilet paper which resulted in tiny pieces of paper being stuck to my chest. I opened the drawers looking for a hair dryer with no luck. A real human couldn't possibly use this bathroom. It was too pristine. With no other option available, I used the immaculate white hand towel and did the best I could to blot the spot and remove the toilet paper decoupage.

Someone banged on the door, so I gave up and stuffed the used towel under the sink. Better the housekeeper found it later than another guest. I splashed water on my face and wrung out the wine from my hair. I couldn't do anything about the smell. Anyone who stood within two feet of me would assume I'd overindulged.

Back into the main rooms, I meandered as if I belonged, arms crossed over my chest to hide the wine residue, all the while furtively searching for Arnie. I passed through the foyer into a living room area featuring a center double-sided stone fireplace that sizzled and popped, sending a blaze of sparks up the chimney.

The conversation in the room hummed with an electric intellectual vibe. I wiped the sweat off my brow. I prayed no one else tried to talk to me. I smiled tensely and quickly looked away from anyone who made eye contact. \

I didn't find Arnie in the professional chef's kitchen nor in the formal dining room which seated twenty. I grabbed another glass of wine to have something in my hand and picked up a shrimp canape. I planned to pop it in my mouth and make appreciative moaning sounds if approached.

I traversed the entire first floor with no luck. Did I have enough courage to ascend the staircase? Maybe not courage but I certainly had enough foolishness. I made sure everyone appeared to be occupied and took one step at a time as if admiring the artwork.

I took one final glance around at the top of the stairs before I hurried down the hall to my right. It was difficult to tip-toe with boots on the marble floor. I listened at each door for voices and kept one eye trained behind me. If I didn't find Arnie, I could eliminate this house as a place where Bailey could be held. Methodically I checked every room. The police had to follow the law. I didn't have the same restriction.

I made my way into the primary bedroom. It was plush and inviting. The king-sized bed was draped in a gold satin comforter and mounded with pillows. My overtired brain imagined a giant vanilla cupcake with cream cheese frosting. I wanted to dive into it, roll around, and smother myself in luxuriousness. The physical and mental exhaustion of the last few days weakened my legs and my resolve. I wondered if five minutes on that bed would hurt. It drew me like a siren's song. I crept closer. Five steps, four, three, two, one, and ah. I flopped down on my back and sunk in like a cocoon. This is how it feels to be rich.

I eyed the ceiling. Any mansion worth as much as this one had to be would have a sprinkler system. Where there's smoke, there are firefighters. If someone sets off a fire alarm, *accidentally on purpose*, it might draw the fire department who would have to do a room-by-room search. If I could set off an alarm, I could be certain Bailey wasn't here. I would burn this place down if that's what it took to rescue Bailey.

I seriously contemplated how to set off a smoke detector when I heard voices. Holy cow, I had to get out of this bed, this room. I scrambled to the other side, hurled myself out of bed, and ducked into the well-appointed bath. It was larger than my apartment but had no exit. If anyone came into the room and didn't leave, I would be stuck. I couldn't hide in the shower as it was all glass. That left the toilet area as the best option.

I heard a man's voice and then a woman's laughter. If they were planning a secret tryst. I was in a bad place. More laughter and then a faucet running in the bathroom. It was now or never. I flushed the toilet and threw open the door. Arnie stood at the sink with a toothbrush in hand, his mouth gawked open in shock.

"Excuse me," I said and brushed past him. I wondered if he thought it gross that I didn't stop to wash my hands. Too late! I wasn't waiting for judgment. I didn't take the time to register who the female was lounging on the bed where I had just enjoyed fantasizing about a different lifestyle. I hit the bedroom door without a backward glance and dashed down the hall. Some super sleuth I was. I couldn't even tell if he was a single or double-ply kind of man.

I flew down the staircase where people still congregated. I was headed to the front door when Matthew snagged my arm.

"Leaving so soon?"

"Yes, I'm not feeling well again."

"You do look flushed. Would you like to share a car back to the resort?"

I looked at his wedding ring. I had to trust that he didn't expect to walk me to my room or be invited in. Since he mentioned his wife, I decided I was probably safe with him. All the same, I wondered if I should slip out the door and check out the garage before I left. I couldn't do that very well if I had a companion. Then again, nothing about this place screamed hostage situation. But what the heck would I know about that?

"That would be great."

Matthew grabbed his coat and led me outside where a line of cars waited to take guests back to their rooms. I sunk into the soft leather seat of a black executive car. Matthew slid in beside me and told the driver to take us to High Mountain.

I rested my head against the seat and closed my eyes. It had been twenty-four hours since Bailey disappeared. I felt as if half my life had passed. Where was she? I refused to consider the possibility she wasn't alive. I believed that I would know if she wasn't.

CHAPTER TWELVE

It was a short drive to the resort—when you didn't get lost and fly off a mountain. To my embarrassment, I still managed to fall asleep on Matthew's shoulder. He shook me awake when we arrived at the hotel. I sleepwalked into the lobby.

"Thanks for sharing the car. I'm sorry I drooled on your coat."

"No worries. I'm sorry I caused you to spill wine all over your nice sweater."

I looked down at the blotches where the wine dried. "I'm sure it will wash out."

"I hope you feel better. Tomorrow's agenda is all fun team-building exercises now that the work part of this trip is done. There actually is a snowman making challenge."

I grimaced. There was no way I could fake a full day around sober employees. "What time does it start?"

"The buses are picking us up at nine. We can meet for breakfast if you want."

I tapped my finger on my cheek. "Let's see how I feel. As much as I would hate to miss any of the fun, I wouldn't want to get anyone else sick."

Matthew nodded. "I can check on you in the morning if you want."

"Er, no I'm sure I can manage," I stammered.

"Well speaking of my wife, I should call her before it's too late. I always talk to my daughter before her bedtime. Have a good evening." He headed to the elevator.

I called out to him. "Hey, I forgot to ask you. How did you know I'm staying here?"

He stepped into the elevator and pressed his phone to his ear. The door closed before he answered.

Was I being paranoid? He never mentioned that he saw me sitting with Bailey at the bar. I shook my head. Probably the employees were housed at the resort and he assumed I was one of them. The town didn't have an abundance of hotel options. I dragged my feet up the path to the lodge and flung myself across the bed. Even though I'd passed the burnout phase hours earlier, sleep wouldn't grace me until almost sunrise.

I was rolled in the blankets like a stuffed sausage when I heard the room phone ringing and ringing. I pulled the pillow over my head. It stopped and then started again. I cursed it and opened my eyes. I wasn't in my bed at home and Bailey was still missing. I didn't want to face another day.

I snatched the handset and pushed buttons until it stopped ringing.

"Hello, Jayne? It's me, Henri. Is your friend back?"

I sighed. "No, she's still missing."

"This is not good."

"It's worse than not good, it's horrible. I hunted all day yesterday for her. The sheriff has a posse out too."

"What can I do to help you?"

I planned to revisit Arnie's mansion while everyone participated in forced fun and check out the garage. I hoped to find something to link him to Harry, at the very least. A person with that kind of money could easily hire a private investigator. The question was why? Unless someone hired Bailey to find security breaches in his company, he would have no reason to hire her and then hurt her. He could have done that while she was in Arizona.

"Hello, are you still there?"

"Um, yes, sorry. Remember when we saw those tracks in the road where we found the scarf?"

"Yes."

"Do you think they might still be there?"

"It's unlikely. I'm sure the plows have been through there by now. If the snow hasn't melted from the salt, it would be packed down hard."

"Do you think you could drive me back there this morning? I would like to take another look around."

"Of course. I don't have any lessons until late this afternoon so I'm at your disposal."

I wondered if I dared ask Henri to take me to Arnie's for another quick look around in daylight. "I can be ready in fifteen minutes."

"I can be there in thirty."

"I'll wait in the lobby. Thanks so much for doing this."

"No problem, Mademoiselle. Henri is at your service."

I jumped out of bed and took a quick shower. I dug through what clothes I had before switching to Bailey's suitcase. I had to plan for possible extended outside time, so I needed multiple layers. There was no way I could fit into any of her pants with the height difference between us, but I could squeeze into one of her oversized sweaters again.

I needed to formulate a plan of action. I made a mental list of what I had done so far and what remained to be investigated. Arnie's house appeared to be clear. However, in my haste, I didn't check to see if there was an attic or basement. Then there was the issue of the garage, and it had been too dark to look for other buildings on the property.

I wasn't getting a feeling that Arnie had any motive. I was sure Bailey hadn't known him before the first night at the bar. If she'd had any concerns that he was dishonest, she wouldn't have bothered to meet with him.

Still, the name Core Logistics hovered at the edge of my psyche. I'm sure it was familiar. Maybe Bailey mentioned the name to me in a conversation. If she was chattering about anything relating to logistics or math I would've spaced out. There was no point in badgering my subconscious. I let the thought go with the knowledge that the memory would come to me eventually.

I dressed quickly and scampered down to the lobby. I didn't want to waste time eating but my stomach growled as a reminder I hadn't eaten much the prior night for dinner. I didn't have time to order anything from the restaurant and besides, the idea of a full meal made me want to retch. I compromised by purchasing two packages of peanut butter crackers in the gift shop and a can of diet soda. I ate one package immediately and stuffed the other in my pocket for later.

As I waited for Henri, I hopped on the resort computer and ran a search for Core Logistics. It was humiliating that I also had to lookup what a logistics company did. Apparently, in this company's case, they warehoused, distributed, and transported goods, specifically antiques. Their website listed rare wines, furnishings, artwork, and much to my shock, cryogenic bodies. The thought of frozen bodies brought Harry's face to my mind, and I shuddered. Even more interesting was the fact that the company was based in Scottsdale. I may have driven past their building on my way to the mall.

How would Bailey have been involved with this company? I could imagine they needed a secure way to manage the data of all their transactions -- not to mention the work involved in the maintenance of frozen heads or body parts. The peanut butter crackers felt lodged in my throat. I took a big gulp of soda and choked on the carbonation. I wondered if one of her home computers would have information worth killing for. I still couldn't make a connection between Arnie Miller, his company Miller Communications, and Core Logistics.

I cleared my search history and exited the computer just as Bailey taught me. My eyes felt like I had stuffed them with cotton balls. I pressed my hands to my temples to try to ease the migraine that danced just under the surface.

I pulled on my ski jacket and watched from the lobby for Henri. I saw his giant pickup through the windows and dashed out to open the passenger door before he pulled to a complete stop.

"Change of plans."

He looked at me over the top of his aviator sunglasses.

"There's another place I need to check out and it's close to where I last saw Bailey."

"Pas de problème. Tell me the way."

I had the route to Arnie's place memorized. There was no chance I would get lost again. The temperature was higher than it had been when we arrived. Rivers of melted snow flowed down the sides of the road. Trees stood taller having released their icy burdens. If the situation weren't so dire, I could have been happily seated in Henri's truck, listening to his stereo blast a soprano singing opera in French.

I directed Henri to the gates of the Miller Communications mansion. The gate was closed, which I hoped meant everyone was busy with the team building exercises, and I would have free rein to investigate until I was satisfied Bailey wasn't being held on-site.

Henri sat with the truck idling and looked at me expectantly. "You know the person who lives here?"

"Sort of. I was here last night."

"And you left your purse behind?" he prodded.

"Yes, exactly! I've come to retrieve my purse which could be anywhere."

"Did your plot include a method of gaining entry?"

Oh boy, he completely got me. and yet kept himself from being an accessory should my plan include breaking and entering.

"It doesn't, but I'll figure it out when I get to the house. If you could just wait here for…" I tapped my finger on my lips. How much time would I need to search the house again and the other buildings?

"I will wait for you until someone comes. At that point, I will explain that I am here to give a private snowshoe lesson to the madam." He reached behind the seat with a smile and held up a snowshoe.

"Wow, you think fast. I'm impressed at your devious mind."

"Do not underestimate someone because you don't think his job is an important one."

"I would never do that."

"If someone comes and I can't drive through the gate, my horn will *accidentally* become stuck as a warning. You must then find your way back to this location where I will pick you up."

I hoped I would be able to hear his horn inside the stone castle. Even if I couldn't, I was committed to my plan. "Okay. I'll hurry."

"If you are not back in one hour, I will find you if it means I have to break down the gate."

"Oh geez, let's hope that isn't necessary. I searched once already and found no sign of Bailey. I need to be sure I didn't miss something." I stepped out of the truck. Before I closed the door, I called to Henri, "Thanks. I couldn't have done this without you."

He waved me off and tapped his watch to indicate the clock was ticking. I waved and walked quickly toward the gate. I knew I was capable of climbing over it as I had done something similar in the not-too-distant past. Luckily, this gate was more decoration than security so I was able to climb through some snow-covered brush and get to the driveway.

I walked as fast as I could but stayed close to one side in case I needed to dart into the trees. This time I headed directly for the garage. It meant I had to tromp through snow which would leave tracks and freeze my toes, but I had no other choice. I rationalized that if I couldn't see the house, no one inside could see me.

The side entrance was unlocked, so I slipped inside as quietly as I could. The garage was dimly lit, but I could make out a Maserati, a Porsche, and a Rolls Royce. I doubted any of those cars would have been used to kidnap someone, let alone driven in the blizzard.

There was nothing amiss that I could see, so I moved quickly to the house. I slipped in the back door off the patio as quietly as possible and listened for any sound. Except for almost running into the housekeeper, the search was a bust. I didn't find an attic entry and the basement held mostly bottles of vintage wine.

I left out the same door I came in and looked around for any place I might have missed. In the distance, I could see a cabin that might have belonged to a caretaker. It was too far to tell for certain. I had started in that direction just as I heard Henri's horn blast three times. I rushed toward the back of the garage and peered around the corner to see a long black limousine pull up to the front of the house. Arnie exited with three other gentlemen whom I assumed were company executives.

Time was up, so I sprinted toward Henri before the driver had time to turn around and catch me. Henri had moved his truck to the side with the hood up. As I burst out of the gate moments before it closed, he slammed the hood down and jumped in the driver's seat. We sped off faster than you could say luge.

"That was a close call." I bent over trying to catch my breath.

"When I saw the limo, I popped the hood and pretended to look at the engine. The driver stopped to ask if I needed help. I said it was a loose battery cable and I would be fine. That's when I blew the horn."

"I'm so glad we had a plan. I generally just charge in and figure it out as I go."

"I guess you didn't find anything."

"No. I ran through the house again top to bottom. Bailey isn't there. The garage is cleaner than my apartment and twice the size. I feel like I'm missing something. I can't put my finger on it. I'm drawn to something connected with this place or its owner."

"Where to now?"

"I guess back to the resort. I'll check in with the sheriff to see if he has any news.

"I need to stop by my house and pick up something before my class. Do you mind a slight detour?"

I slumped down in the seat. It didn't matter if I rushed back to the resort. I didn't know where else to look for Bailey. "I don't mind. I appreciate your help."

Henri drove to his house, left the engine running, and came out minutes later with a small bag. He handed it to me. "Here, these may help you feel better."

Inside were six small milk chocolates. Each had a leafy flower design on top in assorted colors. I popped one in my mouth. "Yum, this is delicious." I swallowed and stuffed in another one.

"You may want to go easy on those."

"Don't worry I've had plenty in my day." I savored the unusual taste and reached for a third. Chocolate was my go-to sweet whenever I was sad, mad, stressed, or happy. Chocolate worked no matter what my mood was.

"Those aren't regular chocolates. Those have marijuana in them."

"What? Are you trying to kill me?"

He laughed. "I promise you won't die from three candies. You are going to be flying high in about thirty minutes."

"Holy cow. I'm going to be sick. I've never done drugs in my life. Why didn't you warn me?"

"I tried, but you ate them so fast. Worst case you'll feel lightheaded. Take a nap and when you wake up, you'll feel fine."

I started to hyperventilate at the thought of drugs in my system. I swore I already felt odd sensations. It was likely the result of my panic. There was no way my stomach digested the candy that quickly. My leg jiggled and I chewed my bottom lip.

"What am I going to do? What if the sheriff wants to see me? I don't want to go to jail again," I wailed.

"Cannabis for recreational purposes is legal in Colorado so you won't go to jail. Wait, did you say 'again'?"

"It's a long story."

We pulled up to the resort and I opened my door. I reached over and hugged Henri. "I'm sort of mad at you for giving me drugs in the form of chocolate. But I know you had the best intentions and so, thanks for all the other stuff you've done to help me." I jumped out of the truck before I got teary-eyed—again.

My mind worked ninety miles an hour. I pictured the videos of stoners that my father, the cop, made me watch all through junior and high school. I was going to be high. I already didn't like the feeling. I wondered why people did this on purpose. I needed my mental faculties working on all burners. The last thing I needed was to zone out.

I dashed up the stairs to the lobby with my head down. I prayed no one would stop me. I needed to reach the safety of my room until the effect wore off. When I stopped long enough to breathe, I realized I didn't feel any differently than before I ate the candy.

I rushed to the gift shop to grab bottled water. Once I reached my room, I planned to lock myself in for as long as it took. As I passed the sitting area near the stone fireplace, I heard my name.

I stopped, too afraid to turn around. Please don't let it be the sheriff, I thought.

"Where've you been?"

"Jonas, what are you doing here?

"I came because I thought you needed me. I'm wondering if I was wrong."

I ran at him and threw my arms around him. "I've never been happier to see anyone in my life."

He wrapped his arms around me, and I felt the weight of the last few days whoosh out of my body. Then again maybe that was the pot kicking in.

"Who was that guy you were with? In the big black pickup?"

"That was Henri. He's my ski instructor. And my friend too I guess."

Jonas released me and held me at arm's length. "I saw you hug him."

"I was thanking him. He is the one who helped me look for Bailey the night she went missing. Today he took me to Arnie's house to see if he was holding her captive. Then he gave me pot candy. Well, I'm not grateful for that part because I already feel weird."

"Oh, Darlin,' slow down. One thing at a time. Who is Arnie and why would he hold Bailey against her will? Did you say you ate pot candy?"

"Come to my room and I'll explain everything."

Jonas grabbed his overnight bag, and I took his hand. Now that he was here, I hoped everything would be okay. He was my Superman.

I unlocked the door to my room and held my breath. I had left the room like a whirlwind with clothes strewn on every surface. Thank goodness the housekeeping here was exceptional. My clothes were neatly folded and stacked on the window seat. The beds were made with the pillows fluffed to perfection. My cosmetics were arranged in the bathroom, and my shoes were in the closet. I was relieved that Jonas would not see the catastrophe I had left in my wake.

He set his bag down and peered out the window at the mountain. I kicked off my shoes, had a second of guilt, and moved them to the closet.

"This place is really something. I'm glad Bailey didn't spare any expense."

"Yeah, it's beautiful, but I would rather be in a no-tell motel right now and have Bailey here."

I flopped down on the bed. He sat down beside me and rubbed my back. "Start at the beginning and don't leave any stuff out this time."

I scooted over and pulled him down next to me. "I don't know where to begin. So much has happened."

"You didn't give me any notice that you were taking this trip, and now so much has happened I'm feeling a bit late to the party."

I rested my head on his shoulder and recanted the trip from the moment we landed. I talked until my eyes became heavy and my speech slurred. When I woke up Jonas was sitting in the chair with Henri's pants on his lap.

"Oh hey, I guess I dozed off." My head felt too heavy to lift from the pillow.

"You left out one part of the story. The part where there's a man's pants in your hotel room."

I propped myself up on my elbows. "I'm sure I told you about those. Those are Henri's. My clothes were soaked when I made it to his house, so he gave me something dry to wear."

He nodded as if it seemed plausible. "I would feel better meeting this guy, so I know he doesn't have an ulterior motive."

"If you met him, you would know you have nothing to worry about. But really, Jonas you have nothing to worry about with any guy."

"A white shirt covered in wine and food, one shoe missing with cactus spines in your rear end."

"Huh?"

"That's what you had on the first time I met you. You were wandering down a road in the dark, alone."

"You remember what I was wearing?" Inwardly I shuddered at the memory of our first meeting. I was accosted by the mayor of Cave Creek and managed to escape his unwanted advances by running through the desert. He was murdered that night, and I was charged. The fact that Jonas remembered every detail still warmed my heart.

"You threatened to hit me with a cow pie. I wanted to kiss you. I knew I'd never met anyone as feisty as you. That insatiable curiosity gets you into troublesome situations constantly. That unpredictable quality makes me crazy. It's also one of the things I love about you." He stood and walked over to where I lay on the bed.

For a second, I thought he was going to propose. My heart pounded and spots danced before my eyes.

"I feel like I'm going to be sick." I ran for the bathroom and leaned over the toilet with dry heaves.

"Well, that's not quite the reaction I hoped for." He held my hair back from my face.

"I'm s-s-sorry. I don't feel well. Dang Henri and his drugs."

"When did you eat last?"

"Besides the candy? I had peanut butter crackers this morning." I sat on the cool tile floor and rubbed my head.

Jonas handed me a wet cloth. "Put this on your face. I'll order room service."

I wanted to tell him to be careful because the cost of a cup of soup could run into the millions, but I didn't have the strength. I heard him on the phone and then he was back sitting on the edge of the bathtub running his fingers through my hair.

I leaned against him. "You are the best boyfriend ever."

"Yes, I am. Now let's get you into the shower and then in bed."

"As much as I've missed you, I don't think I'm feeling very sexy right now."

He laughed. "As irresistible as you generally are, your hair is a tangled mess, and you kind of smell. So, I would agree you aren't your sexiest self at this moment."

"I'm the worst girlfriend ever."

"It's why I came even when you said I didn't need to. I respect your independence, darlin.' I also know when you are in over your head. I'm in this for the long haul in case you haven't already figured that out."

I tilted my head up to kiss him, but remembered I hadn't brushed my teeth since before my peanut butter cracker breakfast. "I just want to find Bailey and bring her home."

"I know. We're going to find her. First, the shower."

He turned on the shower and helped me undress. I felt unsteady on my feet and woozy. I didn't like the feeling of being disconnected from my body. I turned the water temperature as hot as I could stand and scrubbed my body until it was pink. No matter how hot the water was, I couldn't seem to get warm.

I dried off and slid into the fluffy hotel robe that hung on the door. I heard room service come in as I ran a comb through my hair. The smell of greasy grilled cheese and fries seeped under the door. My appetite hit like a frying pan to the face.

I pulled a chair up to the built-in desk and dug in. "This may be the best meal I've had in my life."

Jonas smiled. "Pot will do that to you. Do you feel better now?"

"A little. I don't feel as strange as I did before the shower." I took a big bite of the gooey sandwich. "What do we do now?"

"While you showered, I called the sheriff's office for an update. The unwelcome news is there is no news on Bailey. The good news is they are still committed to finding her. The deputy said they have multiple teams combing the mountains."

"I need to do something to help. I can't sit here waiting or I'll lose my mind."

"I've been thinking about that. We could join in the search."

"I know this sounds crazy, but I don't believe she's out there. My gut tells me someone took her."

Jonas rested his head on his hand. "Who? This Arnie fellow?"

"I thought it might be him. Now, I'm not so sure. I didn't find anything at his house, and I can't see any reason he would take her."

"Okay, so who else?"

"The sheriff thinks it's tied to Harry Schepp's murder. I have to figure out who killed Harry and why. That will lead us to Bailey."

"From what you told me Harry was investigating Bailey. Can you think of anything at all she could have been involved in, even if she didn't know it wasn't on the up and up?"

"I wish I could. One thing's for sure, she wouldn't deliberately do something illegal."

"I agree. I can't imagine Bailey committing a crime. You maybe, but not her." He poked me in the arm good-naturedly.

"Not funny."

Jonas frowned. "This is the time when we need Bailey's skills. I'll bet she could hack into a computer and figure this out in five minutes."

I set my sandwich down. "Jonas, she's been missing almost two full days now. What if I'm wrong and she is out there somewhere in the cold?"

He took my hand. "No matter what it takes, we'll find her."

CHAPTER THIRTEEN

Jonas made a good point. If Bailey were here, she would be able to find herself. That wasn't exactly his point, but it gave me an idea. If I thought as Bailey would have, maybe I could put the pieces together.

"I suspect Sheriff Cox thinks there's a connection to this company, Core Logistics. I didn't find anything that jumped out at me when I searched the internet. I wonder if Jenny can access Bailey's computers to tell me more."

"Do you think Bailey shares her passwords with Jenny? Or anyone for that matter?"

I slouched in my chair. "Probably not. And if she were working on something highly confidential, she wouldn't have involved Jenny. But what if Bailey called Core Logistics and asked to speak to the president?"

"Where are you going with this?"

"If Bailey were to call and ask to speak to, say the president of the company, and he takes the call, we would know she was working for them."

"And I suppose you're going to be Bailey?"

I touched my finger to my nose. "Exactly. So, if I were Bailey, why would I call?"

"I'm no help to you there. I still don't understand what she does."

"Geez, I thought it was just me. Let's think of a valid reason to call."

"Her bill wasn't paid."

"Would you call the president for that?"

"No. You might call accounting. If they investigate it, you will also know she's working for them."

"You're pretty smart for a guy." I threw a French Frie at him. "Can you look up their number on your phone?"

Jonas woke up his phone and opened the browser. He grabbed the complimentary pad and pen off the desk and jotted it down. I cleared my throat and dialed. When the automated voice answered, I punched the number for accounting. But then a woman answered and I freaked. Nothing came out of my mouth but a squeak.

"Why'd you hang up?

"Do I play bad cop or good cop?"

"Huh?"

"Should I be mad that my bill wasn't paid? What if she asks me when I sent it? What if Bailey only bills once a quarter? What if she asks me how much it was?"

"Take a breath. Bailey probably bills monthly. The accounting department can look it up by her name. It's all computerized."

I handed him the phone. "Why don't you call and pretend to be my, I mean Bailey's, accountant. Say you're reviewing her books or something."

He rolled his eyes. "Give me the phone." He dialed and paced the room waiting for a human to come on the line.

I was impressed by what Jonas could do, but never more than at that moment. His voice was strong without the trembling like mine would have had. I heard his side of the conversation. He asked all the right questions. He was perfect, except that he used his real name.

"Holy cow! Why did you give them your real name?"

He laughed, despite the seriousness of the situation, and waved the piece of paper with his notes in my face. "Do you seriously think they are going to look me up? She already gave me all the information we needed."

"Don't keep me in suspense. Bailey works for them, doesn't she?"

"She does or she did. Her last invoice was paid, and the person told me the check cleared. If the check cleared, my guess is that she would have invoiced them at least thirty days ago. Most large companies only pay monthly."

"Okay, now we call the president himself."

"Do you plan to call him up and ask if he kidnapped Bailey?"

"No, no. I want to know if he hired Harry Schepp."

"And you think he'll tell you he hired a private investigator to run surveillance on his contractor?"

"No, but if he thinks I'm Bailey, he might say something that we can use."

Jonas shook his head. I knew it wasn't the best plan, but it was better than no plan.

I hit redial and went through six menus, and three times I was disconnected. On the fifth try, I connected with Walter Caldwell's assistant, who was more of a guard dog than a Doberman. He informed me that Mr. Caldwell was out of the country until the new year and couldn't be reached. When I asked to leave a message, he told me to call back and leave it on his voicemail. I redialed another six times without ever reaching either Caldwell or his assistant's voicemail. I scratched his name off my list in frustration.

Regardless, I refused to give up so easily for the other two names. I went through the process four more times to reach Walter Caldwell, Jr. When I finally reached his assistant, she promised to give him my message but said he was unlikely to return it before the following week due to his schedule.

That left only Lauren Davis from the sheriff's list. By this time, I was a pro at navigating the recorded menus. When she answered her phone, I was so surprised I didn't speak for several seconds. Pretending to be Bailey hadn't made me any new friends. I figured honesty couldn't hurt.

"My name is Jayne and I'm a friend of Bailey Chauncey. I'm calling because she's missing, and I was hoping you might be able to help me."

"Bailey's missing?"

"You know her?"

"Yes, of course. She's been doing work for Core Logistics. When you say she's missing, what exactly happened?"

"It's sort of a long story." Suddenly nervous that I could be inadvertently providing information to a possible killer or kidnapper, I paused. "Do you also know Harry Schepp?"

"Why do you ask?"

"Harry's dead."

"Oh no! What happened to him?"

"It seems he was murdered."

"Oh no. Poor Harry."

"Can you tell me what Bailey was working on for you?"

She hesitated. "I've already said more than I should."

I cleared my throat. I didn't know if I could trust this person. I looked at Jonas for support, but he only shrugged his shoulders.

"Bailey's my best friend. We came to Colorado for a last-minute business trip. She disappeared and we haven't been able to find any trace." I tried to keep my voice steady, but each re-telling was harder because it meant more time without finding her. "I don't need to know classified information. I'm just hoping for anything you can tell me that might help find her."

I could hear her tapping a pen on her desk while she considered my request. "I hired Bailey to revamp our internal security because I suspected something was amiss. I don't want to say more except that she told me that she was remarkably close to not only plugging the holes but also to figuring out who was involved."

I slapped my forehead. I remembered where I saw, not heard, the name Core Logistics. It was on one of the file folders Bailey removed from her suitcase. It was also one of the items stolen from our room. I could see the name in my mind typed on a printed label that was pasted on the file folder as clear as day. I had tried to focus on when I had heard the name, not where I saw it. Someone knew we were here. There had to be a connection.

"I'd like to give this information to the sheriff if you don't mind."

"I'll help in any way I can." She gave me her cell phone number. Before we hung up, she asked me where we were staying. She promised to dig deeper on her end and call me if she found anything that could help in the search.

As soon as we hung up, I called the sheriff and filled him in on what I found. In my excitement, I slipped and mentioned my exploration of Arnie's home. Instead of appreciation at all I'd discovered, he berated me for interfering in his investigation. I held the phone away from my ear as he ranted about civilians who thought they knew more than law enforcement.

"I've been doing this job for more than twenty-five years. What makes you think you know more than I do about how to run an investigation?" Before I could respond he continued, "I'm telling you right now, I've got scores of good people out there looking for your friend. Did it occur to you that I might already be investigating Core Logistics? I do not need you making trouble in my county. If anyone told you it was required that you remain in town, they lied. Feel free to go home."

"Sheriff, I…"

"Listen here little girl, if you aren't going back to Arizona, then you stay in that room and do not, I repeat, do not get in my way.

If I hear about you breaking and entering anywhere, I'm going to arrest you and put you in jail. Do I make myself clear?"

"Er, yes, but I…"

"No buts. I mean it." The dial tone told me he was done with the discussion.

"You might not have told him that you were snooping around someone's house," Jonas suggested with a shake of his head.

"Why didn't you stop me?"

"Do you think I could stop you from doing anything once you set your mind to it?"

I shrugged. I knew not to argue that point. He was right. I could be a tiny bit stubborn from time to time. If I admitted the truth, I was stubborn more often than not. I liked to think it was in a good way if that's possible. Stubbornness didn't sound as nice as tenacity did, but they were the same thing. One girl's stubbornness was another girl's resolve.

Jonas stood and stretched his back. "There's nothing more we can do in this room. Let's take a walk and get some fresh air. It may clear our heads."

"The sheriff told me to stay in my room."

"I don't think he meant it literally." He grabbed my hands and pulled me up. "Get your coat on."

I bundled up and together we went down to the main lodge. It felt good to have Jonas here. I was glad he ignored me when I told him I didn't need him to come.

As we walked, I expressed a concern I had been afraid to face. "What if Bailey isn't being held captive? What if she is out there freezing to death?"

"At first, I was sure she simply got lost trying to find help. Now, the more we learn, I don't know what to make of all of this."

"I don't know what to think anymore. I'm just as scared that someone would kidnap her. What if it's one of those people who take women and do terrible things? Oh my! I can't bear it."

Jonas put his arm around my shoulders. "Let's not go down that road. We have to stay positive and believe she'll be found soon."

He didn't need to say what I knew we both thought. The longer she was missing the worse the situation appeared. Whether she was somewhere lost in the mountains or held against her will, it was all bad. We walked the path to the lobby hand in hand. I took little comfort in his warmth when all my mind could do was fret.

I stopped suddenly. "Darn, I forgot my phone. I'll run back up to the room and grab it. I know I'm the last person the sheriff wants to talk to again, but all the same, I ought to have it handy in case there's any news."

I left Jonas to wander around the outside fire pit while I scurried back to the room. I grabbed my phone and pulled the room door firmly closed behind me. I flipped open my phone to check for any missed calls. In my distraction, I rushed out the building door, headed down the path and ran headlong into Matthew.

He caught me by my arms. "Hi. It's Jayne, right?"

"Er, yes hi."

"You look like you're feeling better." As he stepped closer, I resisted the urge to move away from his overpowering cologne and intense probing gaze.

"Um, yes, better. Thanks."

"I didn't see you at the activities today. I thought maybe you felt worse."

I bit my bottom lip trying to think of a valid reason I wasn't at the company functions. "I decided to work from my room, you know, in case I was contagious."

He stroked his beard. "You've been in your room all day?"

"Well, sort of. A girl has to eat." I looked around hoping Jonas didn't show up and blow my cover story.

"Odd, I swore I saw you get in a pickup truck this morning. You can tell me the truth. I won't tell anyone."

Busted. The question I debated in my head was whether I should tell him the truth or a version that he might believe more easily. If I told him I didn't work for Miller Communications, he would wonder why I showed up at the party. Seconds ticked by. He patiently awaited my answer.

"You caught me. I wanted to take another ski lesson. The person in the truck was my instructor. How often do we get a chance to ski?"

"You spent the day skiing?"

"Sure. I mean, yes. Yes, I spent the entire day skiing."

"Which run did you do?"

I tried to remember the names of the runs. My sole experience had been the bunny slope and I doubted anyone would believe I was excited to spend a day doing that.

When I didn't respond, he suggested, "What is the red diamond slope? I've heard that one is awesome."

I detected a hint of sarcasm in his voice but shrugged it off due to his lack of confidence in my ability. "You know how it is when you're whooshing down the slopes. Red, blue, yellow. They all wind up at the bottom."

He smirked. "So, I've heard. Where's your friend?"

"My friend?"

"Yeah, the one I saw you with at the bar. Where's she at?"

Now I had confirmation that he saw me with Bailey. I wondered why he didn't mention it when I saw him at the party.

"She's around." I looked over his shoulder for Jonas.

"Does she work in accounting too?"

I wondered why he asked about her. "No, she's, um…" I tried to remember what he said he did. Gaming! I watched a house-keeper push her cart up the snow-packed path. "She's in house-keeping."

"I didn't know Miller had a housekeeping department. She didn't look like a janitor."

I started fidgeting under his scrutiny. "She gets that often. She's, like, the head of the janitorial department. You know she makes sure the trash is emptied and the, er bathrooms are clean."

I saw Jonas walking up the hill toward us. I didn't want to give Matthew a chance to ask anything else, especially not about why I brought my boyfriend to a company event.

"I've gotta go. I see someone else from accounting and we have to discuss the upcoming audit."

I gave him a beauty pageant wave and scampered down the hill to intercept Jonas. I could tell Matthew suspected something. I hoped he hadn't figured out that I wasn't an employee. Of course, if I thought about it, by this time all the lodgers at High Mountain probably knew I was the one who found a dead body.

When I reached Jonas, I shook my head and indicated we should keep walking. I didn't want to give Matthew any other reason to quiz me. I was getting way more practice at telling tales than I liked. As much as I could remember odd details, I was a terrible liar. My tendency to spew whatever first came to mind left me with too many details that didn't fit into the big scheme of lies. Eventually, I always tripped myself up by mixing the facts with whatever mumbo jumbo I came up with in the heat of the moment.

I pictured Bailey in an olive green janitor's coverall. Her love of bright colors would have prevented that career choice. However, her passion for organization would have ensured that she did the job to perfection. I reminded myself again to try to think like Bailey. I wondered how she would rescue me if the situation was reversed. Or if she would fail as miserably as I seemed to be.

Jonas and I walked through the back of the restaurant into the lobby. Another problem, actually several, bubbled around in my thoughts like water ready to boil over, and I knew I couldn't avoid them any longer.

"Bailey invited me on this trip. She met with her new client, Arnie, and the rest was supposed to be just us two having fun."

Jonas nodded, but his attention was captured by a fur-clad woman as she entered the lobby. Behind her, the bell captain dragged a luggage cart stacked to the top with designer suitcases. We heard a bark from her purse as a Pomeranian poked his head out.

I continued my discourse. "We were supposed to be here for only a few days. I can't leave here without Bailey."

He nodded and directed me to a sofa beside the fireplace. He took my hand as we sat.

"I can't leave, and I can't stay here." I waved my hand to indicate the hotel. "I'm afraid to find out how much the bill is."

"I have a credit card you can use. Let's find out what the situation is with the bill. Either way, we should check out and move to something a bit less fancy."

"What if Bailey comes back here looking for me?"

"I'm sure if she does the hotel would call you immediately."

I sighed. "There's also the matter of work."

"What about it?"

"I need to get my shifts covered." I didn't add that no work meant no income and I had already given up much-needed shifts to take the trip. Missing a week of work would leave me scrambling to pay bills.

"Call Emmett and let him know what's going on. He would want to know about Bailey. He'll get your shifts covered."

"What about your work?"

"Don't worry about me. I can move my clients around. I plan to be here for the duration."

Relief flooded me. Ever since Jonas had arrived, I feared his departure. I didn't want to be selfish and beg him to stay, but I was grateful I didn't have to.

"Thank you. I don't know what I would have done if you hadn't shown up."

"That's what boyfriends are supposed to do—come to your rescue, hold your hand when you need it, and chase away any bad guys."

"You do all of that and more." I kissed him. "I guess we should check out and hear the bad news."

We walked to the reception area and waited while the woman in fur barked orders at the clerk. I rolled my eyes at Jonas. I'd bet she never worked a day in the service industry, or she wouldn't talk to people that way.

When my turn finally came, I crossed my fingers in the hope the bill wasn't too high. "I need to check out." I gave him my name and Bailey's name.

The clerk's fingers tapped on the keyboard for a minute. "Very well Miss Stanford. I see you had a late checkout for today. Would you like a printed copy of your bill or email?"

"Printed, I guess." I figured why prolong the agony? Better to know now what I owed so I could calculate monthly payments on my credit card. I had only brought my phone and room key. Jonas reached into his pocket for his wallet.

The clerk handed me the bill with a smile. My hand shook as I took the envelope. I opened it and gasped.

"Is there a problem?"

"Um, no. There's no problem." I grabbed Jonas by the arm and dragged him out of hearing distance of the clerk.

"It says the balance is zero," I whispered.

I could see Jonas let out a breath. He was as worried as me about how we would pay the bill if the charges hadn't been covered by Bailey or her client.

"That's great news. Let's grab your stuff and find another place for tonight."

162

He didn't have to suggest that twice. I ran for the door and dashed up the path to my room. I realized I must have either a) gotten accustomed to the elevation or b) gotten in better shape as I wasn't even slightly out of breath. I jammed my clothes into my suitcase, clean and dirty mixed like a jambalaya of clothing. Jonas neatly folded Bailey's into her case. Henri's loaner clothes went into the last dry-cleaning bag. We scanned the room to ensure we hadn't missed anything and then packed everything in Jonas's rental car.

On my last trip through the lobby, I filled two large cups with hot chocolate and took a final look around. Emotions about High Mountain Resort, both good and bad, would forever be imprinted on my brain. The laughter we shared and the adventure we anticipated were clouded by the nightmare of Harry's death and Bailey's absence. One thought was always foremost, where was she?

CHAPTER FOURTEEN

During my short traipse down memory lane, Jonas chatted with the valet. He gave us recommendations for hotels in the area from moderately priced to cheap but scary. We drove into town and stopped at four hotels with no vacancies before we went to the last place on the list.

About a mile on the other side of town and off the main road, we found our destination. The twenty-four-foot-tall sign in front of the Rip Van Winkle Motel flickered as it advertised low rates for daily and weekly rentals. That should have been our first clue.

In my hometown, if someone rented a motel weekly, it meant that all your worldly belongings were packed in your car. Short of sleeping in our car we knew we had to consider it before driving farther down the mountain out of town. Jonas stopped at the edge of the driveway. The engine idled as he looked at me and back at the motel in an *are we this desperate* sort of way. I nodded because we were that desperate.

"What if this place says reservations are required?" I suppressed a fit of hysterical giggling.

Jonas patted my hand, "Well, then we're in trouble because we have no reservations anyplace."

Jonas let his foot off the brake, and as we rolled slowly over the snow-packed road to the crumbling stone archway over which was a sign for the Office, I saw a curtain move in the window.

Jonas stopped under the archway which was so narrow neither of us could open our door fully.

Across from what appeared to be the registration office, I counted ten doors painted neon blue. Each door opened onto the dimly lit central parking area. There were six vehicles, two of which appeared to have not been moved since the last snow, along with one that sat on jacks where the four tires should have been.

I turned the knob for the office to find it locked. The door had a small panel of smudged glass through which I could distinguish light flickering. I pressed my ear close and heard the muffled sound of a television, so I knocked.

Jonas opened the trunk. "There's a sign which says to ring the bell after dark."

My finger hovered over the bell. I looked back at Jonas. "I'm having second thoughts about leaving the resort."

"We both know we can't stay there. Did you notice how much they charged per night? We can drive farther and see if we find anything better, but it's getting late."

I could see the tiredness around his eyes. In one day, he had rushed to the airport, flown to Colorado, driven to the resort, and then cared for me all day. I couldn't ask him to do more.

"No, it's dark and I want to be as close to where Bailey might turn up as we can."

Jonas nodded. I appreciated that he didn't point out we had no idea where Bailey was. For all we knew someone could have taken her miles from here. Or she might still be wandering the mountain alone and freezing. I shivered, pressed the button for the bell, and waited

When no one answered, I pressed it again and knocked.

After ten minutes, with me alternating between bell ringing and knocking, Jonas shut the trunk and climbed back behind the driver's seat. I pressed one last time and turned just as the door opened a crack.

"What do you want?"

"We'd like to rent a room."

The door opened farther to reveal a sizeable woman in a Hawaiian floral print top with chartreuse stretch pants. Her dyed black hair was teased and sprayed to a height that she could have hidden a small child under it. She blinked and one of her false eyelashes came loose and landed on her cheek. She swiped it up and stuck it back on.

"You got cash or credit card? I don't take checks."

"I have a credit card."

She waved me in and shuffled along in worn orthopedic slippers through the semi-darkness. She flipped a switch on the wall, and I blinked as fluorescent light crackled to life.

The Formica was peeling at the corners of the countertop where a lamp with a pull chain stood sentry. Dusty prints hung on walls covered in wood paneling left over from the 1970's. She hefted her weight onto a red vinyl stool and opened a reservation book.

She looked up when Jonas came in the door with our bags.

"I got one room cleaned."

"That's all we need."

She pointed at him, "You two married?"

Jonas paused, before he responded, "Ah, yes ma'am, on our honeymoon."

I suppressed the urge to laugh. If this was his idea of a honeymoon palace, we would be in for an interesting future.

"In that case, you can have the bridal suite. It's very girly." She smiled to show a gold-capped tooth.

She slid a clipboard in my direction and held out her hand for my credit card. I reached for my wallet, but Jonas beat me to it. He bumped me aside with his hip, "Darlin' the husband always pays on the honeymoon."

"How long you plan to stay?"

"We'll rent nightly, but I expect a couple of days."

I filled out our names and Jonas's home address and handed the clipboard back. She handed us a door key on a ring with the number 202 imprinted on it. I looked at her questioningly. As far as I could tell, when we drove up there was only one floor of rooms.

"My ex-husband had an odd sense of humor. It's room 2 across the parking lot. Name's Patsy, but don't bother me unless you break something." She pointed in the direction opposite the office.

We thanked her and dragged our bags to the room, both of us feeling a sense of dread. I prayed that we didn't have to endure bed bugs or other mysterious insects who came in from the cold. People focus on the fact that Arizona has scorpions, but I'd been lucky and rarely seen one inside. Otherwise, there weren't many bugs to battle.

In Maryland, where I grew up, we had bugs, bugs, bugs. Flying bugs, crawling bugs, hopping spider bugs, mosquitos—all of which were drawn to me. I was less bothered by snakes than I was by crickets after accidentally stepping on one barefoot when I got up to use the bathroom in the middle of the night. I shuddered at the memory of the crunchy sound of the skeleton and the squishy feeling under my foot. I always wore flip-flops or shoes around the house after that.

Jonas looked at me as he slid the key into the lock. "If it's horrible, we'll stay tonight and check out in the morning." He nodded in the direction of the other cars. "Someone else stayed here and concluded it's not too bad."

He opened the door deliberately and we both peeked our heads inside. He reached around until he found the light switch. I could smell a strong familiar odor which reminded me of Bugsy's cat box. A single bulb flickered from the ceiling which scarcely illuminated the room. Jonas took my hand and we took two tentative steps inside.

The floor was covered with a dark threadbare carpet, which might have been red at one time, but now was brown as if from years of ground in dirt. To our left was a two-pane stationary window covered by a sheer curtain through which the on-off blinking of the outside light gave a strobe effect. A small student-sized desk sat beneath it with a metal folding chair. Four steps across the room the full-sized bed, shrouded in a tattered pink gingham bedspread, lay in wait for a desperate guest. Beside it was a crooked nightstand with a single bulb lamp without its shade and a mustard push-button telephone. On a credenza with one leg that appeared shorter than the rest balanced a nineteen-inch television with rabbit ears style antenna.

I cautiously stepped to the bathroom and turned on the light. Inside in coordinating Pepto Bismol pink, were a rust-stained sink affixed to the wall, a toilet, and a tub with missing ceramic tiles.

Using a piece of single-ply toilet paper, I lifted the seat on the toilet. Short of finding a dead body, the toilet was almost the worst thing I had ever seen. A thin transparent plastic shower curtain clung on four hooks and barely hid the black ring around the side of the tub. Foil covered the twenty-four by twenty-four-inch window and, despite my curiosity about what was underneath it, I was afraid to peel back a corner. There were no bath towels. I recoiled and backed out of the bathroom.

Jonas rolled in our suitcases. "No place like home, is there?"

I wrapped my arms around my chest and shivered. "It's freezing in here."

Jonas closed the door, as I held my nose. "I suppose it's freeze or get used to the smell."

"It makes me miss my kitty." My eyes welled up. "Can you turn up the heat?"

Jonas looked around the room and found a radiator in the closet. He shook his head in amazement. "I've never seen anything like this. It looks like they built the closet right around the radiator." He turned the knob and soon we could hear the unit wheeze and gasp and finally spit out steam through the pipes. "There should be a thermostat to control the temperature. This unit is so old that either I don't see one or it's on the other side of the wall." He moved into the bathroom. "Aha!"

I peered over his shoulder. There was a small area cut through the wall of the bathroom where the edge of the radiator was wedged beneath the sink. He tried to turn the knob to manage the temperature, but it was painted over, and the knob was so built into the sheetrock that it wouldn't budge.

He gave up, stood, and rubbed his back. "I guess any heat is better than none."

"Maybe we can find another place tomorrow." I patted his shoulder. "Let's try to get some rest."

I opened my suitcase, dug around for my toothbrush, and carried my pajamas into the bathroom. I stared into the cracked mirror at my reflection. Worry lines creased my face and I saw something else I didn't expect. It felt odd to be in a motel room with Jonas. I'd spent the night at his house and he at mine. I'd always expected our first trip together would be romantic. Walks on the beach holding hands, dinner by candlelight, plush robes, and champagne on the balcony. A king-sized bed with Egyptian cotton sheets with rose petals scattered on top of a fluffy pristine comforter.

Worse than jealousy was disappointment. I didn't want Jonas to see I was disappointed that our first night in a hotel was a roadside motel with sheets that may not have been washed in six months. He was here and that was all that mattered.

Jonas had slipped out of his jeans and pulled the bedspread off the bed. He lay on top in just his boxer shorts and a smile.

He patted the bed beside him. "Come over here and let me hold you in my arms."

I didn't need to be asked twice. I slid onto the mattress and rested my head on his broad shoulder. The mattress sunk so low I swore I could feel the floor beneath me.

"I don't think I told you how happy I am that you came. I've missed you."

Jonas smiled, "Why don't you show me."

I took his face in my hands and kissed him. All the emotions I'd felt since Bailey's disappearance flowed from me into him. The feel of his lips on mine made me forget where I was until I felt something extra crawl up my leg.

"Geez Louise, what the heck is that?" I reached down, felt it move, and flung it across the room. I leaped from the bed and jumped on the chair, which wobbled from my weight.

Jonas stood and pulled on his cowboy boots. "We may have company."

"Heaven help me. I'll never sleep if something might crawl on me." I jumped off the chair long enough to grab my clothes. I sat on the desk and pulled my pants over my pajamas. "I have to sleep in the car."

"Hold on a minute. Let me look around. Maybe it was just a cockroach."

"Do you seriously think a cockroach rates any higher on my grossed-out scale than a mouse?"

Jonas shook his head at me and peered under the bed and behind the credenza. He laid on his belly and poked a wire hanger under the radiator. A gray mouse the size of a spool of thread popped out and jumped on top of Jonas's head. He shrieked loud enough to shake the window and hopped onto the desk beside me.

I held my stomach and quaked with laughter as tears rolled down my cheeks. "That was the funniest thing I've ever seen. I can't believe a big, strong cowboy is afraid of a tiny little mouse."

He shuddered, "Not funny. If that mouse jumped on your head, you'd be halfway home by now. Not funny at all."

170

"Oh my gosh." I wiped my eyes with my sleeve. "I wish I had that on video. If you could have seen the way you flew up off the floor in your boxers and cowboy boots, you would die."

"Yeah, yeah. I would have made a fortune on one of those stupid video shows." He nudged me. "You're so brave, you find him."

"I'm not going to find him. You find him."

"Darlin' there's a lot I will do for you but I'm not going to find that mouse."

I let out a sigh. I looked around the floor and saw no movement, so I jumped off the desk and threw open the door to the room. "Maybe he'll just run out."

"Either that or he'll invite his family in to warm up. One thing I know for sure is that the mouse is not leaving voluntarily."

I eyed the ancient telephone, "Should we call the front desk?"

He laughed. "You think Patsy will come over here and get rid of the mouse?"

"Do you think she might?"

"She might charge us extra for a third body in the room. To be honest I would be too embarrassed to even ask."

"That leaves you or me. We have to do something it's getting cold in here."

He heaved a sigh. "I suppose I have to man up. I'll chase it out, but I won't kill it."

"No! I don't want you to kill it. Just make it leave, and I promise I'll make it up to you."

Jonas slid off the desk, closed the door, and dressed. He took the car keys, and I heard him digging around in the trunk. He returned with a crowbar and an ice scraper. I put my hands over my eyes and bit my lip. I wished I had a smartphone to record the scene before me.

He methodically swept the room from the bathroom to the door with no sign of the mouse. He turned off the overhead light and

171

cracked the room door to allow only the parking lot to illuminate the room. He traversed the room again, as quietly as a mouse or in this case, a six-foot-three man in boots could do. I heard a squeak and then a shout and the door slammed.

"He's gone. You can come out from hiding now."

I peeked out between my fingers. "Are you sure?"

"I'm sure." He took my hand and presented the room with a wave of his hand. "Harper pest control at your service."

We undressed and climbed back into bed. All thoughts of romance were completely erased from our minds. Mouse or not, it felt good to feel his arms around me. In minutes, I heard the soft whistle of his snoring in my ear. I couldn't think of a nicer sound except maybe my cat's purr of contentment or the sound of Bailey's voice telling me she was okay.

CHAPTER FIFTEEN

I rolled over in bed and felt around for the warmth of Jonas. Not only was he not there but the bed was cold. I imagined the mouse, his family, his grandparents, and cousins had come in the night and carried Jonas off to their secret spot. Muffled sounds crept into my dream. Thump, thump, thump.

I sat up in bed and looked around the room. The bathroom door stood open and empty. More thumps and what sounded like moans came from the other side of the wall. Ugh, it sounded like someone was on a real honeymoon in the room next door. I laid back down and pulled the pillow over my head.

I heard the key turn in the lock and peeked out to see Jonas coming in with a bag of greasy fast food, coffee, and a large soda for me. He was my hero. I loved the smell of coffee but couldn't stand the taste. It took a can of diet soda to get me going in the morning and one in the afternoon to get me through a shift.

"I found a mini market down the road so this is the best I could do." He handed me the soda and laid out napkins on the bed. "It's not the fanciest but it is breakfast in bed."

"You sure know how to spoil a girl on her fake honeymoon." I bit into a mini glazed donut.

Jonas unwrapped a tortilla with an egg concoction that oozed cheese down his chin, which he quickly wiped away. "I checked out the area and there aren't many options. Ski season keeps the better places booked through next year. We're stuck here for the duration."

I took a large gulp of soda. "I'm not giving up on finding Bailey so if it means staying here, then I'm in." I looked around the room. "Patsy said this room was clean. If this is the best she has, there's no point in changing rooms."

"I thought of that too." He reached for another bag. "I picked up some bathroom cleaner and paper towels."

I suppressed a smile. Jonas was a neat freak. If I thought this room was bad, he must have been disgusted. He didn't disappoint me, for as soon as he finished his gooey breakfast, he started cleaning.

The fumes were so strong that I tried to open the window, but it appeared to be painted shut. I didn't want to leave the door open as a welcome gesture to the mouse. Instead, I stood guard and waved my hands to move the odor out and the fresh air in. Jonas pulled the bathroom door closed and sang while he worked. I admire a man who enjoys cleaning.

It was snowing lightly, and I watched as it melted on the still-warm hood of the rental car. With the caffeine kicking in and my sugar fix from the donut, I was twitching with energy. With Jonas to help me, I was sure we could make progress today. I refused to let negative thoughts creep into my mind. I could feel that Bailey was alive, but I knew time was likely running out.

I was lost in thought when I heard the song "I'm Too Sexy" blast out of Jonas's cell phone. I knew immediately it had to be his ex-wife.

I could feel the muscles in my neck tighten. I slammed the door shut and marched over to his jacket. I dug in the pocket and pulled out his phone. Her picture made a kissy face at me. What the heck?

I looked at the bathroom door and back at the phone. My first instinct was to throw it outside and hope she smothered under the snow. It stopped ringing and then started up again. I debated if I should answer it and tell her he was busy—that *we* were busy. Ultimately, I didn't want to be that type of girlfriend. After all, Jonas was here with me, and he came to help me. She was old news. No matter how hard she tried to get back in his good graces or get back into his pants, I wasn't going to shove him in her direction by being too jealous.

I carried the phone with me and knocked on the door. "Is it safe in there yet?"

He opened the door. Sunshine yellow rubber gloves strained over his large hands, sweat dripped down the side of his face and the fumes almost made me feel faint. I handed him the phone.

He swiped to answer it and pressed it between his ear and shoulder.

I knew I should step away and let him have a private conversation. I didn't. There was a limit to how patient I could be with her.

I could hear the mumbled conversation on the phone. Jonas pulled off the rubber gloves and walked into the bedroom. "Did you try calling Smitty? Okay. Okay. I'll see what I can do." He hung up and sat down on the bed.

"What's going on?"

"I have an emergency. I'm going to have to go back." He patted the bed beside him.

I sat and tried to calm the jiggling of my legs as the sugar fix churned in my stomach. "What kind of emergency?"

"That was Caroline. The renovation I'm doing on the Rutherford house has a problem. It seems the new plumber I hired made a mistake and they had to turn off the water to the entire house. Smitty can't fix it, so I need to go back on the next flight."

"Can't the plumber fix what he messed up?'

"He had a family emergency and left for California."

My legs jiggled faster. "Can you call someone else?" I hated the whine in my voice.

175

Jonas pressed his hand on my knee to settle my nerves. "I'm responsible. The Rutherfords have friends who have plenty of money to spend on renovations. This job could be the turning point for my business."

I understood how important it was for him to be considered not simply great at what he did but reliable. It was one of the numerous traits that made him so wonderful.

"Why did Caroline know about this? Why is she calling you, not Smitty?"

"That's what I was going to talk to you about when you came home. I hired her to manage bookkeeping, set up appointments, and work with my suppliers. I've been so busy that I can't keep up."

"Why her?"

"She used to work with me when we were married. She needed a job, and I didn't have to spend time training her. It's temporary until she finds something permanent."

He patted my shoulder and the simple act felt so condescending that I felt my anger at all her antics reach the boiling point. "You could have asked me for help."

I knew as soon as the words left my mouth that it wouldn't have worked. First, I already had two jobs. My night shift server position at Wild Bronco paid my bills and my part-time gig at the senior assisted living center gave me a little spending money. Secondly, and probably more significantly, I could barely balance a checkbook let alone keep track of his income and expenses. All that didn't matter at that moment. I felt as if Caroline had slowly but surely edged her way back into his life and I would be the item written off the books.

"Darlin,' you already have more on your plate than you can handle. Between your two jobs and mine, we barely see each other. My day starts practically when your night shift ends. Our time together is better spent on other things. Besides she's in the office and I'm on the road all day. It's not like I'll be with her."

I hung my head and breathed in and out slowly to curb my temper. Jonas was naïve when it came to Caroline. I could picture her showing up at his home office wearing something too tight and too short and flaunting her perfect body in front of him. Neither of us said a word while I tried to digest the information like I was cramming a forty-eight-ounce slab of beef into my gut.

I sat there in my goofy-only-my-girlfriend-will-see-me-in-these pajamas with the pink kittens stamped all over them. The saggy socks that I brought to sleep in were a men's size ten so they would be loose but keep my feet warm. I hadn't even considered combing my hair yet, so it stood out in every direction as if I'd just escaped from the electric chair.

I wanted to tell him that he should have at least asked me. He should have considered that I would have given up something to help him. But would I have?

I loved my job at the restaurant. Every night was different. We never knew who might waltz in the door. It could be a celebrity or a couple celebrating their fiftieth wedding anniversary. The servers pranked each other all night so you had to be alert and never let your guard down for what might pop out at you—it could be a fake mouse in your locker or a piece of chocolate cake that was made of rubber.

I also loved the residents at Sunset. They were my adopted family. Everyone had a story and I rushed to work to hear them. I learned more from time spent with the seniors in a day than I ever did in a month of formal education. I wondered if I was willing to sacrifice time with them to answer the phone for Jonas. I wasn't. I didn't want Caroline to do the job either. If only there was someone else that I could trust to do the job and do it well.

I rolled my shoulders to unlock the tension. It was bad enough that I was frantic over my best friend's disappearance, but now I added worry about what Caroline was up to behind my back. If I missed too many shifts, I might be searching for another job when I returned home. And somehow, I had to pay for this runaway vacation turned horror story, and Jonas wouldn't be here to have my back. All because of her! As much I as knew Caroline had nothing to do with my troubles, she made an excellent scapegoat.

"Fine. Go home. Let's not keep Caroline waiting." I stood, brushed past him to the bathroom, and slammed the door. I knew I behaved badly but, in that moment, I needed to be irrationally angry at someone. Jonas was handy. I squeezed a dollop of mint toothpaste on my toothbrush and scrubbed my teeth with passion.

He knocked on the door. "Come on. I know you're upset about Bailey. I'm sorry I can't stay. You know, I have to go home to resolve the plumbing emergency. I promise, if she isn't located, I'll turn around and come right back.

I rinsed my mouth, splashed icy water on my face, and ran my fingers through my tangled hair. Slightly more presentable, I opened the bathroom door. "I'm sorry. I appreciate that you flew here with a moment's notice. All the same, I wish you hadn't hired her because you are the only person who doesn't realize her agenda."

He shook his head. "You aren't giving me enough credit. I'm not blind."

"Then why do you let her manipulate you?"

"There's more going on with her than I can tell you right now."

"What does that mean?"

"It means just what I said. Caroline confided something to me that I promised not to share."

"She asked you to keep secrets from me? That totally burns my bacon."

"Listen, let's not spend our time arguing about Caroline. Please"

He looked so sincere that all my resolve to be angry melted. I didn't want her to win and causing us to argue would mean exactly that. "Come here, cowboy." I pulled him to me and kissed him.

"If you keep kissing me like that, I'll never get back to Arizona to fix that plumbing issue."

Reluctantly, I stepped back from our embrace and allowed him to hurriedly pack his small bag so he could catch a flight back to Arizona.

We decided that I would go with him to the airport and either rent another car or keep his. I positively did not want to be stuck in the Van Winkle without any means of getting around.

Assuming snowless roads, it was a two-hour drive each way. We got lucky heading to the airport with Jonas's driving. He'd grown up in Prescott which is north of Phoenix and attended Northern Arizona University in Flagstaff. While Prescott didn't get much snow, Flagstaff which was at a higher elevation, received enough to keep skiers busy from October through March.

With Jonas by my side to help with car selection we decided to return his sedan, and I rented a four-wheel drive jacked-up Jeep. It felt comforting to sit higher and have extra metal surrounding me. I dropped him at the curb with only forty minutes to get through security and get to his gate. No time for a lengthy goodbye.

"Promise me you'll be careful driving and call me as soon as you get back to the motel."

I nodded as my lower lip trembled. There were so many things I thought about on the drive to Denver. I wanted to tell him I cared about him. Each time I opened my mouth, I stopped in fear. I wondered if I told him I thought I was in love with him if he would say the same back to me. Would he think I said it only to stake my claim on him? I blinked back tears as he hugged me tightly.

"Jonas, I wanted to say…"

He hugged me tighter. "I know. Me too. I'm praying Bailey's found soon." He released me and took my face in his hands. "Promise me you'll stay safe. Don't do anything crazy."

"I promise. But I was going to say…"

"Call me when you're on the road. No wait. Call me when you stop. Don't drive distracted. I just need to know you made it back safely. And check around the other hotels. Maybe something better has a vacancy."

"I'm okay at Rip Van Winkle. It's not so bad since you cleaned the bathroom." I didn't add that it was likely all I could afford.

"I have to go so I don't miss my flight." He kissed me quickly and dashed inside.

I stood on the curb by the shiny black Jeep. Jonas had insisted I get a G.P.S. which was an additional fifteen dollars a day. Even though he insisted on putting my rental on his credit card, I was tempted to return it. On the other hand, despite my concern over the cost, the last thing I wanted was to get lost.

I heaved myself into the metal monster, fiddled with the radio to find a country station, and rolled away from the man I loved. I had at least two hours alone behind the wheel to think about a whole lot of Jayne stuff that caused a collision between my head and my heart.

I thought it was time to make changes in my life. Bailey constantly encouraged me to go back to college and get my degree. I couldn't argue the fact that I had rambled around for the last couple of years with no real plan. Was I going to work two jobs forever? What would it be like to still be a server when I was older and not as charged with energy as I am in my somewhat youth? Maybe I should sample a class or two at the community college? The problem was I had no idea what I wanted to do. Didn't every child have a dream to be something? I had been contented living in the moment—until now.

It irked me that I wasn't the one who could help Jonas in his business. Caroline made no secret of the fact that she had a degree in accounting. Well, la dee da. I didn't want to spend my days hunched over a calculator. I wondered if anyone still used calculators.

I tapped my finger on the steering wheel in time to the music and forced myself to take a hard look at my life. Accountant, no way. Astronaut, out. President of anything out. I didn't envision myself in a leadership role. I preferred to remain in the background, more of a soldier than a general. I loved animals and my job at the senior residence. I didn't faint at the sight of blood, but never would I ever be able to poke a needle into a body, animal, or human, so that eliminated veterinarian, vet tech, or nurse. Contemplating my future made the miles fly past, but in the end, I still didn't have a plan for a new career nor was I any closer to figuring out where my best friend was.

When I got back to the motel, I pulled my phone from the bottom of my purse to call Jonas and let him know I was okay. It was weird to see that I had missed a text message. No one ever texted me because my flip phone made it almost impossible to figure out texts. Everyone who had my number knew to simply call me rather than message me.

After a few minutes, I finally figured out how to read that the message was from an unknown number. It was probably a spam message or a bill collector, but I opened it anyway.

The message said, "Hey girlfriend. I'm okay. Go home. I will fill you in when I get there. Bailey"

I was so excited to know Bailey was okay, I dropped my phone. I spent another five minutes trying to get back to the message. I read it again, wondering why my stomach was doing strange flips as if I had been hit where I stored my chow by a heavyweight boxer instead of being thrilled to have a message from my missing friend.

The bed springs creaked in protest as I sat down and read the message three more times. Something didn't ring true to me. Bailey, of all people, would never text me. She knows how frustrated I get when I have to figure out something technical. The words were odd. In the year we had known each other, she never once said 'Hey girlfriend' to me. Bailey would never, ever, ever tell me to leave her in a text. I was as certain of that as I was that I would never leave here without seeing her face. What did this mean?

If it had been Bailey, she would have asked where I was and how I was. In the end, I was convinced that someone else sent me the message. I suspected it was whoever had taken Bailey, and that person was trying to get me to back off. Maybe I was closer to finding her than I thought, or maybe they just wanted me to stop looking.

I took a deep breath to focus. Think, Jayne, think. I needed to run through the facts I knew and determine a better plan than searching randomly. So far that had yielded zero results. Also, I needed to stock my room with snacks and soda. I could, and had, survived on Diet Dew and cupcakes for days when necessary. My budget was tight and I couldn't afford to eat many meals out. I wasn't going to run ramshackle around the town. I refused to risk getting in the Sheriff's way and give him a reason to detain me. I'd been on the inside of a jail cell, and it wasn't a place I ever wished to visit again.

I found a scrap of paper and started a list. The first was to stock up on supplies. I couldn't think clearly on an empty stomach. Second, check in with Arlene and make sure she was okay to keep my cat, Bugsy, until I returned. Third, call Emmett and ask him to cover my shifts. Fourth? Find Bailey. My gut said she was being held someplace. There was a connection in her disappearance between Harry's death and Core Logistics. I needed to call Lauren back and see if anything else had occurred to her.

I tapped the pen against my cheek. Who else did I know besides Bailey who could navigate around the mysterious world of the internet? Maybe the odd duck I met at Arnie's party, Matthew! He said he was in the gaming department which meant he knew computers. I didn't know when the employee team builder was going to end so I had to get moving immediately. If he had already checked out, I would have been at a loss as to who could help me.

I jumped into the jeep and hauled my butt back to the resort with no plan as to how I would find Matthew, but I knew that if he was there, someone would have seen him. Those bow ties were unmistakable. On the way, I considered that I also had Travis and Henri who would help in any way they could. Until I could convince the Sheriff to start looking at places Bailey might be held against her will, all the locals would be concentrated on the snowy mountains. Unless that changed, I was alone in this quest. I hoped I was up for the challenge.

CHAPTER SIXTEEN

I parked my car in the guest parking lot at the resort and hurried inside. My plan included asking every staff person, other than the people at the reception desk if they had seen someone matching Matthew's description. Alternatively, if I happened across anyone I recognized from the party, I would know Miller Communications was still on site. Then it was a matter of waiting for Matthew to enter or exit via the lobby so I could exert my powers of persuasion and convince him to help me.

No one in the restaurant had seen him, nor the valet guys nor a random housekeeper I cornered while she tried to roll her cart down a hallway. I camped out in the lobby with a cup of hot chocolate and a cookie, or three. The thought crossed my mind that I could sit in the lobby every day and supplement my meager food budget with free snacks.

While I watched for Matthew to pass by, I made calls to Arlene and Emmett. Arlene was happy to keep Bugsy as long as needed. After Emmett stopped yelling at me for getting myself into yet another predicament, he agreed to cover the shifts he could, or coerce someone else into doing it. I also checked in with Jenny even though I had no news for her. Bailey would never forgive me if I didn't make sure Jenny was doing okay.

My last call was to Lauren to see if she remembered anything else that might help. Her phone went to voice mail, and I left a message for her to call me as soon as she could. With nothing else productive to do, and a belly full of cookies, I decided to find a grocery store where I could buy a few items that would be okay in my motel room. I would probably store anything that wasn't in a soda can in the car to ensure my mouse friend didn't find a reason to move back in.

I used my car navigation and found a Stop and Shop small grocery store between my new abode and the resort. The day was getting late, and I didn't want to be driving around the mountains at night ever since the ride with Bailey ended in disaster.

There weren't many cars, so I was able to park close to the door under a streetlight. I grabbed a cart and drifted down the aisles in search of groceries I could store in my car; things that had a baseline nutritional value and didn't require cooking. I picked a can of tuna, *eew gross,* and some bread. Then, I put the tuna back and got peanut butter and jelly, donuts, and cheddar cheese chips. I topped it off with fruit and a twelve-pack of Diet Mountain Dew.

As I rounded the last aisle to check out, I smelled him before I spotted him. Mathew!! I hurried to catch up to him.

"Hey Matthew, remember me?"

His eyes opened wide, and his mouth hung open. "No, I don't think we've met," he stammered and turned his cart as if to leave, but I was quicker and grabbed his arm.

"We met at the company party a few nights ago. That guy knocked into you, and you made me spill my wine all over my sweater. We shared a car back to the resort. We've run into each other a couple of times since. I'm sure you remember."

His face turned three shades of red and he licked his lips.

After a long pause, he sighed, "Yes, I remember you. Jayne, *from accounting.* I checked and there isn't anyone named Jayne who works in accounting. Why are you following me?"

I looked down at my cart, "I'm not following you, but I do really, really need to ask you a favor."

"You're kidding me, right? I know who you are. Everyone at the resort knows you're the one who found the dead body and I know you don't work for Miller Communications. Why would I help someone who is a liar?"

"Look, I'm sorry I lied to you. I'm desperate. My friend went missing and I'm sure she's been kidnapped. I'm trying to find out who might have taken her and why. I hope you will use your computer skills to help me investigate. I think there might be a connection to Miller Communications or this other company called Core Logistics."

"Did you say Core Logistics? Why would you ask me? I don't know anything."

"The sheriff and I both think there's a connection."

"I don't know anything. You need to leave me alone."

"Wait, what are you doing grocery shopping? Aren't all your meals paid for by the company?" I peered into his cart and started digging around. "Alcohol wipes and cotton balls?"

Matthew yanked his cart away from my prying eyes. "It isn't against the law to buy groceries and it's none of your business why I'm here. Why are you here? Shouldn't you go home where you belong?"

I held up one finger, "Number one, I have to eat and, you're right, I don't work for Miller, so no one is paying for my meals." I held up two fingers, "Number two, I can't leave until I find my friend and I thought maybe you could help me – would help me. And number three, well, actually, I don't have a number three."

He let out a long sigh. "You still haven't told me what you think I could do. I don't know your friend and I won't snoop around my company. I have a wife and daughter to take care of."

"I honestly don't know if you can help me. I'm here and I'm not a computer wizard like my friend Bailey is. If I had her skills,

I could probably find me if I were missing. I'm desperate. The sheriff hasn't found her, but he thinks she's lost in the woods, and I'm pretty sure someone kidnapped her because she had the dirt on someone at a company she was working for."

Matthew fidgeted. "Kidnapped! That's a serious charge."

"Well, it's a serious situation when your friend, who is like a sister to you, vanishes without a trace."

A woman with two kids in her cart and an exhausted expression us a wide berth, likely due to my raised voice.

Matthew pulled me to the side of the aisle. "Keep your voice down. I had a sister too. I know what it's like to lose someone you love, but I can't help you. If your friend found something out, then she's the only one who knows what it is and why someone would want to shut her up." At that he hurried away, leaving his cart behind.

"Geez, a simple no would have worked," I called to his quickly moving back.

I crossed Matthew off my list of helpers although I didn't think he needed to be so reactive. I had to figure out a better plan. I paid for my meager food supply and headed back to my temporary housing. I missed Jonas already. I knew he was in the middle of solving the plumbing issue, but I wished he could fly back right away. I felt grounded in his presence and not my usual scattered self.

Back at the motel, I tried Lauren's cell phone again and this time was lucky when she answered on the third ring.

"Hi Lauren, it's Jayne Stanford. I was wondering if you remembered any more information that might help me find Bailey."

"Hi. I'm just getting off a flight in Denver. I do have information that might help. I have a meeting with Sheriff Cox in the morning, but I want to meet with you in person first. It's not something I can discuss over the phone."

"Thank you! There's been no new information about Bailey since we spoke, and every minute that she is still missing makes this situation seem more frightening."

"I'll be at the resort by seven. Can we meet?"

I didn't relish the idea of hanging out in my sparse room waiting to see if the mouse returned, but I was also nervous about driving back to the resort in the dark. Despite that, I knew Bailey would have moved mountains to find me if the situation was reversed, so I had to suck it up and drive.

"I'll be there. I'll meet you in the lobby."

She hung up. I flipped through the television channels to try to distract myself. All the earlier driving back and forth to the airport left me exhausted. Despite my anxiety about sleeping alone in the room, I stretched out on the flimsy bedspread and tried to rest my mind so I could be fresh when I met with Lauren.

I prayed she had legitimate information that would help find Bailey. The situation was like a bomb with only seconds left before it exploded. Every minute she was missing was like another weight pressing down on the detonator. All the tragic experiences I'd ever had in my relatively brief life, including the moment when I watched my father drown, swirled in my mind. I asked myself again if I had what it took to find my best friend.

I awoke with a start to sounds coming from the room next door. Thump, thump, thump. Why did I have to get a room next to someone who made strange noises at all hours of the day or night? I hadn't planned to fall asleep and felt a heavy fog that only a shower would clear away. Thank heavens Jonas had done a full-on sanitizing of the bathroom so it was usable.

After a quick shower, I pawed through my clothes and Bailey's to find something respectable to wear to meet Lauren. I changed clothes twice and dropped my mascara three times trying to get ready. This meeting could be the key ingredient to help find my friend. I wasn't sure if the shaking of my hands had to do with hunger pains or the outcome of tonight.

As I exited my room, I saw an odd couple hurrying into one of the rooms at the end of the row. It was too dark to make out their faces but he had his hand on her back as if to rush her inside. I hoped their room was in a better state than mine. On second thought, I wondered if this was one of those pay-by-the-hour types of place based on the noises I kept hearing from the room next to mine. I shook that image off and climbed into the jeep.

My pulse raced at the thought of what news Lauren might have to offer, I hoped it would bring me closer to finding Bailey. I drove as quickly as I dared. Without the comfort of streetlights to show me the way, the night was as black as coal, and I felt as if I were driving down into the depths of the earth. I felt a sudden chill and pressed my foot on the gas. There wasn't a minute to lose. I slowed for the turn from Route 40 onto the small road that would lead me to the resort.

Around the first sharp bend in the road, I was blinded by the flashing lights of multiple emergency vehicles. My stomach clenched and my mind flashed back to the accident on the night Bailey disappeared. I bit my lip to quelch the urge to scream. It had happened days before, but I felt the sensation of going off the road as if it was happening in the moment. My body reacted again to the memory of feeling weightless for seconds before plummeting down the cliffside.

At the sight of a car wrapped around a tree, I pulled over to the shoulder and rested my head on the steering wheel. I squeezed my eyes closed and focused on slowing down my breathing. I almost jumped out of my seat when there was a rap, rap, rap on my window.

"Roll down your window ma'am."

I powered down the window, "Yes, officer."

"Why are you stopped here? This is an accident scene. You need to move your car down the road."

I sniffled, "I'm sorry. All the lights freaked me out. Is everyone okay?"

He shook his head, "I'm not at liberty to say." He leaned closer. "Have you been drinking this evening?"

"No, I promise you I have not had anything alcoholic to drink in days." I wiped my sweaty palms on my pants. Even when not guilty of a crime, I immediately felt that everyone believed I was.

"Move along ma'am."

Part of me wanted to correct him that I was a Miss not a Ma'am but what was the point? I put the car in gear and rolled slowly past the EMTs as they loaded a woman from the car onto a stretcher. They were speaking to her, so I knew she was conscious, and I took that as a good sign.

I drove more slowly the rest of the way to the resort. The parking lot was almost full, so I was forced to park the Jeep in one of the spots farthest from the lobby. Whisper-light snowflakes fell on my cheeks. In another circumstance, I might have held out my tongue and caught them, but tonight I wanted nothing more than to meet with Lauren and crawl back to my frugal abode.

I inquired if Lauren had checked in at the front desk, but they refused to confirm or deny. The clerk did agree to take my name in case she called. I dropped into a seat near the crackling fireplace and sat with my head in my shaking hands. My stomach was doing a succession of flip-flops. I suspected it had nothing to do with a lack of food. There was so much at stake if Lauren really had information to lead to Bailey. If this fell through, I couldn't imagine what I could do next.

A deep sigh escaped. I was failing at the most important challenge of my life. Yes, the Sheriff was looking for Bailey, too, but she was my best friend and I felt the personal responsibility deeply.

I watched people coming and going in the lobby for the next hour. Where was Lauren? I checked my phone, but there were no calls since she and I spoke. I tried calling her number, but it rang until it rolled over to her voicemail. I wondered if the snow had slowed or stopped her progress. I decided I would wait until she showed up regardless of the time.

The ticking of the massive grandfather's clock helped slow my heart rate, and I stopped jiggling my legs. I sipped a hot cocoa to soothe my frayed nerves and quiet the turmoil in my stomach.

I dozed off in the chair and was roused by the stern voice of the Sheriff.

"Wake up Miss Stanford. I need to speak with you."

I jumped to my feet. "Did you find Bailey?"

"No, but we are still looking. We need to talk about another matter."

"Sheriff, I swear I haven't done anything. I've been in my room except when I went to the grocery store."

"It's nothing you have done. This time anyway." He sat in the oversized chair beside me that barely fit his girth.

If he wasn't here to give me news about Bailey, I couldn't imagine what else we had to discuss. I slumped back into the chair. I rubbed the back of my neck to release the tension that kept creeping into my body.

"Go ahead, Sheriff. Give me whatever bad news you've come here to tell me."

He cleared his throat and shifted in his seat before he began. "You spoke to a Miss Lauren Davis."

"Yes, I did. I've been waiting here for her to arrive."

"You won't need to wait any longer. She won't be coming."

"What? Why?"

"I'm afraid to tell you she's been in an accident this evening."

My pulse raced and the image of the accident I passed flashed through my mind. "Where did this happen?"

"Just a few miles down the road from here."

"Oh no! Is she…?" I couldn't finish my sentence. I refused to let the thought complete in my mind.

"She was taken to the hospital. I'm not at liberty to discuss the extent of her injuries but she regained consciousness and asked me to contact you."

"Thank goodness. I was afraid you were going to tell me something horrible. Not that having an accident isn't bad enough but at least she's alive."

"Ms. Davis had an appointment to meet with me in the morning to go over some information she thought might be relevant to Harry Schepp's murder as well as your friend's disappearance. Unfortunately, she is likely to be in the hospital for a period. I'll have to wait to speak with her at length until her doctors release her."

"Sheriff, I've been meaning to tell you that I'm certain someone kidnapped my friend. I know you've spent a lot of time and effort in finding her, but my gut tells me she isn't out there. Maybe she's closer to us than we know."

He sighed. "While I appreciate your theories, I've been doing this job for as long as you've been on this planet." He held up his hand to stop me from interrupting him. "This isn't my first murder nor missing person investigation. Just because this community seems quiet doesn't mean crime doesn't happen here too."

"What does that mean in relation to Bailey?"

"It's my job to follow every lead. My priority was to confirm that Ms. Chauncey wasn't wandering around in the snow or injured – despite there being no tangible evidence to support that. Although it's **not** my job to keep you in the loop with our investigation, you might be on the right track."

I almost jumped out of my seat. This was good news. Not that Bailey had been kidnapped, because that still wasn't great news, but that she wasn't someplace wandering the snow-covered mountain alone. My heart told me she was alive, and she wasn't freezing to death. The Sheriff didn't confirm my suspicion, but he didn't deny it either.

"Do you have any idea of who kidnapped her?"

"I can't tell you that. However, there is a way you might be able to help the investigation."

"I'll do anything you need. You can use me as bait for the kidnapper. Or I'll get a billboard with her picture on it. Or I could go door to door."

"Stop right there. I want you to think about those names I showed you before. Lauren Davis was on that list. We know she had a relationship with Harry Schepp. We also know that she had a relationship with your friend, Bailey. We have three pieces to the puzzle."

"Lauren told me about Harry and Bailey. But she didn't tell me anymore about why someone would hurt them."

"I need you to think about anything Bailey may have said or done that seemed out of the ordinary." He held up his hand again when he saw that I was ready to jump in with more ideas. "I want you to think about anything you've seen or heard since you left Arizona that might be relevant. I know we've been through this before, but I need to be sure you focus on the connection between your friend, Harry Schepp, and Lauren Davis."

"Lauren told me she had more information and that's why we were meeting tonight. I can go see her and find out what she wanted to tell me."

"No, you will not," He ordered.

"But Sheriff. We don't have any time to waste!"

"I forbid you from going to the hospital. I thought I made myself clear about your participation in my investigation before. I want you to stay put and focus on what I instructed you to do. Not one iota more. Do not bother Ms. Davis. Do not stick your nose into this and potentially destroy evidence or alert the unknown subject."

I shook my head, "How can I avoid someone unknown?"

"Don't play cute with me or I will detain you to keep you in line."

I took a long drink of my now cold cocoa and tried to steady my voice. Being detained was a nice way of saying he would lock me up and then I couldn't continue my search for Bailey.

I nodded. "I'll do my best to stay out of the way."

The Sheriff stood, satisfied for the moment by my response and the fear I was sure he saw in my eyes. "I'll be in touch in the next few days. Stay in town for the time being in case I need you to come into the office."

"I'm not leaving until Bailey's found."

"Very well. Remember my warning. Stay out of trouble."

"I don't plan to get into any more trouble than I've already had since I've been here."

I watched him stomp out of the lobby. His heavy toolbelt was loaded with his gun, taser, pepper spray, and handcuffs. If I had one immediate goal in my life, it was to avoid giving him a reason to use any of those on me.

I exhaled the breath I didn't realize I'd been holding. Every encounter with the Sheriff left me drained. I gazed at the clock as it progressed to the top of the hour. I knew I *should* go back to my motel room and try to get some rest. I also knew what I *would* do instead and that was to visit Lauren. I wouldn't be able to close my eyes until I saw her and convinced myself she would be okay. I told him I would do my best to stay out of the way, but I did not tell him I wouldn't go to the hospital. Sheriff or not, he wasn't the boss of me.

I didn't know which hospital she was at but a quick check on the hotel computer showed me that there was only one in the area. It was five miles in the opposite direction from my motel. I grabbed a handful of cookies and wrapped them in a napkin, as well as a to-go cup of steaming hot chocolate and plodded out the door.

It didn't take long to warm up the Jeep, and having seats that heated my rear was particularly enjoyable. The rental was cleaner and more luxurious than my motel room, and if I ran the engine all night, it may be a better option.

I plugged the hospital address into the GPS and followed a distinctly British voice that directed me which turns to take. Thankful that the roads were clear of the earlier snow flurries, I made good time.

The hospital was a three-story modern building with rows of windows on every floor. The parking lot was full of cars with plates from every state. I imagined I wasn't the only person who slid down the snowy mountains on her rear end, but maybe others were worse than me for the wear.

The lobby had a pungent antiseptic smell, but it was nicely decorated in soothing shades of blue and green. On the left was a spacious waiting area with rows of chairs and a television on the wall playing a cooking show. Signs pointed to where X-rays, Labs, and Pediatrics could be found.

I approached the rosy-cheeked woman sitting at reception. She smiled as she asked me if she could help me.

"I'm looking for Lauren Davis's room. She came in a little while ago after a car accident."

"She's in room 310, but I'm afraid visiting hours ended at 9."

I looked at the clock behind her which read 9:05. "Do you think I could just run up for five minutes to let her know I'll be back in the morning? She flew in today just to see me, and I know she's wondering if I know she's okay."

"Are you family?"

"Yes," I lied. "She's my, ah, cousin."

She looked around at the people in the lobby and the security guard who stood nearby. "I guess it's okay if you just run up for a minute. Promise me you won't stay long."

"I promise. I'll just dash in and see how she's doing and dash back out."

She pointed down the hallway. "Take the elevator up to the third floor and follow the signs."

"Thank you so much. I can't tell you how important this is."

I moved with measured steps. My heart said hurry, hurry but my head said slow down and don't act like a crazy woman. The sheriff didn't tell me how serious Lauren's injuries were, but since she wasn't in the intensive care unit, I sensed it wasn't life-threatening.

I entered the elevator behind an elderly couple. It was heartwarming to see how carefully the gentleman pushed her wheelchair and turned her so that she could push the button for the second floor. He smiled at her and held her hand while we waited as the doors closed and the elevator began its excruciatingly slow ascent. My toe tapped and I stifled an exasperated huff of breath. It would be 9:30 by the time I made it to Lauren's room at this rate.

After what felt like an hour, the elderly couple disembarked the elevator on the second floor. Slowly the doors closed and I counted to one hundred until they opened again on the third floor.

I paced the hallway until I found room 310. The door was closed and the room was lit only by a florescent light that shone over the bed. I could see through the small window that there was only one occupant. I took a couple of quick breaths and pushed the door open.

A woman lay with her right leg in a cast propped up on pillows. Her left arm was wrapped and covered by a sling. Her short brown hair was tousled around an ashen face marked by jagged stitches on the forehead. I could see that dark bruises had already formed below each eye. The machines by her side emitted a constant beep indicating a steady heart rate. I had learned a few things, besides who didn't like peas, by working at the senior living center.

I stepped to the bedside and softly rested my hand on her good arm. Her eyelids fluttered open and she turned to look at me.

"Lauren, I'm Jayne. We talked on the phone. I'm so sorry about your accident. Is there anything I can do?"

"It wasn't an accident. Someone forced me off the road," she whispered.

I gasped, "No! Does the sheriff know this?"

"I told the officer at the scene and spoke briefly to the sheriff."

"This must be related to Harry's murder and Bailey's disappearance. How would anyone know you were coming here?"

She slowly shook her head, "I don't know the answer to that. I had documents in my rental car that might provide help to figure this out. I'm not sure if they're still in the car or if the police have them. I can only think that someone in my office must have a stake in this."

"Do you have any idea who that is?"

"I have a suspicion, but I can't accuse someone without the information that Bailey was working on."

"It must have been in the folders she brought on this trip. They were stolen from our room right after we got here."

Lauren's eyes fluttered shut. "I'm so tired."

"I'm sorry. Is there anything I can get for you? Are you in pain?"

The only answer was the sound of her breathing and the machine beeping.

I considered stuffing myself into the small chair in the corner and staying the night in case she awoke with more information. Those plans were dashed when a nurse strode into the room.

"Visiting hours are over. You'll have to leave."

"Please tell her I'll be back in the morning."

I slumped down the hallway to the elevator. I was no closer to finding Bailey than I had been the first hour she disappeared.

Granted, I did know there were other people connected and Bailey was one piece of the puzzle. I felt the clock ticking the time away. The longer she was missing the more danger she was in. Why couldn't I figure this out? I punched the elevator button for the first floor. First thing in the morning, I was going to set up my own posse and recruit local help. Together we would find Bailey or die trying.

CHAPTER SEVENTEEN

My head was pounding. The same thing happened every time I fell asleep. Thumping from the room next door continued on and off all night long. I banged on the wall, but whoever it was didn't care. The noise would stop for a while and then begin again as soon as I dozed off. Once it was it was daylight, I was going to talk to the manager. Good old Rip Van Winkle may not be a deluxe motel, but my money should have ensured I could sleep for more than an hour at a time.

I gave up and decided to shower and get dressed while I waited for it to be an appropriate time of day to start making phone calls. I needed to touch base with Jonas and Jenny and give them both updates. After that, I hoped to recruit Henri and Travis to help me solve this mystery.

I was worried because the sheriff hadn't stationed a guard outside of Lauren's room. I feared that whoever ran her off the road might return to complete the deed.

I called Jenny first and gave her what little information I had. I did my best to assure her that neither the sheriff nor I believed that she was lost in the woods. Although possibly being held captive by a deranged person wasn't good news, it was better than being lost in the woods to freeze to death. I did my best to give her a silver lining for a grave situation. I also asked her to look around Bailey's office to see if she could find anything related to Core Logistics. She promised to call me immediately if she found anything.

I called Jonas next and left him a long rambling voicemail. I missed him more than I ever thought possible. I wanted to tell him that I needed him desperately and beg him to drop everything and fly back to Colorado. I wanted to tell him that, even though I hadn't been able to say the words yet, I was in love with him. I wanted to tell him how safe he made me feel whenever he was near. I wanted to promise him that I would be neater and would stop leaving clothes all over the floor.

But I didn't tell him any of those things. Instead, I told him about not being able to sleep and how I hadn't seen the mouse since he left. I kept my message lighthearted so he wouldn't worry and could focus on getting the plumbing job completed that he flew back to finish.

When I hung up, I felt the exhaustion that had been building since the car crash with Bailey. I knew I should eat something, but the thought of food made my stomach turn. I felt a hollowness in my chest and considered crawling back into the bed and pulling the thin blanket over my face, but I knew I couldn't. I sat in the rickety chair with my face in my hands and tried to summon the energy I needed to keep moving forward.

I went into the bathroom and stared at my reflection in the mirror. Disheveled black hair framed a pale face outlined with dark shadows. Despite being in my twenties, I could see frown lines and creases on my face that hadn't been there days before. I plucked at what looked like my first gray hair and wondered if gray hair could shoot out of my head due to stress.

I pointed at my reflection. "Stop being a baby, Jayne. You have a job to do so get busy. You've been in worse situations than this and you got out of it. You can do this too. You *have* to do this."

I pressed my lips together and, with my chin held high, marched out of the bathroom. The time for action was now. I needed to ask for help because I couldn't do this alone.

I called Henri, grateful when he answered immediately.

"Bonjour Jayne. Do you have good news to tell me?"

"No, Henri. I wish I did. I don't know where Bailey is, but I'm sure I know where she isn't."

"Where is she not?"

"Neither the Sheriff nor I believe she's lost in the woods. He didn't say it exactly, but I sense he agrees with me that Bailey was kidnapped. I don't want to go into it all over the phone. I'm hoping we can meet and maybe brainstorm together."

"A votre service. Henri would be honored to help. I have two lessons this morning. After that, I'm free all afternoon."

"Perfect. I have one more call to make to someone else who knows this area. I'll call you back with a meeting time and place as soon as possible."

"Au revoir."

I didn't have a phone number for Travis, so I had to dial the main resort number. The phone rang several times before I was directed back to reception. I felt antsy in my room, so I decided it was time to hop in the jeep and look for Travis in the barn.

On the way, I pulled over at the spot of Lauren's accident. Her car had been towed, probably to the only service station in town, which was also where my rental had been towed. I wanted to check the surroundings to make sure the deputies hadn't missed any clues. As unlikely as I thought that would be, I suspected they weren't working the case as a hit-and-run at the time. She told me she had files related to the situation in which Harry and Bailey were involved. On the off chance that they were ejected from the car during the accident, I examined the area.

I assessed the damage to the tree her car slammed into and the surrounding area where the emergency crews had tromped the snow into slushy piles. Nothing jumped out to me as a "Here I am - the evidence you've been searching for." I gave up and drove the rest of the way to the resort barn.

The hotel van parked in the lot told me Travis might have taken the sleigh out with guests. In the paddock next to the barn, the mules we rode on our search for Bailey contentedly munched their breakfast of hay while covered with heavy horse blankets. Candy lifted her head at my approach and gave me a snort. *Yeah, after our bear encounter, I'm not thrilled to see you either,* I thought to myself.

Chickens clucked and scratched for bugs in the aisle between the stalls. I inhaled the aroma of leather and horse and felt a sense of calm. I rolled my shoulders and relaxed the tension I had been holding in my jaw. Some people loved the ocean and some people loved the mountains, but for me, my happy place was wherever there were horses.

Ever since I was a little girl, I'd dreamed of having my own horse. Being with Jonas helped that dream come true in part because he and I rode his horses whenever we could. I rested my face against the nose of a two thousand pound bay gelding who gave me a deep nicker.

After a moment to recharge my soul, I went in search of Travis. Four of the stalls were empty and the sleigh wasn't parked ready for the next excursion. I decided to check the office to see if Travis had posted a schedule for sleigh rides. Based on that I would either wait for his return or go back to the hospital to check on Lauren.

John Whiteskunk leaned back in the rolling desk chair with his muddy boots propped on the desk. His dark eyes seared into me, and it felt as if he knew my deepest secrets.

His weathered appearance was etched with the lines of wisdom and experience earned over a lifetime. His face, marked by the passage of time, bore the traces of a life lived close to the land and in harmony with nature. In his deep and knowing eyes I saw the stories of generations past, reflecting the resilience and strength of his people. More than anything at that moment, I wanted to sit quietly by his side as he told me his stories.

I sunk into the brown leather chair which had softened over time, forming a comfortable nest that molded to the contours of my body. The arms of the chair bore imprints of countless elbows and hands, smoothed by constant contact. Despite its age, the chair retained a sense of character.

Neither of us spoke for several seconds. The aromas of the barn and John's calming presence relaxed me. My breathing slowed and my body relaxed. I released my grip on the arms of the chair and stretched my legs out in front of me.

"Hi, John. It's good to see you again."

"Welcome back Jayne."

"You remember me?"

"Yes. Did your spirit guide show you the path to take?"

"Er, I guess he did. A lot has happened since I last saw you."

"I can see that you are different, and your burden is heavier."

"My friend is missing. I have a feeling someone kidnapped her— someone she found incriminating information about. I don't know which way to turn. I have to find her."

John removed his boots from the desk and stood. My people have a saying. It is, "When your heart and the earth sing the same song, you know you're walking the right path."

"I don't know what that means."

"You must listen. Listen to the sounds around you. What do you hear?"

I closed my eyes and focused. "I hear the chickens cluck and scratch. I hear a horse chomp on feed. I hear the hum of the computer on the desk. I hear myself when I take a deep breath." I stood and faced John, "None of that helps me find Bailey."

"Keep listening. Listen with your heart."

"I'm sorry John. I know you're trying to help me meditate or something to find the answers, but I've never been good at that. I'm a jump-in and figure out how to swim kind of girl."

"How is that working for you?"

"Well, to be honest, it hasn't worked out too well in the past. It's gotten me into trouble, but I usually find a way out."

"No man is an island."

"Is that more wisdom from the Ute people?"

"No, it's a quote from John Donne. "No man is an island, entire of itself; every man is a piece of the continent, a part of the main.'"

I put my hands over my face. Why was he talking in circles? It was giving me a headache.

He continued, "Ask for help, Jayne. You are not alone. In your life, have you ever been alone?"

I thought about his words, "No, I guess I haven't ever been really alone. There's always been someone I could turn to for help. Bailey was someone I turned to recently. She can't help me find her when she's the one who is missing."

"Maybe she can."

John walked to the door of the office and turned to me before he left. "Remember what I said. Listen with your heart and it will guide you."

I closed my eyes for a moment and when I opened them he was gone.

I heard sleigh bells ringing and people laughing. I stepped out of the office and John was nowhere to be seen in the barn.

I called out, "John, wait. I have more questions. I don't know how to listen with my heart."

He had disappeared as quickly as the breeze that blew through the barn, taking small bits of straw and swirling them into the air. I shook my head. I wondered how a man of his age moved so fast.

Travis pulled the team to a stop just outside the barn and helped the rosy-cheeked guests step down from the sleigh. I waited at the entrance until they said their goodbyes and he unhooked the horses.

John reminded me of my goal in coming to see Travis. I needed to recruit his help. He knew the area better than anyone. If there was a good place to hold someone captive, I hoped he would be able to point me in that direction.

Travis shook his head at the sight of me as he brought in two of the massive draft horses.

"I've been riding out every day looking for any sign of your friend. She's not out there or I would have found her. Are you sure she didn't just leave you here?"

"I'm one hundred percent sure. I have more information about her disappearance which is why I want to talk to you."

He put the horses in their stalls and dropped a leaf of hay in each feed bin. "Let me get these ladies settled and we can talk in the office."

I busied myself with formulating a plan. If I had Travis and Henri on my team, we had a better shot of finding Bailey than I did alone. No man is an island. Nor any woman. I knew it would take a village and I planned to recruit one.

Travis lumbered into the office and plopped down in the chair vacated by John.

"Okay, tell me what new intel you have."

"Bailey was investigating an employee of Core Logistics. I don't have all the information yet, but I should know more today when I go back to the hospital."

"The hospital?"

"Sorry, Let me start from the beginning. Bailey is a computer geek. She has lots of clients and she makes sure their site is safe from viruses and stuff like that. One of the employees named Lauren hired Baliey to dig around in their system because she suspected someone was stealing. Lauren also hired Harry, the guy whose body I found."

"Don't remind me about that. I still have nightmares about seeing him."

I shuddered, "Me too. I can't stop thinking about him. I worry about his family and what they must think about him being found by a stranger. Anyway, Lauren was coming here to meet with the Sheriff and also to tell me something that I hoped would help us find Bailey. Someone ran her car off the road before she had a chance to talk to us. She's in the hospital with a broken leg."

"Whoa. Do you always get wrapped up in so much trouble?"

"I think whoever kidnapped Bailey is still here. My gut tells me she wasn't taken far from the resort. That's why I'm here. You know this area better than anyone. I'm hoping we can put our heads together and think of places the sheriff wouldn't think to look or can't search legally. I don't have the same restrictions."

"I want to help you. I really do."

"I sense an objection coming."

"I don't want to go up against the Sheriff."

"I'm not suggesting we cause any problems for him. We can do our own search which doesn't interfere with his. I have someone else to help us too. His name is Henri and he gives skiing lessons. Before he came here, he did search and rescue missions in Canada."

"Didn't you say you don't think she's lost on the mountain? How can he help?"

"We need to search for Bailey and rescue her. It makes perfect sense that he should be part of the team. Besides John said no man is an island which means we need more help."

"John who?"

I point to the photos on the wall, "You know John Whiteskunk. The guy in those photos."

Travis gave me a sideways glance, his eyes questioning me. "That guy has been dead for twenty years."

"What? No way! I spoke to him a few minutes ago. He was sitting in that exact chair with his muddy boots on the desk."

Travis looked at the desk, "Muddy boots, huh? There's no mud on the desk. There's no mud anywhere around here. Just snow and more snow."

I collapsed onto the sofa. "Am I going crazy? Is this some sort of bad dream and I'm going to wake up to find Bailey isn't missing at all?"

"If I didn't know that you found a dead body, I might agree with you that you're crazy. But you did. I don't know why you think you had a conversation with a dead guy, but I know for sure that your friend is missing. I'm on team Jayne. Call your friend, Henri, and we'll figure this out as best we can."

I jumped up and wrapped Travis in the biggest hug I could. "You don't know what this means to me. Thank you!"

I grabbed my phone and called Henri. He agreed to meet us at the barn in two hours when he finished his last lesson. I told Travis I would be back and rushed to the hospital to check on Lauren. If she had any details that might help my ragtag crew find Bailey, it would be a momentous day.

CHAPTER EIGHTEEN

I drove as quickly as I dared to the hospital and dashed up to Lauren's room. I found it empty. After a moment's panic that Lauren had taken a turn for the worse, I asked at the nurse's station. Fortunately, she was released earlier as the doctor didn't need to keep her for observation. The only place I thought she would go was High Mountain. As far as I knew, she still needed to meet with the Sheriff.

Changing direction, I zipped over to the resort. Breaking all the rules about distracted driving, I called Lauren on my way so I could confirm that she was there and doing okay.

She answered and gave me her room number which was on the first floor. I parked in the visitor lot again and galloped to her room as fast as I could go. I couldn't suppress the grin that split my face. I had a feeling that today would be the day when something good happened.

I knocked on room one-oh-one just off the lobby and waited for Lauren to answer. I heard a clump, clump sound as she made her way to the door with crutches.

Finally, she opened the door, and I was taken aback by her appearance. The bruises on her face had fully bloomed into a map of black and purple trails from forehead to chin. Her eyes were swollen to the size of overripe tomatoes and the skin surrounding the stitches was red and puckered.

"Oh my gosh, you look terrible!"

"I feel as bad as I look. Everything hurts in my body. Come in."

She half hopped; half limped back to her bed.

"I'm so sorry this happened to you. Does the Sheriff have any idea who ran you off the road?"

"I don't think he believed me."

"I know the Sheriff can be a tough guy but he seems fair."

"Well, I've been under a massive amount of pressure lately. Core Logistics has been in the news. We're trying to go public and we've had big league players interested. I stopped at a dispensary and picked up a few gummies to help me sleep. I swear I didn't take any. I know better than to take them and drive, especially at night."

My mouth formed an 'o' but I couldn't think of any words. After the experience I had with Henri's *little candies*, I never wanted to get near medicinal marijuana again.

Lauren continued, "So the Sheriff found the gummies and assumed I was high when I ran off the road. They took blood, and I know it will come back clean. Until that happens, I don't think the Sheriff is on my side."

"I don't know what to say."

"I swear I wasn't using drugs. A vehicle ran me off the road."

"Did you get a look at the driver or what the car looked like?"

"It wasn't a car. It was an older van. I couldn't be sure, but I thought I saw a woman in the passenger seat. She smiled at me just before they swerved in front of me. Why would someone run me off the road and keep driving?"

"Are you sure they did it on purpose? Maybe they didn't know you had an accident."

"They knew. The driver cut in front of my car so fast that I only had time to whip the steering wheel to the right. They couldn't have missed seeing me fly off the road."

"That's so strange. Don't you think this must be related to Harry's murder and Bailey's disappearance?"

"I do. I don't know how someone would know I was coming here, unless…"

I leaned forward, "Unless what?"

"I went through our travel department to book this trip. It's possible someone in that department alerted someone else."

I held up my hand, "You think there might be more than one suspect?"

"It's possible. I don't have any solid information, but I have my suspicions."

"Why don't you tell the Sheriff about this?"

"I will when I see him. He's sending a deputy later today to pick me up. I hope he has the results of my bloodwork so he knows I wasn't driving impaired."

"Can you tell me anything to help me find Bailey?"

"This is what I know. I hired Bailey because I heard she is the best at finding computer viruses that have invaded a system. We oversee delicate information at Core Logistics – information which is very personal to our clients. We store priceless works of art, wine collections worth hundreds of thousands of dollars, and cherished antiques. We also manage cryonics."

"Cryonics?"

"Cryonics is the practice of preserving human bodies or brains at extremely low temperatures with the hope of future revival or medical treatment. It's a niche and controversial field that operates in select locations worldwide."

"Are you saying you have frozen body parts stored in your facility?"

"We do. Certain people hope to be able to have their brains implanted in the future into a human or non-human body."

"That's just creepy and gross." I shuddered thinking of what that must look like. "What part did Bailey have in this?"

"Her research wasn't completed, but she told me she was close to determining who might have installed a virus on our main frame. That virus could move valuable items we have stored there to other locations."

"So, someone was stealing people's brains?"

"Well, not those, but someone has been moving other valuables. They appear on the computer to be safe in our facility, but when we did an actual inventory, items were missing."

"Thank heavens they didn't steal someone's brains. I can't get that out of my head." I slapped my face. "Sorry, I didn't mean to say that. Sounds like a bad pun."

"It's a serious situation, and we were very close to discovering the person or persons' identity. I had some suspicions, which is why I brought Harry into the investigation. He had narrowed it down to a few possible suspects."

"So, Harry came here, not because of Bailey, but because he followed one of the suspects?"

"Originally I asked him to keep an eye on Bailey for her protection. If this person is capable of this level of crime, Bailey might have been at risk. The last time he contacted me, he was sure he had figured out who was involved and he planned to give me a final report."

"But he never got the chance because someone murdered him first. Someone who knew he was investigating the criminal activity." Internally, I wondered if Harry's report was in the envelope Bailey never had a chance to review.

"That's what I assume."

I slumped into the chair and nibbled a fingernail. This was more serious than I suspected. Whoever didn't want to get caught killed Harry because of it. Would that person have already killed Bailey to keep her quiet?

"There's one piece of good news."

"Oh please. I need good news right now."

"Bailey made backups of everything she did. Most of it was stored on the Cloud, but she also made backups on a separate drive from her PC."

"Yes, I've seen her office. She has backups of backups."

"If you can get that backup drive, I know someone who can access it. Then we'll have the last piece of the puzzle which is what I need to take this to the police."

I had no reason to doubt Lauren, but suddenly the hairs on the back of my neck stood up. How could she know Bailey had backups of everything? Would Bailey tell her that? Maybe, but was I sure I could trust this person? After my recent experiences, I had the feeling I should be a little cautious. The room felt oppressive and stagnant. Sweat dripped down my back and I struggled to catch my breath. What if she wasn't who she said she was? Maybe she needed to find Bailey to shut her up.

I jumped to my feet. "I have to go. I forgot I am meeting someone and I'm late."

"Can you get me those backups?"

"I'll see what I can do."

"Hurry because time is running out."

I rushed to the door, removing the bolt she set when I entered. I needed time to think. Whatever else Lauren said, she was right about time running out. I felt it in my chest.

Once in the hall, I slowed my pace. I would repeat my conversation with Lauren to Henri and Travis and get their take on the situation. Was Lauren part of the mystery or the solution?

I decided a sugar fix would help me focus, which I never planned to have frozen, to focus. I grabbed a couple of warm chocolate chip cookies from the lobby and fixed a piping hot cup of cocoa.

As I turned with my bounty, I saw Matthew seated by the fireplace. All his attention was focused on the phone in his hand. I dropped the cookies, which crumbled into pieces like chocolate chip pebbles all over the lavish rug at my feet. I knew that phone. There was only one person I had ever seen with a phone cover like that. A large brown and pink anime cartoon cat with a pink bow. I walked, as if in a trance, to where he sat.

"Hi, Matthew. I'm surprised you're still here."

Matthew was startled and dropped the phone. We both reached for it at the same time and I accidentally spilled the hot cocoa all over his lap.

"Watch what you're doing! That's scalding! You've probably given me third-degree burns."

He jumped up to grab napkins and while he was not looking, I snatched the phone and stuffed it into my purse. If it wasn't Bailey's I would apologize later.

When he returned, he began his search for the phone. I stood innocently, holding my almost empty cup while he looked around and under the chair.

"Did you lose something?"

"My, my phone," he stuttered.

"What does it look like?"

"Did you take it? Is that why you dumped hot chocolate all over me?"

"I don't know what you mean. I was only coming over to say hello to you. I didn't see a phone."

"You're lying. Give it back."

"I'm sorry but I have to go. See you around."

I scurried out the lobby door as he continued crawling around on the floor. I practically ran to the Jeep. My pulse raced and my palms were so sweaty that I dropped the phone on the floorboards trying to see it. I locked the doors and decided to move my car in case Matthew followed me out to the parking lot.

I drove away from the resort and pulled into a fast-food drive-through. I needed fries and a chocolate shake. It was my go-to energizer when my stress level reached its maximum. I ordered a cheeseburger too since I hadn't eaten much.

I pulled into a parking spot with my food and the phone. It certainly looked like Bailey's phone. What were the odds that a guy would have the same phone that went missing from our room? Pretty small to none, I would guess. I took a huge bite of burger and washed it down with a gulp of shake.

I pressed the power button to wake the phone, and sure enough, I was greeted with a photo of my arch nemesis, Bailey's attack rooster. I didn't know her password but to make sure I was completely convinced this was hers, I dialed her number from my phone and watched it vibrate in my hand. What was Matthew doing with Bailey's phone? Did he kidnap her? If so, what reason would he have? He worked for Miller Communications and as far as I knew, there was no connection between his firm and Core Logistics. I did believe that he had the computer know-how to hack into a company's system.

Would Bailey have notes stored on her phone that would answer my questions? I punched in numbers I thought might open it. None worked. The next option was to call Jenny and hope that she knew what the code was. At least if I could get into the phone, I might have more information. Either way, I bet the Sheriff would want this information.

I left Jenny a message to call me as soon as she could. I scurried back to the resort barn to meet with Henri and Travis. Together we would figure out what to do next.

A short while later we were all seated in the barn office. I paced, while Henri and Travis tossed out different ideas.

"Should we turn the phone in to the Sheriff?" Henri asked.

"If we turn it in, then we must tell him that Jayne stole it from the person who may have stolen it to begin with. What if that guy just found the phone and was trying to figure out who it belonged to?"

I shook my head, "He claimed it was his phone. I'm sure he knew it was Bailey's because he took it from her. I want to know why he had it and what he did with her. I want to know now!"

Henri jumped to his feet, "We must kidnap him and force him to tell us what he did with Bailey!"

"Absolutely not. I am not going to jail for kidnapping someone," Travis declared.

I pounded my fist on the desk, "I don't care what it takes, I'm finding Bailey. We need to grab Matthew and wring the truth out of him."

Henri patted my back, "Let's not go crazy. I didn't really mean we would resort to violence."

I felt tears well up in my eyes and when I spoke my voice quavered, "Please. I have to do something. She's been gone for days and I don't know if she's even alive. I can't stand the thought that someone hurt her."

Travis took over my pacing on the worn wooden plank floor. "Let's go over the facts we know for certain."

I scrounged around the desk until I found a pen and paper. "We know, or at least we think we know, that Bailey isn't wandering around lost."

"I've covered everyplace I could on horseback and snowmobile and so has an entire team of volunteers and no one has found her. The Sheriff had helicopters and dogs looking for her. I'm sure she's not out there," Travis said in a firm voice.

"I too have looked everywhere I thought she could have wandered to no avail," said Henri.

"So, we agree she is not lost. That leaves the kidnap theory. I suppose the Sheriff is also going in that direction. I don't think Arnie Miller or his company is involved. At least not based on my searches of his property. Although that mansion might have rooms I missed, it doesn't make sense that he would be the one holding her."

Travis continued pacing while Henri looked over my shoulder. He pointed to my list, "Let's make a list of suspects."

"Matthew is top of the list. He had Bailey's phone so he had to have found it or taken it from her. We agree he didn't find it, so that makes him our number one suspect." I wrote his name at the top of the page in capital letters with double underlines.

"What about this Lauren person? She has ties to both Bailey and Harry."

I shook my head, "I'm not sure about her. If she was involved, who would have a reason to run her off the road? She told me there were at least two people in the van that caused her accident. At least one was a woman, but we don't know if the other was a man or woman."

"Is it possible she is working with the person who took Bailey and that person decided to double-cross her?"

Travis rubbed the back of his neck, "Don't most kidnappers want money? We haven't heard about a ransom request, right?"

"If there was one, the Sheriff would have mentioned it. No one would ask me for money because I can barely pay my rent most months. Jenny would have told me if anyone had contacted her. I don't know about Bailey's parents. She never talks about them."

I thought about my conversation with Bailey when she told me about the accident that killed her sister, Lilly, and her friend Melissa. It was the anniversary of the accident. Could it be related to what happened here? I rubbed my temples. A small army had started a march through my head.

Henri brought me back to the present with a snap of his fingers, "Earth to Jayne."

"Sorry, I was just thinking about something Bailey told me on the way here. I don't think it's relevant."

"Let's put Lauren's name on our list because we don't have anyone else to consider," Travis suggested.

216

"Back to the facts we know." Henri pointed to the paper, "Write these down, Jayne. We know Bailey is missing. We know at least one person had to have taken her. We know she hasn't been able to contact you or anyone else so she's being held against her will."

A shudder ran through my body. "Or she can't contact me because it's too late."

Henri patted my shoulder, "Now, now, let's not consider that as an option."

Travis stopped pacing and stood with his hands on his hips, "Let's go with someone who has her prisoner. Where is the best place to hide someone?"

Henri rubbed his chin, "Not at the resort. Housekeeping would know."

"Obviously, not at the barn, because look around you. There's no place to hide anyone here that I wouldn't have seen."

"Not at Arnie's place, because I searched it."

We spent another half hour tossing around possible places to hold someone against their will and came up empty. Feeling dejected, we promised to meet again and focus on Matthew. Henri had lessons to teach and Travis had sleigh rides scheduled for the next two days.

I walked to my car with slumped shoulders. My head throbbed and my nails were ripped to the quick from my constant picking at them. We had accomplished nothing. I didn't know which way to turn. Do I trust Lauren and try to work with her to find Bailey? She had the most information of anyone at this point. Do I confront Matthew? Other than the phone, I had nothing. What the heck was the Sheriff doing?

CHAPTER NINETEEN

My spirits plummeted. I felt as deflated as an overcooked souffle and as useless as a steak knife in a vegan restaurant. Why did I imagine I could figure out a problem of this magnitude when someone as experienced as the Sheriff hadn't?

I heaved myself into the Jeep and rested my pounding head against the steering wheel. I could feel each heartbeat as it sent blood surging through the veins in my head. Bang, bang, bang, just like the rude neighbor in the room next to mine. Pounding and banging at all hours of the night. If I could just get one good night's sleep maybe I could think straight.

With nothing left to do and darkness settling like a heavy blanket around me, I decided to return to the motel. As I drove around the parking lot to the exit, I saw an older model green van backed into a spot in the far corner. On a whim, I pulled up in front of it and climbed out.

The front bumper was dotted with spots of rust. Deep dents in the driver's side door made it look as if it would be a struggle to open. The windows were tinted but not to the point where I couldn't peek inside. The tan interior was ripped and the dash had cracks. On the passenger side were more dents and scratches with a rainbow of different paint colors. Lauren's description of the van

218

that caused her accident popped into my foggy brain. I took out my flip phone and used the basic camera to snap pictures of the outside and the license plate.

The van was far enough away from the main entrance that someone could come and go without anyone noticing. Based on every scary movie I had ever seen, this type of vehicle would be excellent for holding someone hostage, at least long enough to take them from point A to point B.

My heart rate accelerated and I felt short of breath. I had no proof but I felt certain this van was connected to everything. It was getting late and I doubted the Sheriff would take my call to rush out and fingerprint it based on my intuition. Still, at least I had photos and a tiny bit more to work with. I vowed this would be my last night without finding Bailey.

After a dinner of potato chips and cupcakes, washed down with a diet soda, my headache abated slightly. I lay down on the lumpy mattress and examined my short list of suspects. After seeing the van, my belief was stronger that Lauren was here to help. I struggled through the process of sending a text to Lauren with the photos. If she recognized it as the one that ran her off the road, it would be more evidence for the Sheriff.

That left only Matthew, who had no apparent motive. I threw my useless flip phone across the room in frustration. If I had a real phone, I could have used it to search for his name. Social media tells volumes about a person's life.

The rickety television had only one channel that played anything other than static. I watched a few minutes of a reality show about rich, desperate women which made me feel even worse about my current situation. Finally, even though it was too early to sleep, I had nothing else to do. I turned off the television and pulled the thin bedspread over my head.

I awoke with a stabbing pain in my neck from the awkward position I had twisted myself into. The noise was getting more frequent from the room next door. It was as if there was a pattern. Three thumps, followed by a pause, then three thumps, another pause, and three thumps. It was so familiar, but confusing. My mind raced through all the options that could make that sound. I felt like the caller to a radio station that played "Identify the Sound to Win a Prize." The prize in this case was my sanity. The thumping was driving me crazy. Despite knocking on the door and pounding on the wall, it didn't stop. It increased in frequency.

"It's one o'clock in the morning for goodness' sake! Can you just stop banging around over there so people can sleep," I hollered at the wall.

The only response was more thump, thump, thumping. I had enough. I didn't care who was in the room next door or what they were doing, I was going to bang on the door until someone answered.

I hated to get up because it took me time to get one small space warmed in the creaky bed. I had every item of clothing piled on top of me to keep the heat in. There were only two temperature choices in this room: steamy hot with rivers of moisture running down the walls or cold enough to see my breath. I alternated between the two extremes.

The neighbor's inconsiderate behavior put me in a foul mood. I considered if I needed to get dressed but hoped the confrontation would only take a minute. I pulled on my hat and ski jacket and stuffed my feet into my boots. I may have looked ridiculous, but I was going with guns loaded for action.

I stomped out the door and let it slam behind me. For a moment I regretted my decision. I wasn't normally a person who looked for conflict. I would go out of my way to avoid it. Tonight, I needed rest. I'd been running around in full panic mode for days and my shoulders were slumped and my feet felt like cinderblocks. There was only so much caffeine and sugar a body could take before it crashed.

I took a deep breath and knocked at the door. Gently at first and then harder when no one responded.

"Come on. I know there's someone in there. Answer the door and tell me what you keep banging around in the middle of the night while some of us are trying to sleep."

I swore I heard something inside. Not a voice, but a muffled sound. I banged one more time and then decided whoever it was would not cooperate and open the door. That person disliked conflict even more than I did.

I trudged the few steps back to my room and turned the doorknob. No, no, no, no! I didn't bring the room key. I shivered in my thin pj's and looked around for anyone who might be able to help me. The parking lot was dimly lit by one streetlight and the randomly flashing vacancy sign. Besides my rental car, the only other car belonged to the couple I had seen going into their room at the far end. I doubted they could help me, but despite that thought, I knocked on their door. There was no answer, but my gut told me someone was there. I pommeled it again but still no response.

There were no lights on in the office and Patsy's car wasn't parked in its usual spot. Despite the odds, I walked over and banged on the door. With the current temperature likely hovering around twenty degrees, I would be a popsicle in less time than it took my neighbor to thump out the tune to a song no one knew.

I moved back to my room and jiggled the knob. I tried the window, but it was locked. Jonas made sure of that before he left me alone to fend for myself. How I wished he was here now. But he wasn't so I needed to get myself out of yet another predicament of my own making.

I remembered the small window in the bathroom. I had never checked to see if it was locked since it was covered with some foil-like material. Fingers crossed; I made my way around the end of the building. If I counted the doors correctly, my room would be the third from the end. I hoped every room had the same basic layout.

In the cold and dark, the front of the motel was less than friendly. I rounded the corner of the building and stopped in my tracks. Barely visible in the dim light were letters painted on the cinderblock wall. I swallowed the lump in my throat as I read the words, "I've been waiting for you."

I backed away. Could I survive the night outside? My fingers were getting numb, and my teeth chattered. The answer was no. I wouldn't make it an hour. I had no phone to call for help and there was no one within walking distance. I had to suck it up and hope I could get in the window. If that plan didn't work, I would rack my mind for another one. With no other options, I had to at least try.

I rounded the corner again, this time with more resolve. Thigh-high weeds with prickly thorns grabbed onto my pajama legs like tiny claws. I stayed close to the wall where I could because the snow was sparse. I tripped over a tire hidden by weeds and landed with my face almost in a discarded toilet with brown liquid frozen in the bowl. I gagged and righted myself. After that, my progress was slow but steady.

I couldn't be sure in the dark which window would lead to my room, so I said a silent prayer that I picked the right one. Even at my height of five feet nine, the window was too high to reach. I backtracked to the toilet to see if I could drag it, but it was frozen to the ground and heavier than I could manage. I felt more than looked to see if there was anything else that I could stand on. A short way farther down I found an old rattan chair. The seat was gone but the frame appeared to be solid. I fought my way back through the jungle of weeds, dragging the chair with me.

I propped it against the building just below the window. I would need to balance on each side of the frame and hope I could hoist myself into the window. That is, assuming I could even open it. As the cold seeped into my bones, it became harder for me to steady the shaking of my hands. My feet were numb, my nose dripped, and I felt as if I couldn't focus clearly on the task at hand.

It was now or never. I grasped the back of the chair, put my right foot gingerly on the side, and then quickly drew my left up. I immediately crashed backward onto something that screeched as loud as I did. I wrestled the furry creature for a second before scrambling back to my feet. A pair of dark eyes stared at me from a masked face. I stepped back from the raccoon as he stood up to me and hissed. Much to my relief, he quickly decided it was safer to turn and scramble away.

I shook off the snow that coated my soaked pajama bottoms. Wet, tired, and frightened of what other creatures I might encounter, I felt the urgency of my situation. I had to get inside my room, or any room, before it was too late. Freezing from the cold was not on tonight's menu.

I took a deep lungful of air and bit my lip. You got this, Jayne. Carefully, I placed my right foot on the side of the chair. Slowly I placed my left foot on the chair trying to balance my weight between the two. The chair rocked back and forth but I persevered. Gradually I stood on trembling legs. With my bare hand, I pushed against the sliding window frame. Years of peeling paint sloughed into my face. I clawed at the frost on the glass to find a way to pry it open. I could see there was no lock on the inside. The panel wouldn't budge but I suspected that if I had something to give me leverage, I could make it work.

Carefully, I climbed down and searched the area for any kind of tool I could use. With each passing moment the icy cold bit into my bones. My actions were slower, and my thought process was muddled. If I could tolerate five more minutes, I vowed to myself that I would be inside and I would blast the radiator until the room felt like a sauna.

I used my boot to dig through random piles of snow-covered junk. I found parts to an oscillating fan, a bucket with no bottom, a broom handle, plastic shower curtains that were frozen to metal shower rods, and bags of garbage that I refused to dig through with my bare hands. I seized the broom handle. If I couldn't pry the window open, I would break it and climb in. My survival depended on heat and at that moment I didn't care what it cost to replace the glass.

Once more I gingerly climbed onto the chair. It was tricky to maneuver my balance and the broom handle. I held onto the small ledge with one hand and rapped at the frame with the stick. At first, it didn't budge but after a few tries, it moved ever so slightly. Emboldened by my minute progress, I gave it my all and jammed the window as hard as I could with the handle. I heard it slam open as I fell backward off the chair.

I lay on the ground in the snow and trash with the wind knocked out of me. Something hard dug into my back but at least it wasn't screeching and hissing at me. I rolled over and slowly got to my feet. I was so cold I considered giving up, but I had made it this far. I righted the chair for what I hoped was the last time. Carefully, I climbed up and peered in the window. Heat blasted my face through the modest opening.

The last hurdle was to heft myself up while not falling off the chair. I paused for a minute to think about the best way to negotiate this obstacle. If I had the upper body strength, I would simply lift myself up and duck inside like a gymnast. The only exercise I got was carrying heavy trays around the restaurant.

My body had never seen the inside of a gym, but at that moment I wished it had. Vaulting into the window like a gymnast would never happen because I struggled to simply walk a straight line on a good day. I was not known as the most graceful server, a fact which my friend Emmett teased me about mercilessly.

It was do or die, literally. I stood on my tiptoes and wedged my head and arms into the small space. I could see the outline of the bathroom. If I fell as I climbed in, I would land in the tub with no way to break my fall. I would have to move slowly to ensure I could prevent landing on my head.

I wedged my hands on either side of the wall and wormed my way inch by inch. I got as far as my hips, face down with my hands on the edge of the tub before it occurred to me that the bathroom in my room was pink, and this one was yellow. And the foil that covered my window was missing. I had broken into someone else's room. I said a silent prayer in my head. Please don't let it be a serial killer or someone with a gun. My miscalculation could end in death.

There was no turning back, so I slithered the rest of the way through the window, listening as I did for any sounds coming from the bedroom. It was eerily quiet so I assumed the room was empty. At least, it was silent until my hips popped through the opening and I toppled headfirst into the scum-filled tub with an ear-splitting shriek that I'm sure was heard for miles.

I scrambled out of the tub and wiped my hands on my pajama bottoms. I shuddered and gagged at the rotting smell that came from the tub drain. The bathroom door was closed but I heard muffled sounds from the other room. I had two choices; walk out the door and face the consequences or crawl back out the tiny window to the bone-chilling cold. I picked the first one.

I took a deep breath, placed my hand on the rust-covered doorknob, and turned it as slowly and quietly as possible. I hoped the person or persons inside would be asleep so I could quietly leave through the front door. If they were awake, I could explain my situation and stay with them until dawn broke and I could find a way into my room.

The warped door was stuck and groaned when I tugged it open. I poked my head out to assess the situation. The room was dimly illuminated from the streetlight which filtered from outside through the thin curtains over the window. A beam of light showed under the exit door as if to guide me out.

I surveyed the room which had a similar layout to mine. On my left was a small console table with a late-model television. Directly in front of me was the exit door and to the right of that was the window. I bit my lip and turned to the right to see who or what was in the bed. What I saw caused a scream to escape from me that would have awakened the dead. It was Bailey!

CHAPTER TWENTY

"Holy shit! Bailey, what are you doing here?" I ran over to where she was tied to the bed.

Bailey's eyes were wild and she struggled against the duct tape that covered her mouth. She wore the same clothes she had when I last saw her.

Her hair was tangled and knotted around her face. I started to yank the tape off but then considered that might be painful. She mumbled words that I couldn't understand.

"Should I yank it off all at once?"

She nodded vigorously. I grabbed one side and wrenched the tape from her face.

"Ow!"

"You told me to yank it off."

"Quick get this duct tape off my hands before they come back." She thrashed around on the thin mattress while I tugged at the tape.

"I can't get it undone!" I scavenged around the room looking for something sharp enough to cut the tape.

"Hurry, Jayne. We may not have much time,"

"I can't find anything to cut it with," I hollered from the bathroom.

I dashed back into the bedroom and spied a glass with murky liquid on the television console. I remembered in the one Stephen King book I read, a wife lay handcuffed to a bed after her husband died suddenly of a heart attack during their romantic getaway. She finally escaped by breaking a glass and using it to slit her wrists to make them slippery enough with blood to slide out of the handcuffs. I didn't need to slit Bailey's wrists. I just needed to cut the tape.

I dumped the liquid on the brown, formerly known as shag, carpet and smashed the top of the glass against the table. It shattered into large chunks. I grabbed a piece and ran over to the bed. It took me several minutes to hack through the tape and free her left hand. I crawled over top of her to saw through the tape on the other hand.

Bailey sat up and rubbed her wrists. Gingerly she moved her legs to the side of the bed and wiggled her toes.

I grabbed her and gave her a bone-breaking hug, "I've been so worried about you. I've been searching everywhere, and we all thought you were lost in the mountains freezing to death. I'm so glad you're safe."

"We aren't safe yet. We need to get out of here and call the police." Bailey tried to stand but her legs gave out and she collapsed on the floor before I could catch her.

"Wrap your arms around my neck."

I half dragged her to the door without a plan of where we would go once, we were outside. I had no room key, no car key, and no phone. But at that moment, any place seemed safer than where we were.

As we reached the door, I heard the key turn in the lock, Bailey and I looked at each other.

"They're back. Quick Jayne, hide!" She whispered.

I dumped her at the door and rushed back to the bathroom, closing the door behind me. I heard a man's voice and a scuffle. My body trembled and my muscles tensed. I felt beads of sweat on my forehead. My brain raced. Should I rush out and use the element of surprise to overtake the perpetrator? Should I wait to see if they would leave and then stealthily sneak her out? If I waited and the person or persons came into the bathroom, I would have no way to defend myself or Bailey.

I considered trying to squeeze back out the bathroom window and running for help. I tiptoed to the door and tried to slide the bolt into place. If I made any sound, I knew I would give my whereabouts away. I bit my lip and with shaking hands reached for the lock. I pressed my ear against the door and listened. Bailey's voice sounded as if she was trying to reason with someone. There was a muffled voice that sounded familiar.

At that moment, I knew it was a now-or-never dilemma. Instead of locking the door, I threw it open with a loud bang and sprinted out as if shot by a gun. I launched myself into the air and landed with a solid thud on the kidnapper. The sudden collision sent a jolt through his body, eliciting an involuntary "oof" as the air rushed out of his lungs. There was a dull thud accompanying the sound, like a muffled echo reverberating through the room.

We rolled around on the floor, each trying to gain the advantage. In the semi-darkness, I could make out his dark eyes and bearded face. He put his thick hands around my throat and shook me until my head snapped backward like a doll. My eyes bugged out and my airway started to collapse. I clawed at his hands to loosen his grip. I heard Bailey screaming my name.

Time slowed and everything around me blurred. I heard John Whiteskunk's words, "Listen to the sounds around you."

I closed my eyes and heard my father's voice. He would say to me, "Jayne, what do you do if someone grabs you?"

My little girl self would answer, "Go for the eyes."

"That's right. Don't forget it."

I stopped trying to break his grip and instead jabbed my finger into his left eye. He howled and grabbed at his face. I scrambled out from under his weight.

Bailey was furiously trying to undo the duct tape he had affixed to her left wrist. I seized the small wooden lamp off the nightstand and yanked it cord and all from the wall. With all the force I could muster, whacked him over the head. He screamed as he felt the impact and fell forward onto the carpet with a heavy thump.

I stood over him with the lamp held high in case he moved.

"Did you kill him, Jayne?"

I dropped the lamp on the floor and bent over. "I can't breathe."

Bailey escaped her bondage and stumbled over to me. "Let's get out of here while we can."

"Sh-should we check to see if he's breathing?"

Bailey reached down and cautiously rolled him onto his back.

"It's Matthew! I knew he was involved," I cried.

"He's breathing. Get the duct tape. We'll tape him up and go for help. Better he doesn't get away before the police come."

I grabbed the tape from where it had rolled in the scuffle. We tore off long strips and wrapped them around his feet first and then his hands. Lastly, we taped his mouth.

"See how you like that buddy," Bailey said as she slapped the tape over his mouth and beard.

His head was bleeding, but it was a trickle and not a gush. I figured he wouldn't bleed out. I'd seen worse injuries than that, and those people had survived. Nevertheless, I stole the pancake flat pillow from the bed and put it under his head. I might be an almost killer but I wasn't a mean person.

"And where do you think you two are going?"

Bailey and I looked at each other.

"Uh oh," I said.

I twisted around to see a woman in the open doorway behind us with a fully loaded revolver pointed at our heads. Her dyed white hair was shaved on the sides and spiky on top. I looked down from my height of five feet nine inches and guessed her to be at least four inches shorter. A baggy black turtleneck and leggings hung on her celery stalk-thin frame. The tattoo of a spider crawled across the wrist of her gun hand.

She directed the gun to my face, "This must be the pesky Jayne, I've heard about from Matteo."

"Who are you?"

"Not that it's any of your business, but I'm Audrey, Matteo's wife."

I shook my head, wondering where I had heard that particular name before.

"I'm so confused. Who is Matteo and why did you kidnap Bailey?"

She waved the gun around and leered at me. "Not so smart after all are you? Call him whatever you like, Matthew, or Matteo. It's the same outcome for you two."

She pointed at Bailey, "Bailey, since your friend has decided to join the party, she can take your place on the bed. Tape her up. Now!"

Bailey sighed and we walked over to the bed. There was no chance for us to figure out a signal or a plan to attack her. Bailey was weak from her time as a captive and my adrenaline was sapped after my tussle with Matthew.

I sat down on the bed and she bound my hands behind my back. She left the tape loose and I hoped it was enough that I could work myself free.

When that task was completed, Audrey instructed Bailey to cut the tape from Matthew. His eyes flickered open and he scrambled shakily to his feet when he saw Audrey.

"How did you let these two overtake you?"

"Jayne jumped me from the bathroom. She almost took my eye out!" He rubbed his head, "I'm bleeding."

"Stop whining and tie that one up again. This time make it tight enough so she can't get loose." She paced and waved the gun around, "I need to think about how to dispose of their bodies."

"What do you mean, dispose of their bodies? I never agreed to kill anyone."

"Listen, Matteo, they know your face and mine. I'm not going to jail for this."

I bit my lip, "I don't know what's going on. I couldn't tell anyone anything even if I wanted to."

"Shut up or I'll gag you."

"Audrey, we could get away. Let's leave them here and make a fresh start someplace new. We could go to Canada or Mexico like you always wanted. Please, let's get our daughter and go. I destroyed Bailey's computer and deleted the files she had on the cloud. There's no evidence left of what we did. Core Logistics won't ever know who took the money."

"I'm sure she has backups. We have to get our hands on her hard copy backups."

Matthew/Matteo looked at Bailey, "Why don't you just tell us where they are and we can be done with this? We don't want to hurt you," he whined.

"I told you. I don't have any other backups. Everything was on the cloud and I gave you access. Just let Jayne go and I'll help you cover your tracks. Audrey, Matthew is right. I can help you escape. You have enough money from the sale of the inventory you diverted from the company to live comfortably the rest of your life. No one has to find out that you stole that billionaire's brain and sold it on the illegal market."

"I'm going to be sick," I gagged.

"All of you stop talking. I need to think." Audrey paced and waved the gun around.

Matthew placed a hand on her shoulder, "We can't go to jail, Audrey. What about our daughter?"

"I'm not going to jail." She pulled an envelope out of her pocket and handed it to Matthew.

"What is this?"

"It's your confession and a suicide note."

Matthew's uninjured eye opened wide, "Audrey, no! You can't mean to kill us all."

"I do. It's your fault, Matteo. You made me do all of this. Your constant whining. Your antiquated ideas about women and family. All you talk about is computer games."

"No, no, no. I didn't make you steal, Audrey. I did my best to provide a good life for us." His voice was high-pitched, almost to a squeal.

"A good life, ha! Your idea of a good life isn't the same as mine. I want more."

"I won't do it. I won't kill anyone, not even for you."

"It doesn't matter. I will kill them and then you. I had your suicide note typed up and now your fingerprints are on it."

He put his hands over his ears, "But I love you. We're a family. Why would you do this?"

"Because for years all you talked about was how Bailey Chauncey killed your sister and you wanted revenge. I gave you your chance for revenge. You should be grateful for that. I'm taking our daughter and we'll be far away from here, living the good life."

I looked from Bailey to Matthew as reality dawned slowly in my mind. I needed to find a way to convince Matthew to join our side or we were all doomed. I started working my hands free of the tape while creating a distraction to buy myself time.

"Matthew, you know it was an accident that killed your sister. Bailey was just a kid herself and she has been paying for her mistakes her entire life. If you do this, your daughter will suffer. I know you're not a bad guy and she needs you. Think of what will happen to her if we're all murdered. You can't let Audrey do this."

Audrey stormed over to where I sat on the bed and pressed the gun to my temple. "Do you ever shut up?" She looked back at Matthew and growled, "I told you to tie Bailey up. Do it now!"

233

Matthew stood looking from Bailey to Audrey while he fidgeted with the roll of tape. Bailey took a small step away from Matthew. Her entire body trembled and her face was ashen. Despite the icy air that wafted in from the open door, sweat ran down my back. The eerie quiet of the night contrasted with the acrid smell of fear.

I may be clumsy and I make bad choices more often than not, but there is one thing I wasn't and that's a quitter. If today was my last day on earth, I vowed to go out with the fight of my life.

As surreptitiously as possible, I wiggled my hands-free of the tape while watching the drama play out between Audrey and Matthew. Audrey's attention was laser-focused on Matthew. Her eyes narrowed and a scowl lined her face.

"Audrey, if you let us go, I will plant a virus on Core's hard drives so no one ever has to know about what you've done. It will send their entire system into a meltdown. I know someone who can make fake passports for you and you can all be living in another country by tomorrow. Jayne doesn't know anything. Give me access to a computer and I promise I'll do it," Bailey begged.

Audrey looked from Bailey to Matthew. "Can she do that?"

Matthew nodded his head slowly, "It's possible. She's the best there is. Miller Communications wouldn't even consider her if she couldn't deliver."

Audrey paced while Bailey edged closer to me. I worried she would throw herself in front of me if Audrey decided to eliminate me as a witness. I knew that if Bailey gave Audrey the chance to live a new life, she would still kill us. The only good witness in a criminal's mind was a dead one.

CHAPTER TWENTY-ONE

There was only one way to end our standoff and that was to get the gun from Audrey. I didn't like guns, but my cop father made sure I knew how to use one. I didn't want to shoot anyone but I would if I didn't have a choice. It wouldn't be the first time I had to make the decision to survive.

I cleared my throat to get Bailey's attention. I needed to convey to her what I planned. If she could impede Matthew long enough for me to get my hands on the gun, we might have a chance.

When she didn't respond, I took another tactic. "It doesn't matter what you do to us. Lauren Davis already knows about you, Audrey. I saw her tonight and she has all the evidence she needs to have you arrested. She's meeting the sheriff in the morning. If you leave right now, you might escape." Another thought occurred to me. "She saw you in that van that ran her off the road."

Audrey stood with her face inches from Matthew's. Spit flew from her mouth as she shrieked. "I told you she saw me. You weren't going fast enough when you ran her off the road. You can't do anything right!"

Without a second to waste, I knew this was my chance. I launched myself off the bed and onto Audrey's back. The force of my impact knocked both her and Matthew into the television console which crashed down onto all three of us where we all scrambled for the gun.

I was laser-focused on the spider tattoo and the skinny hand that clung to the revolver. I bit down as hard as I could on her hand. Audrey screamed and the gun went off with an ear-shattering crack that felt as if it shook the walls. She released her grip on the gun, but before I could grab it, someone else snatched it from the floor.

"It's over. Stop right now or I will shoot you. Jayne, get up."

I crawled from the pile and dragged myself up with the support of the television console. Bailey stood next to me, her hands shaking as they held the gun.

"Let me have that, Bailey," I said as I delicately pulled the gun from her hands.

Audrey rolled off Matthew and started to stand.

"Stay on the floor. Bailey might not shoot you, but I definitely will. We need to get a phone and call the police."

"Mathew has a phone." Bailey stumbled over to where he sat on the carpet, his head hung. She pulled a smartphone from his jacket and pressed a button to wake it.

"What's the code," I demanded.

He gave her a series of six numbers that corresponded to a date a few days prior. I watched as he and Bailey exchanged glances and then she punched in the numbers. Between the two of us, we gave the 911 operator enough information to send the entire police force hurtling in our direction. It was only minutes until we heard the sirens blasting and saw the flashing lights.

Sheriff Cox was the first to rush through the door with his gun drawn. "Drop the gun now!"

I slowly set the gun on the floor and put my hands behind my head. "If I can explain…"

"Do not talk. Do not move."

I obeyed.

The sheriff picked up the gun with two fingers and handed it to a deputy. "Are you Bailey Chauncey? He asked.

"Yes, I am. These people kidnapped me and have been holding me hostage. Jayne rescued me."

"We'll take all of your statements at the station. First, let's get the paramedics to take a look at you. It seems you've been shot."

I gasped and turned to look at Bailey, who had a stain of blood blooming on her left arm. And then I fainted.

My eyes fluttered open. A man was leaning over me. I tried to sit up but he held me down.

"Take it slow, Miss. We need to get your blood pressure back up to normal, so I don't want you to sit up too quickly."

"Where's Bailey?"

"She's being treated by another paramedic but she'll be okay."

Gradually, I felt myself return to normal so he helped me sit up. Matthew and Audrey were gone. The room was a shambles. The console was tilted on its side, and the television screen cracked. My teeth chattered and my body shivered violently.

The paramedic pulled a blanket around my shoulders. "We're going to take you to the hospital to be checked out."

I examined my arms and legs, "Did I get shot too?"

He chuckled, "No, but we prefer to be on the safe side. It looks like you have a scrape or two. You may have bruises from what your friend described as your heroic assault against those two alleged abductors."

"I'm no hero. I didn't have a choice."

"You may not think so but, from the looks of it, you saved both of your lives."

"I need to see Bailey."

He helped me walk to the ambulance that waited outside. A slew of emergency vehicles lit up the parking lot like a July Fourth carnival of flashing red, white, and blue lights.

Bailey was propped up inside the ambulance, covered by a blanket and with an IV in her right arm. Her sweater had been cut away and her left arm was swathed in a bandage. Her red hair had been pulled back off her pale face.

I stood motionless for a moment and looked at her as relief washed over me. Bailey was alive. My gut kept telling me she was. and for once, I listened.

She gave me a weak smile and held out her hand. The paramedic moved over and let me climb in beside her.

"Are you okay?" I asked when she winced.

"Yes. Fortunately, the bullet only grazed my arm."

"I'm so sorry it took me so long to find you."

"But you did find me and you saved my life."

I couldn't stop the tears from running down my cheeks. "I almost didn't find you. I looked everywhere I could think."

"How did you find me?"

"Well, it was an accident. I locked myself out of my room and climbed into yours by mistake."

"Your room? Are you staying here? Didn't you hear my S.O.S.?"

"Is that what all that banging was? Geez, you were driving me crazy with all that noise."

Despite the obvious pain on her face, Bailey smiled. "Only you, Jayne."

Sheriff Cox interrupted our reunion to request my presence in his squad car. I followed him on trembling legs. What now, I wondered.

To my surprise, he opened the front passenger seat door. He hefted his sizeable body behind the steering wheel and gave me a long hard look.

"Discharging a firearm in town limits, breaking and entering, interfering with an investigation, assault." He ticked off my crimes with his fingers.

"But Sheriff, I…"

"Those are all charges I could press against you, Miss Stanford."

"If you let me explain…"

He held up his hand. "I could charge you, but I'm not going to." He shook his head in frustration and I thought he whispered a curse.

"Thank you."

"Once the hospital clears you, I want you and your friend on the next plane out. We'll be in touch when we need you to testify. Until you do testify, I don't want you back in my jurisdiction. And when you do *have* to come back, I don't want to hear about any shenanigans. Do I make myself clear?"

"Yes, sir."

"I hope you finally understand I will not tolerate this behavior from you again."

"Yes, sir."

"Okay get out of my car and go to the hospital before I change my mind."

I opened the door and looked back at the Sheriff. "What will happen to Matthew and Audrey? They have a little girl."

"That's up to the jury to decide if they are convicted. Social services will take charge of the child until someone can be appointed to foster her. I understand she's with grandparents right now so it's likely they will keep her, at least until the trials are over."

"For what it's worth, I don't think Matthew's a bad guy. He made some bad decisions trying to help someone he loved, but haven't we all done that?"

He looked at me. "Some of us more than others. One last thing, Jayne. You did good tonight in saving your friend."

I smiled as I closed the car door. I was ready to go home.

§§§§§§§§§§§

The next day, we were on our way back to Phoenix. Bailey sat beside me in first class with her arm in a sling. On the outside, she looked the same. Her long red hair was neatly braided but the bangles on her wrist shook when we touched our glasses of sparkling wine in a toast.

"We made it. We survived," I said.

She nodded. "I hoped this trip would be a fun girlfriend getaway. I never expected it to be so life changing."

"You went through a lot. Do you think Matthew blamed you all these years for his sister's death?"

"Yes, he did. It was an obsession for him which Audrey used to her advantage. She worked at Core Logistics and started diverting stored inventory a few years ago. She knew I was getting close to discovering her actions. When he told her I was coming onboard with Miller, it was her perfect chance to try to get rid of the evidence she knew I had on her."

"Did she really steal someone's frozen brain and sell it?"

"I'm not sure if there ever was a stolen brain, but regardless, Core Logistics will be in court for years dealing with the fallout. They were supposed to have state-of-the-art security, but Audrey used Matthew's computer skills to divert funds and sell off priceless works of art. Matteo, or Matthew as he goes by now, was convinced he was saving his marriage."

"Lauren hired you because she suspected something was up?"

"She did. She also hired a private investigator. I didn't realize who he was until it was too late."

"This has been the craziest trip of my life."

Bailey looked at me, "If I ever ask you to travel with me again, will you think twice before you say yes?"

I laughed, "Nope, no reservations."

The End

ABOUT THE AUTHOR

Leslie Rager draws upon her experience in the restaurant business, and love of the Arizona desert, to create the characters for her cozy mysteries. As a technical writer, she has written software manuals for online and print. She

Menu for Murder and Cocktails at Sunset, both received five-star reviews on Readers' Favorites, Amazon, and Goodreads. No Reservations is the third book in the series. Next up Leslie is writing her first romance, Reunion in the Desert.

She spends her limited free time hiking in the desert, savoring wine, and spending time with her husband, family, and friends. As a breast cancer survivor, she volunteers for EBeauty, a non-profit organization created to support women undergoing treatment for cancer.

Website: www.leslieragerathor.com
Facebook: www.facebook.com/lesliekellerbooks
Email: LeslieRagerAuthor@gmail.com